P9-DWH-738

DEADLY CAMARGUE

ALSO BY CAY RADEMACHER

Murderous Mistral

DEADLY CAMARGUE

CAY RADEMACHER

TRANSLATED FROM THE GERMAN BY PETER MILLAR

MINOTAUR BOOKS NEW YORK

This is a work of fiction. All of the characters, organizations, and events portrayed in this novel are either products of the author's imagination or are used fictitiously.

www.minotaurbooks.com

Designed by Omar Chapa

Library of Congress Cataloging-in-Publication Data

Names: Rademacher, Cay, author. | Millar, Peter, translator.
Title: Deadly camargue : a Provence mystery / Cay Rademacher ; translated by Peter Millar.
Other titles: Todliche Camargue. English
Description: First U.S. edition. | New York : Minotaur Books, 2018.
Identifiers: LCCN 2018013875 | ISBN 9781250110725 (hardcover) | ISBN 9781250110732 (ebook)
Subjects: LCSH: Murder—Investigation—France—Provence—Fiction. | Private investigators—France—Provence—Fiction. | GSAFD: Mystery fiction.
Classification: LCC PT2678.A238 T6313 2018 | DDC 833/.92—dc23
LC record available at https://lccn.loc.gov/2018013875

Originally published under the title *Tödliche Camargue* in Germany by DUMONT Buchverlag

First U.S. Edition: November 2018

10 9 8 7 6 5 4 3 2 1

The cruel law of art is that people die.

—*Marcel Proust*

DEADLY CAMARGUE

Blood on the Road

In twenty years of service with the gendarmerie, Captain Roger Blanc had never seen so much blood: a dead black fighting bull blocking the road, a dark colossus with at least two dozen 9mm Parabellum gunshot wounds. A few yards behind it lay the horribly ripped-open corpse of a man. The blood of both man and beast had mingled and dried into a cracked brown crust on the stinking tar surface of the road.

It was late afternoon, but the sun still hung above the horizon like a poisonous flower. A battered white street sign indicated the way to Saint-Gilles down the *route départementale*, a minor road branching off to one side. I know the name of that place from somewhere, Blanc thought, but in the heat there was no way to remember where or when he had heard it. Someone had fired a gun at the sign a long time ago, and the edges of the holes had gone rusty. The winding roads were narrow gray ribbons in a world of sand, salt, and tough grass: the Camargue.

Brackish water pooled like leaden mirrors the size of lakes and as calm as puddles, some of them an almost chemical blue, others bright red like diluted watercolors. Yellowish white bubbles of foam clung to their marshy edges. The grass was knee high, every blade as sharp as a dagger, swaying slightly up and down, up and down, in a gentle westerly breeze that brought no relief from the heat. Dragonflies danced over the surface of the water. Blanc noticed elegant pink silhouettes stalking along the blurred horizon and realized with astonishment that they were flamingos. He had only seen them once before, an eternity ago, in the zoo at Vincennes, when his children were still young and his marriage still intact.

Bright flashes of light boring into his eyes like needles diverted his attention to the macabre piece of theater lying at his feet. Rays of sunlight were being reflected by the steel watch on the wrist of the man who had been tossed by the fighting bull's horns. His body lay some fifteen feet beyond that of the shot animal.

Blanc bent down over the man's body. He was in his midfifties, between 5'7" and 5'8" tall, slim, and suntanned. An ultralight angular pair of sunglasses covered the upper half of his face; long gray hair already turning white spilled out from under a helmet that looked as if a computer-game designer had made it with a 3-D printer. The dead man was wearing black cycling shorts and a sports T-shirt in cobalt blue and neon yellow. Not that there was much of either color visible given that one of the bull's horns had struck the cyclist in the abdomen while the beast itself had thrown up its head, ripping him open as if with a butcher's knife from his navel almost to his throat. The edges of the wound were jagged, and the man's small intestine bulged out of the opening like some pale garden slug. Blanc spotted the end of a broken rib as well as a few other organs he wasn't too keen on identifying. Gorged bluebottles were crawling all over the corpse. The smell of blood and partly digested food mingled with that of the brackish water. Blanc felt faint and got quickly back on his feet.

He looked around, squinting despite his sunglasses. Just a handbreadth higher than his immediate surroundings a luxuriant green meadow glistened, enclosed behind a sturdy fence of square wooden beams and iron posts, with only one access gate, which was made of wood in a massive steel frame. It lay wide open.

Blanc looked back at the dead man. He had been riding an expensive-looking mountain bike that had skidded maybe thirty feet until the front wheel had ended up in the drainage ditch at the side of the road. Then Blanc looked at the bull, its legs stretched out like the imploring arms of a beggar, its heavy lilac-colored tongue hanging from its mouth, the lines scraped in the tarmac by its horns, each one as long as a man's arm, and the side of its massive body ripped open by the bullets.

An older gendarme, sweating profusely, came over to him, the name RONCHARD on his badge.

"Was it you who shot the bull?" Blanc asked.

"Yes, *mon Capitaine.* A witness reported the accident. My colleague and I were the first on-site and found the body." Ronchard nodded toward another uniformed gendarme, who was using a compact camera to take photos of the road and the victim. He was holding the camera at arm's length as if afraid it might explode at any moment. Blanc doubted he would produce a single usable photo of the scene.

"The bull was still standing next to the victim," Ronchard went on. "At first we didn't dare get out of the car. I wasn't keen to tackle that half ton of bone and muscle with just my service pistol. It just so happened we had a UNP-9 in the car because we were on the way back from the shooting range. I'm a hunter in my spare time and . . . *eh bien . . .*" He hesitated, then gave a humorless laugh. "It wasn't exactly a marksman's shot. I rolled down the side window and emptied the magazine."

Blanc glanced back at the bull and nodded. "Maybe you'll get the sawed-off head as a trophy. Bit different from a pheasant."

"I'll be in the papers, that's for sure. I can't remember the last time a tourist in the Camargue was impaled on a bull's horns."

Blanc nodded toward the open fence. "Was that gate already open when you got here?"

"As open as a flasher's fly."

"So the bull was grazing in a meadow that had been left open," Blanc mused. "Why wasn't the gate closed? And how long had it been open? *Bien*, one way or another, a cyclist just happens to be coming down a country road on his mountain bike."

"These animals are bred to fight, *mon Capitaine.* They are extremely aggressive and very fast. Maybe the animal got disturbed and it felt threatened. Or maybe it was just bored and hot with that black pelt in this sun. Maybe the screech of the brakes irritated it. Those things are monstrous beasts. In any case the creature must have seen the cyclist. There was nothing in between them. The bull lowered its head and charged. Hits him straight on. It'll be in the pages of *La Provence* in the morning."

"Maybe the front page," Blanc murmured gloomily, removing the victim's sunglasses. "Have you taken a closer look at him, Ronchard? Do you know him?"

The man coughed. "The helmet and sunglasses covered up most of his face, and in any case I wasn't that close."

"Try to ignore the ludicrous cycling outfit he's wearing. Imagine him in designer jeans and an elegant dark jacket, wearing a shirt so white it hurts your eyes, with always one button too many undone. That's how this gentleman normally appears on his frequent television appearances."

It was Thursday, August 4, the seventh day of a heat wave that felt as if God had dragged the Midi away from Europe and planted it in the Sahara. Every day the radio was predicting temperatures of 95 degrees—a political move, Blanc figured, made not to panic people. If the temperature gauge in his run-down old Renault Espace still worked, he expected the little display would show 100 degrees from morning to late in the evening.

On Wednesday he had given up trying to inspect the roof of the old olive oil mill he had been living in for several weeks. The curved terra-cotta tiles had been heated by the sun to the extent that he had been forced to put on gloves just to touch them. After a few minutes, covered in sweat and dehydrated, he had retreated down the rickety wooden ladder he had found in a Dumpster near the house. But he had been careless enough to go up there with his shirt off and had come back down with sunburned shoulders. He cursed his own stupidity later when the burning from his neck to his upper arms stopped him from falling asleep. Born a northerner, always a northerner.

On Thursday morning he had sat in front of the nearly useless monitor of his antique computer staring at the screen saver. The heat had sapped the destructive energy of even the usual suspects in the criminal fraternity, so there was not much to do. He had tried to move as little as possible, which wasn't easy given that the chair was too small for his nearly six-foot-six frame. The shabby little concrete office block in the center of Gadet had air-conditioning, but it was less than inadequate and hadn't been serviced in years with the result that the whirring metal box emitted nothing more than a few waves of lukewarm air stinking of mildew. To get any fresh air at all the gendarmes had to open the windows from time to time, even if it did feel like they were opening the doors to an oven.

As always Blanc had gone to work in dark jeans and a black T-shirt and felt as if even the light cotton was scraping the sunburned patches of his skin.

His partner wasn't doing any better. Lieutenant Marius Tonon was also sitting staring apathetically at his screen, though at least he wasn't plagued by sunburn. His massive subordinate's olive-colored skin had long since become immune to the rays of the sun. But he blinked continuously, and there were big inflamed rings around his eyes while spiderwebs of tiny burst veins had exploded across his eyeballs.

Blanc had had lunch with his colleague in the shade of the plane trees in Gadet's Le Soleil restaurant, watching Tonon knock back a pastis "to cure my thirst." And then another. Only then did the landlord silently deliver his usual carafe of rosé wine.

When they were just starting to nod off in the office later, Blanc and Tonon jumped at the ring of the telephone. "*Merde*," Blanc muttered when he glanced at the display and saw that it was their boss calling.

Commandant Nicolas Nkoulou as ever lorded it over them in his office at the opposite end of the corridor, his immaculate pale blue uniform contrasting perfectly with his gold-rimmed glasses and chocolate-colored skin, on which there was not a single bead of sweat. He looked at Blanc and Tonon for longer than usual and for a moment it seemed as if he was about to say something totally different than what he was supposed to say to them. But in the end he collected his thoughts and pushed a piece of paper across his desk to them.

"This has just come in. It would appear to be"—the commandant cleared his throat—"a rather bizarre accident. A cyclist, a bull, and a real mess. Go check it out, purely pro forma."

"*Putain*, what does he mean pro forma?" Tonon whispered as they closed the door to the boss's office behind them.

"That he's given the job to us because everybody else thinks it's too hot," Blanc replied, requisitioning a squad car. "How long will it take us to get down to the Camargue?"

His colleague rolled his inflamed eyes. "Have you ever looked at a map?"

"The only map I know remotely well is the street map of Paris."

"Welcome to the real world."

As he walked out into the glaring sunlight, Blanc pulled the cloth armband bearing the word GENDARMERIE onto his left arm. Even that hurt. "I never would have thought that I'd feel better in that moldy hunk of concrete than I would outdoors," he grumbled, looking back at the gendarmerie station and noticing a blind twitch. Almost certainly a gloating colleague. *Merde.*

"You'll feel at home in the Camargue: it's salty, flat, and boring. Just like the north, only a bit hotter."

"I don't recall mad fighting bulls careering down the streets back home," Blanc replied dismissively.

His colleague flopped down into the passenger seat with a groan and fiddled with the dashboard until Radio Nostalgie filled the Renault Mégane, which was a bit of a relic from the past itself. Patricia Kaas. "*Reste sur moi.*"

"I'd like to know whether it is a Provençal or Spanish fighting bull," Tonon said, unconsciously mouthing the words of the melody so it looked as if he was singing along. It annoyed Blanc and he concentrated on looking at the road.

"A bull is a bull," he replied, driving slowly out of the gendarmerie parking lot. There was hardly any need to rush.

Tonon gave him a sympathetic look. "You wouldn't say that if you were a bullfighter. In the Spanish corrida it's a matter of life and death. Usually it's the animal that gets stabbed, but sometimes the bull can win. Spanish bulls are bred so that their horns point lower—that makes it easier for them to get you."

"That's only fair."

"Provençal *cocardiers*, however," Tonon went on, "are smaller than the Spanish animals, faster, more nervous, more mobile—and their horns point upward."

"Nice for the *torero.*"

"We call them *raseteurs.* Their job is to seize the rosettes fixed between the bull's horns, tiny little things tied to the base of the horns, right above the powerful skull. No normal person would do it of their own free will. A *raseteur* doesn't wave a red cape or play around with a sword or prance around the arena like some fancy Spanish fairy. A *raseteur* has no weapon save for the *crochet,* which looks a bit like an outsize knuckle-duster with hooks on it. That's what he uses to snag the rosettes from the horns if he's skilled enough and can get that close to the bull. A *raseteur* is dressed all in white and has to be quick on his feet. That's why we call it the *course camarguaise*; it's really more like a race than a fight. It can end in bloodshed, but it doesn't very often, and if it does, it's the man's blood. Throughout the spring and again in the autumn the spectacles are held in arenas such as those at Arles or Istres, sometimes Spanish-style but more often Provençal-style. But even the best bulls end up in the abattoir. Their meat has a gamy taste."

"All your thoughts come back to the kitchen," Blanc teased him. "If there are that many beasts, how come cyclists don't get gored more often?"

Tonon laughed. "Because there's enough free space to get out of the way most of the time. The Camargue is nearly eight hundred square miles, full of swamps, meadows, rice fields. The town of Saintes-Maries-de-la-Mer has a Mediterranean coastline with beaches, gypsy music, happy tourists. Saint-Gilles is a hick town with a huge church, Aigues-Mortes is a sort of medieval Disneyland. But apart from those three towns, the whole area is more or less deserted. In the middle of the wasteland there are a couple of places where Parisians and the English come down to bust their balls on the backs of the famous Camargue white horses. There are the little *cabanes* that used to be lived in by the *gardians*, the cowboys of the Camargue with their black hats and tridents, the guys who look after the bulls but who can't afford the huts anymore. They're lived in by the Parisians and English who cool their balls off in them after they've been out riding. The cattle just wander freely through the wasteland, but the fighting bulls are kept in enclosed meadows behind strong fences. As a cyclist, there's normally just you and a few thousand uninterested flamingos."

"You sound like a great fan of the Camargue."

"You might say that."

Blanc turned onto *route départementale* 113, which ran mile after mile straight ahead between fields and lines of cypress trees. It felt a bit like driving down an endless airport runway without ever taking off. He was glad to see the traffic get a bit heavier as they approached Arles or else he might have fallen asleep at the wheel. His colleague nodded at the road sign that read SAINTES-MARIES and said wearily, "That way, just keep straight ahead. We're bound to come across the whole mess sooner or later."

It only took a few minutes before the patrol car was in a whole different world, driving through an ocean of grass and silvery water. Blanc spotted a *cabane* a few hundred yards away from the road. The straw roof had gone dark, but the walls were whitewashed to the extent that they were almost blinding. The northern end was narrow, rounded, and without windows. Blanc had experienced the mercilessly icy mistral and could imagine why these huts out in this unsheltered expanse presented it with a streamlined, wind-resistant face. There didn't seem to be a track across the marshland to the *cabane* and he wondered how anyone was supposed to get there from the road. A few white horses were tied to a wooden fence near the building. Paulette Aybalen, who lived near Blanc's dilapidated oil mill, also kept Camargue horses on her land. Sometimes she would ride out alone and sometimes with her daughters through the forests that lay on the other side of the mill. A wild, attractive woman. A woman . . . And then his thoughts went back to Geneviève and why she had left him. He wondered if she was still on vacation in the Caribbean with her new lover. Or whether she was back in Paris with him. Looking out the window of *his* apartment, cooking in *his* kitchen, falling into *his* bed in the evening . . . He wasn't paying attention to the road and almost drove into a drainage ditch when a few miles down the road took a sudden turn.

"The Camargue is better than Valium," Tonon commented, as soon as he had gotten over the shock. "As soon as you get here, your thoughts drift off elsewhere. What were you thinking about?"

Blanc was too worked up to give him a bland, inconsequential answer. "My wife," he replied.

"Your ex-wife."

"We're not divorced yet."

"Dream on. Is she still crying her eyes out, or has she found a new guy?"

"She's on vacation with him in the Caribbean."

"I'm sure your ex spends every day lying under the palm trees thinking about you." Tonon punched him so hard on the shoulder that Blanc came dangerously close to driving into the ditch again. "Believe me, I'm speaking from experience. One cop is enough. A woman who's been hitched to a gendarme doesn't make the same mistake twice. Get her out of your head."

"We have two kids."

"Grown up?"

"They're allowed to vote. But at times they act as if they are still in kindergarten."

"*Eh bien.* They chucked you out of Paris and sent you down here to the farthest province. Your wife left you. Your kids don't want anything more from you except a bit of money now and again. Sounds like ideal conditions for a new beginning."

Blanc thumped the steering wheel. "My career is shit and I'm driving through a swamp to see the only cyclist in France stupid enough to get his guts ripped out by an ox. You call that a new beginning?"

"Whenever you reach the bottom, you have to go up again. It's the law of physics."

Blanc looked at his overweight, exhausted colleague who hadn't been promoted in decades and didn't bother with an answer. He put his foot on the brakes because there was a line of a dozen cars in front of him, stuck behind an RV with Dutch license plates. The van's driver was doing under thirty miles per hour through the plains. Every time there was nothing coming from the other direction, two cars would pull out and pass the RV. When it was his turn, Blanc pulled out and roared past the huge white slug, even though there was a group of brightly clad cyclists coming toward him. One of them flipped him the bird.

"Flat land. Good for cyclists," Blanc muttered, pulling out again to overtake another pair of cyclists, an overweight middle-aged couple on mountain bikes.

"All you have to do is watch out for fighting bulls and mad drivers," Tonon replied.

Blanc declined to reply and instead nodded up ahead to where a blue light was flashing rhythmically and a uniformed gendarme was using a paddle to wave traffic around a lane that had been blocked off with tape. "We're there," he announced.

Ten minutes later he was standing alongside Corporal Ronchard in front of the horribly mutilated corpse and realizing that he was staring at a celebrity.

"Albert Cohen," Blanc muttered.

Ronchard forced himself to take a closer look. "So it is," he conceded after a few seconds, his face having gone pale beneath the heat flush. "I would have bet he would have met his end somewhere in Afghanistan or Syria, not here in the Camargue. What was he doing here?"

"Maybe he was working on a report about cattle," Blanc replied grimly. Cohen was a well-known reporter for the weekly magazine *L'Événement* and the handsomest man in the small circle of Paris's fashionable intellectuals. Blanc, who had worked on corruption cases before his ignominious exile, knew more about that group's dirty laundry than their glittering public façades. As far as he knew, there was nothing more to Cohen than the façade: he had heard of him but he had never come under suspicion by the police.

In the eighties Cohen had made his name in social reportage. Blanc recalled a piece about North African drug dealers in the *banlieue*, one of the few magazine articles that had stuck in his head. Cohen had won prizes and had been on television a few times. Then at some point, Blanc couldn't remember exactly when, Cohen wasn't so much on television occasionally as all the time, broadcasting his opinion on anything and everything. He had continued to write for *L'Événement* but had been focused on commentary and essays instead of reportage. He had been in favor of French intervention in every global crisis, preferably sending in troops, whether it was Libya, Mali, the Congo, or Syria—it seemed no country was safe from Cohen's calls for intervention. At one stage he had even advocated the use of force in Tibet, which had led to ructions in Beijing and more than minor panic at the foreign ministry on the Quai d'Orsay.

Tonon had by now come up to them after having spent a long time looking at the gunshot-riddled body of the bull. "It was a Provençal fighting bull," he said abruptly. Then he stared indifferently at the corpse and said, "At least he didn't suffer long."

Blanc wasn't sure if these sympathetic words were intended for the bull or the cyclist. He told his two colleagues what he knew about Cohen, if not quite everything.

Albert Cohen had become more and more involved in domestic politics over recent years. At the last presidential election he had outspokenly campaigned for one of the candidates, who had nonetheless gone on to suffer a crushing defeat. Then Cohen had appeared a few times with the minister Jean-Charles Vialaron-Allègre, who belonged to the other party and was popular as a hard-liner in the Ministry of the Interior. He was also unfortunately the politician who had put Blanc's career on hold and exiled him to the Midi.

And now here was a friend of the politician he had to be most careful not to offend lying with his guts spilled out on a rural road in the Camargue. Blanc was worried Vialaron-Allègre would want to get involved in this peculiar death and might end up bringing out all sorts of things. But obviously he couldn't tell that to the other two gendarmes.

"Were there any witnesses?" he asked, not really expecting an answer. To his astonishment, Ronchard nodded.

"The car driver who called us on his cell phone."

"He actually saw the accident?"

The man's face went deep red. "Not directly."

Blanc sighed. "Bring him over anyway, Ronchard."

The gendarme went over to a dented pale red Renault Kangoo

by the edge of the road. It had PATRICK GIREL, ELECTRICIEN, ARLES, on the side door along with a cute illustration that looked a bit like Mario clutching a bundle of lightning bolts. Blanc was reminded of the state of the ruin he lived in and was tempted for a moment to take down the man's telephone number but then thought better of it. Did he really want to entrust the complete rewiring of his home to a lightning-bolt-hurling comic character?

As it happened, the man the gendarme introduced bore only a distant resemblance to his advertising symbol: Patrick Girel was in his early thirties, already bald, and rather chubby. His pants pockets were overflowing with insulated screwdrivers, wrenches, and various metering devices.

"Monsieur Girel, can you tell me what you saw?"

"A bull, where it shouldn't have been: out in the middle of the road. I was on the way back from a job and saw the animal. When I got a bit closer I saw"—he struggled for the right word—"this man here." He waved his right hand vaguely in the direction of the corpse without actually looking at it. His hands were shaking slightly.

Blanc nodded understandingly. "So the cyclist was already lying dead on the road when you arrived."

"He wasn't moving anyway."

"But you didn't see the bull attack him? Not even on the horizon before you got close? Maybe you noticed some movement but didn't realize what was happening? The land around here is flat as a pancake."

"You're not from here, *mon Capitaine*, are you?"

"Did I ask a stupid question?"

Girel gave an embarrassed smile. "*You* said that, not me. The air in the Camargue at midday is so hot that everything shimmers in a haze. I drive out here from Arles almost every day to the ranches and to Saintes-Maries. If I looked at the horizon all the time, I'd have had cancer of the eyeballs years ago. No, it's better just to concentrate on the road immediately ahead. Then you can see things in time, even escaped bulls."

"You say 'escaped.' Are you sure that the animal was always in the field?"

"That bull's been there for over a year. I've driven past it so many times, we could even be on first name terms."

"And the gate was always closed?"

Girel hesitated for a fraction of a second. "Oh yes," he said, sounding, however, as if he wasn't totally happy.

"But?"

"Just in front of that gate is one of the few places on this road where you can turn right. There's usually a drainage ditch, or you run the risk of going into the swamp. But the land in front of that gate is firm."

Blanc looked at the piece of land Girel was talking about: dusty, light-colored earth with tire tracks and a few small-looking imprints. The animal's hooves, he suspected.

"Tourists stop there a lot to take photographs," Girel continued. "Some of them stand there with huge telephoto lenses and take pictures of the flamingos. And a few others"—the electrician shrugged—"take photos of the bull. And occasionally, they can be, *eh bien*, a bit loud and act the clown."

"Clown?"

"They wave their arms, stick their tongues out. On one occasion, one of them even started waving a red beach towel. A *torero* in his swimming trunks. He would have been in trouble if the animal had really gotten mad."

"It wasn't an aggressive animal then?"

"Oh, it was aggressive. Perfectly trained, if you know what I mean. But not stupid, not stupid at all. It knew it couldn't break through the gate. It just stood there staring at the tourists, snorting and pawing the ground with its hooves, as if it knew it just had to pose."

"But if the gate was left open often . . ."

". . . then the bull would have known straightaway." Girel nodded. "If you ask me, this guy was a tourist who'd opened the gate so he could get a photo a bit closer. Then he discovered just how quick a fighting bull can be, tried to run back to his bike, but didn't make it. End of story."

Blanc was thinking that Cohen's body had been ripped open from the front and not from the rear, as would have been the case if he had been running away. And that there was no camera to be seen. And that his mountain bike had spun off into the ditch, which suggested that the bull had attacked him from the front while he was riding it. But then it wasn't the electrician's job to explain what had happened.

"Did you see anything else?"

Girel shook his head and made a dismissive gesture with his hand. "There was a car maybe a hundred yards farther along the road beyond the bull. It was a light color, maybe white or yellow or beige. But I didn't notice anything else. It accelerated and then it was gone."

Immediately Blanc forgot about the heat and the stink of blood and brackish water and the droning of the bluebottles. All of a sudden his head cleared. "The car drove off?" he asked, to be sure. "And it was already beyond the bull? That means it was going in the same direction as you were, which means it had somehow driven past the animal and the corpse?"

Girel hesitated for a moment, then gave an embarrassed smile. "I guess so, *mon Capitaine.* He was going toward Arles. And he was definitely beyond the bull, at least several hundred yards. He was going pretty fast."

"Not even tempted to stop and help," Tonon muttered under

his breath. "Typical for people around here. Not my problem. Somebody's lying there in his own blood on the road, but they prefer to turn around and get out of there rather than report it."

"Did you see the light-colored car turn?" Blanc asked.

Girel shook his head. "I saw the fighting bull, then the dead body. I only glimpsed the car out of the corner of my eye. No more."

"Nothing really," said Tonon.

Blanc held up his right hand to tell him not to be so hasty. Then he felt a sudden pain beneath his arm and slapped his left hand against his side. He had indeed killed a horsefly as big as his thumb, but not before it had bitten him. It had already swollen up red and itched. "When did you call the gendarmerie?" he asked irritably, trying to suppress the urge to scratch himself like a maniac.

Girel looked understandingly at where Blanc had been bitten, then shrugged and said, "In the afternoon, I finished work early . . ."

"The call from Monsieur Girel's cell phone was registered at 3:01," Ronchard interjected punctiliously.

"At least we have something," Blanc stated with some satisfaction. He dismissed Girel and then suddenly stared into the distance. There was a car approaching the scene of the accident from the direction of Arles.

A light-colored car.

For a second Blanc was so nervous that he involuntarily reached for the gun he had, against regulations, tucked into the belt of his pants. Then he relaxed as he recognized the vehicle. The car in question was an ancient, scratched Jeep Cherokee with an eight-cylinder engine that rattled so loudly the *contrôle technique* tester who had let it through the inspection must have been deaf. The 4×4 came to a halt only just before running into the police roadblock. A woman in her midthirties opened the door, her features hidden behind a bizarre forty-year-old pair of sunglasses.

"Nice to see I'm not the only one who has to work through the summer," Blanc called out, walking over to the Jeep. "Welcome to the battlefield, Dr. Thezan."

Fontaine Thezan, *médecin légiste* at the hospital of Salon-de-Provence, kissed him on both cheeks, bathing him for a moment in a cloud of expensive perfume and marijuana. By now Blanc was used to the aroma of drugs that accompanied the pathologist and was actually grateful for it shielding him briefly from the other smells around them. He glanced briefly at the passenger seat where a bored-looking man slouched, his unkempt hair framed by a pair of giant earphones connected to an iPad balanced on his knees. He was wearing a T-shirt with the British flag and was at least ten years younger than Dr. Thezan. He didn't look as if he was her assistant. She made no effort to introduce her companion, just picked up the briefcase with her instruments in it and strolled over to the corpse, pulling on her protective gloves.

Blanc only knew the doctor in her professional capacity and knew nothing about her private life. The way she handled the body was precise and professional; it almost seemed as if she was being particularly careful, almost tender. After a few moments she turned the body on its side, removed the helmet and the ripped remnants of his vest. Cohen's eyes were closed, his lips pressed together. But to Blanc, looking over the doctor's shoulder, there was no wound to the head or bruising evident.

"Serious internal injuries. Massive blood loss," Fontaine Thezan muttered as she got back to her feet.

"Yes, I can see that, too, now that you've spelled it out," Blanc said.

"Watch out that you don't get struck by the heat, or struck by anything else, *mon Capitaine*," the pathologist replied, pulling her gloves off.

She rooted around in her bag and brought out a tube, squeezed out some clear gel, and without asking permission, smeared it on Blanc's lower arm. He smiled gratefully: the gel had cooled the sting of the bite.

"It would appear that his lungs, stomach, and liver were all gored," Dr. Thezan said without further comment. "I'll give you a full report after I've got him laid out on the table. I'll need to have the bull's horns, too." She turned to Ronchard, who was looking more unhappy than ever.

"I'll be interested to see if there are any traces of drugs," she added.

"What makes you think there might be?" Blanc said, taken aback. "Just from touching the body briefly?"

"Because I read *Paris Match*," the pathologist replied with a disarming smile. "It's not just my patient's innards I look at. I recognized Monsieur Cohen immediately, *mon Capitaine*. And two or three weeks ago I read a piece in *Paris Match*, which you obviously didn't, that said he was supposed to have had a minor heart attack. He spent a couple of weeks in a convalescence home somewhere in Brittany. The journalists were less than discreet, however, and mentioned the possibility of cocaine abuse. After he left the clinic he went down south to see his publisher and continue his convalescence."

"It doesn't seem to have worked."

"His publisher won't be unhappy. They're firing more journalists every day in Paris because nobody reads the papers anymore. Here's one more expensive celebrity he won't have to fire."

"Sounds almost like a good motive for murder," Blanc replied, only half jokingly.

With the pathologist finished, Blanc pulled on a pair of gloves himself and carefully examined the corpse. No documents, no money. In the left pocket of his cycling shorts Blanc found a half-used salve for reducing the pain of horsefly bites. That's not stupid, he thought to himself, clearly not the first time Cohen had been cycling in the Camargue. He could see the familiar shape of a cell phone in the other pocket and pulled out an iPhone: the latest model, no headphones. Maybe Girel had been right: Cohen had stopped, opened the gate, and gone to take a few photos. Miraculously the phone had survived the bull's attack without even a scratch. It was locked with a code, so Blanc couldn't check if Cohen had taken a few photos before his death. He would leave that to his colleague Fabienne Souillard, who was an expert at hacking cell phones. He would be interested to see if there were any photos of a raging bull.

Apart from that there was nothing else on the dead man's body, not even a key. The mountain bike had a full bottle of water and a compact air pump attached to the frame. It all gave the impression that Cohen had just been intending to take a short exercise ride through the Camargue. But he couldn't get Girel's story about the car vanishing in the distance out of his head.

Half an hour later, as the pathologist was stowing her bag on the rear seat of the old Jeep and beginning to fill out a form with her initial observations, a BMW 3 Series came roaring up and almost crashed into the off-roader. The sedan was a shimmering metallic silver with dark glass in the side windows. The driver didn't even bother to turn off the engine before he opened the door and burst out of the vehicle. He was a lean guy of average height, between forty and fifty years old, the sort, Blanc immediately thought, who acted calmly most of the time but could explode in a ferocious rage when provoked. Like right now. He had a thin cigarette, stinking of cheap tobacco, in his shaking left hand. He was wearing jeans and a long-sleeved black shirt decorated with embroidery down to the waistband.

"Aurélien Ferréol," Ronchard whispered. "The bull breeder. We called him."

The man strode over to the bull and stood there a long time staring at the corpse. Then he hurried over to Blanc, without so much as glancing at the dead cyclist.

"Tassou was four years old!" he shouted. "It cost me a fortune to get a bull to that age. He's been fighting for two years and has already been named *meilleur taureau* three times, the best bull in the show. He was already fit for the arena this autumn. Next month is the *course camarguaise* in Pélissanne, the posters have already been printed, *merde*. And now you people come and just shoot him dead! *Connards!* I'll see you in court."

"Then we might be standing in front of the judge together, Monsieur Ferréol," Blanc replied calmly. "Because this animal was your responsibility." He spoke politely, but at the same time he eyed the bull breeder coolly.

Ferréol took a step backward, stared at Blanc, and for the first time looked at the dead man, then back again at Blanc. Clearly a man who lost his confidence if someone responded calmly to his outburst.

"The gate meets all the regulations," he replied defensively.

"The gate was open."

"Then you damn well need to find out who opened it!"

"That's what I intend to do," Blanc promised. "Where were you during the last hour, Monsieur Ferréol?"

The breeder went silent, taken aback. Then he shouted furiously, "You're actually accusing me?"

"Just answer my question, please."

"*Putain*, I was at an official meeting of the Club Taurin,"

Ferréol said, pointing at his embroidered shirt with the motif of a club on the left breast. “Don’t you see this? I’m vice president.”

Blanc shook his head. He’d never seen an item of clothing like it.

“It’s the club for *raseteurs*, plus the breeders and all bullfighting aficionados,” Tonon interjected. “They organize the annual bullfighting program. The shirt is a sort of uniform.”

“We had a meeting in Alleins,” Ferréol continued. “Began this morning.”

Blanc nodded to Tonon, the gesture meaning he should check it out later.

“When were you last here?”

Ferréol shrugged. “I don’t have to be here all the time. The bull can take care of itself.” Then he thought for a moment. “Two days ago. And I didn’t go into the field but stayed out here.”

Blanc closed his eyes. There was no obvious reason to think the breeder was lying. And if what he said could be checked, which wasn’t exactly hard, then he had a concrete alibi. “Have there been any threats?”

Ferréol looked as if he’d like to punch Blanc in the face. “Against me? I have no enemies, but I do have a lot of friends around here,” he snarled.

“No blackmail? Send me five thousand euros or I’ll set the bull loose? Something like that. Or maybe,” Blanc recalled a case he had dealt with in Paris six months earlier, “maybe from militant animal-rights activists? There are people who aren’t so fond of bullfights.”

“Those green crazies let chickens out of cages, but even they aren’t stupid enough to tackle a bull. And in any case most *manades* wander freely around the Camargue.”

“*Manades?*” Blanc said questioningly.

“The herds of cattle. The black cattle of the Camargue are

the last real wild animals in Europe. They don't need some farmer herding them into a stall and massaging their udders. At the most they need a *gardian* to keep them in a herd. Otherwise they just wander through the marshes and heathland as free as God made them. The cows even calve out in the open."

"But this bull was in an enclosed meadow."

"I was training him for the fight. And I didn't want anything to happen to him so close to the start of the season, *merde*!"

"Where do you live?" Blanc asked. "Just in case we have more questions."

"And so you know where to send the check. I'll be charging you for the loss of the bull." Ferréol pulled a slim silver box from the pocket of his embroidered shirt and handed Blanc a business card. It was made of heavyweight cardboard with two bulls as a sort of insignia above his name and an address in Saint-Gilles.

"Probably best not to invite the breeder to the ox roast," Tonon said as Ferréol roared off in his BMW.

Blanc took a last walk around the whole scene of the accident. In front of the gate he got down on his haunches and ran his fingers through the sandy soil. He could smell earth, salt, and cattle. Most of the marks in the earth were weather-beaten, but at the edge of the piece of ground were two broad lines. "Somebody was in a hurry to get out of here," he muttered. "Those were made by spinning tires."

"Watch out you don't start going round in circles yourself," Tonon replied. "This sun isn't good for any of us."

Blanc ignored the comment and knelt down to examine the tire marks more closely. The tracks were blurred at the edges. There was no way of identifying the tires' profile, which meant they had no means of identifying the car that had sped away from the scene.

The driver took off so fast he skidded, Blanc surmised.

"We should take off just as fast to get back to Gadet, I'm dying of thirst," Tonon said.

Still down on his knees, Blanc suddenly glanced up at the open gate. A tiny silvery flicker had caught the corner of his eye. He took a closer look. A sparkle, a reflection of the sunshine, like a splinter of glass lying in the dust.

But there was no glass to be seen.

A Mas *in the Camargue*

"You're going to have to be thirsty a bit longer," Blanc muttered, getting to his feet. "There's something in the dirt down here."

"*Putain*," Tonon exclaimed.

Blanc hurried over to the open gate and just beneath the bottom edge, lying in the dust, he found a strip of black leather about the length of his finger. One end was frayed, but on the other was a metal prong, a prong that had reflected the sunlight.

"Looks like part of a buckle," said Ronchard, who had come a bit closer out of curiosity.

"A watch buckle," Blanc suggested.

"Or part of a handbag. My daughter has handbags that are nothing but straps and buckles."

"Does she carry them with her out walking in the Camargue?"

Ronchard didn't reply.

Blanc smiled. "A watch strap," he repeated to himself. There had been a time in his life when he had found the energy and enthusiasm for a hobby; the children were no longer that small but not grown up yet, his marriage was so sound that he thought only death would part them, and the apartment in Paris was paid for. That was the stage when in his few moments of spare time he began to get interested in mechanical things. He had found himself fascinated with the art of putting together the most complicated devices with little more than feathers and cog wheels, so that they would work without batteries or chargers or thousands of cables. He had used the money earned in doing overtime at night to buy an old Leicaflex SL and take black-and-white photos of the Eiffel Tower. A colleague on the forensics team had given him his private photo lab equipment and he had developed the prints himself. A divorced colleague, with older children.

He should have taken it as a warning. The old camera and the laboratory equipment had to be somewhere in the heap of junk he had piled into the car and driven south with after splitting up with Geneviève.

Blanc had also gone around to the secondhand markets looking at old watches: Heuer, Rolex, Jaeger-LeCoultre. He had become as familiar with the names of the Swiss manufacturers as other men were with the names of bars. He had bought collectors' magazines and even a book or two. But he had never bought one of the watches. What would his colleagues have said if one day a corruption investigator had turned up in the office with an Omega Speedmaster on his wrist?

Even though his knowledge of chronometers was only theoretical, he was still certain that the fragment he had found in the dust was part of a wristwatch band. Blanc nodded toward the gate. "Somebody lifts up the iron lever on the gate, someone who knows how dangerous a fighting bull is. He's acting quickly, nervously, in a rush. He tears the band of his watch on the lever, gets the watch free but leaves part of the buckle on the gate because he doesn't have the time to worry about it. The bull is getting closer, and Cohen is coming down the road. Our unknown suspect leaps into his car and with tires spinning roars off. A second later the animal storms out of the field and catches the surprised cyclist on his horns. A few minutes later Girel the electrician comes along. He sees a dead body, a bull, and a light-colored car on the horizon. It could have happened exactly like that, it all fits. The question is: Did our unknown suspect free the bull just for the hell of it and it was purely a tragic accident that the animal took out Cohen? Or was someone deliberately out to get the journalist and had waited until he was coming? Was it a terrible accident? Or was it a treacherous murder?"

"It was bullshit," Tonon said grumpily, sweat shining on his forehead and his hands shaking slightly. "It may well be that some *connard* opened the gate deliberately. But that on its own does not turn this bloodbath into a murder. It was a stupid accident, one way or another. Open-and-shut case. Done and dusted."

Ronchard looked as if he was about to agree with Tonon, but then realized that Blanc was the ranking officer and so said nothing. Blanc looked over at Fontaine Thezan, who had long since finished filling in her forms but had sat there in the driver's seat listening to their conversation. The sunshine reflected on her extravagant sunglasses meant Blanc couldn't make out the expression on her face. "What do you think, Madame?" he asked her.

"I think I've never heard such a far-fetched theory as yours, *mon Capitaine*. Definitely worth following up."

Blanc didn't know the pathologist well enough to work out if she was encouraging or mocking him. "Nice to see we always think alike," he replied sourly.

All of a sudden he was tired and felt the heat of the sunburn on his shoulders. He had the feeling he was going to have to deal with everything on his own. "Ronchard," he called out, "secure the area until the hearse arrives."

"And the cattle truck," Tonon added.

"We're going back to Gadet."

Tonon's features visibly relaxed. He pulled his ancient cell phone out of his pants pocket. "I'll book us a table at Le Soleil, the table under the plane trees."

"You can book me a place on Commandant Nkoulou's waiting list. I want to talk to him about this case."

"This isn't a case, *merde*!"

An hour later Blanc was standing in front of Nkoulou's desk. The sun looked as if it had been glued fast to the same spot in the sky, as if even it was too exhausted to move. The commandant had a white Dyson Ventilator standing on the floor, looking like a giant tuning fork. He was the only policeman Blanc knew who would spend his own salary on designer equipment for the office. He laid out all the facts for his boss and told him his own theory.

Nkoulou stayed silent for a while. Eventually he said in a cool voice, "Given everything we have at the moment, we have to assume it was an accident."

"Whatever the case, a third party is to blame. Somebody opened the gate."

"Even that is just a theory at present."

"It would be absurd if it happened by chance. A fighting bull has been in that field for at least a year. The breeder Ferréol was there two days earlier. If there had been anything wrong with the fencing, he would have noticed and done something about it, if only out of self-interest. The animal was a gold mine on four legs. Ferréol would have had the gate fixed immediately. Two days before it was in perfect condition, then today it's open. And precisely at the moment when a celebrity Parisian journalist is passing on his bike. That would have been a pretty unusual coincidence."

"So in your opinion somebody had planned to murder Cohen? A murder attempt where the accomplice is an unpredictable fighting bull, carried out in broad daylight, in the middle of a flat landscape where you can see for miles in any direction? Excuse me, *mon Capitaine*, but that doesn't sound any less absurd than the idea of a chance accident."

"The haze in the air reduces visibility. And the animal was not unpredictable. I have a witness who says this animal was aggressive and perfectly trained to be so."

"Your witness is an electrician, not a veterinary surgeon."

"That just goes to show that everybody who knows what's what in the Camargue knows how dangerous the bulls are."

Nkoulou closed his eyes. "Here in Gadet we are one of eight brigades in the region. Three thousand five hundred square miles, one hundred and twenty thousand people, and just one hundred and seventy-four gendarmes. Half of whom are on vacation."

"There's not exactly a civil war going on."

His boss opened his eyes and gave Blanc a look of curiosity. "Do you really want to go around to every *cabane* in this great swamp and ask people for their alibis? Do you seriously want to go around asking everybody, anybody, if they let a fighting bull free so it would gore one particular cyclist? If a journalist were to find out that we were spending our time . . ."

"I haven't got much to do otherwise. Let me just spend a few days going around the Camargue. I'll be discreet. Look at it as a sort of training exercise until the criminals are back from their summer vacations and you can set me on another case."

"This isn't a vacation camp."

"What else am I supposed to do?"

Nkoulou stared at him. Blanc knew that his ambitious boss didn't appreciate him: Blanc was the officer whose dubious reputation could damage Nkoulou's immaculate career. He could guess what was going on behind that wrinkle-free forehead: If he set Blanc out to investigate the death of a celebrity, he could cause trouble. On the other hand if Blanc were to spend days, maybe even weeks, looking into this obscure death, he wouldn't be able to get involved in other possibly more sensitive cases.

"Get on to it," Nkoulou said in the end. "But don't crop up on anybody's radar. I will tell the press that we are looking into the circumstances surrounding this tragic death. That way everyone will think it was an accident, even if I don't expressly say so. But if you don't keep quiet and somebody produces the headline 'Bull Murder of Parisian Celebrity,' I'll have a horde of hysterical national journalists descend on me. And hysterical animal-rights activists. And hysterical mayors worried that bullfights in their towns will be banned. And eventually a hysterical minister asking what the hell we've been thinking."

"It could get busy here at the gendarmerie."

"I would put the hysterical horde in your office. You wouldn't be needing it."

When Blanc returned to his office, the seat opposite was empty. Tonon's computer was in sleep mode. He shrugged and was about to get down to work when the door opened and a fit young woman came in: Second Lieutenant Fabienne Souillard. She had her long brown hair up to keep her neck bare in the heat and was wearing jeans and a flame-red T-shirt with DUCATI printed on it—the make of her motorbike, Blanc recalled, kissing her on both cheeks.

"You didn't offer Marius an alcohol-free beer, did you?" she joked. "He charged out of here like a raging bull."

"You've heard, then?"

"A black-horned monster as an instrument of murder. Only a Paris cop could come up with such an oblique idea."

"A former Paris cop. How did you find out?"

"I hacked into Nkoulou's Mac," Fabienne replied flippantly. She was the best computer expert they had and for a moment

Blanc was tempted to believe her. "Marius was swearing so loudly, they must have heard the whole story in Salon," she eventually explained.

"His version of the story."

"What's yours?"

Blanc liked his colleague. Fabienne lived with her girlfriend in *PACS*, a civil partnership. She didn't make a big deal of it and woe betide the cop who made some stupid joke about it. She rode her motorbike like a lunatic and could rattle away on a computer keyboard so fast it made Blanc dizzy just watching her. She knew all about fashion and music and films, and raved about drinks Blanc had never even heard of, be they alcoholic or obscure Asian teas. She was everything he should have been as a young cop, except for his obsession with spending even weekend evenings getting his teeth into corrupt politicians. He pushed Tonon's chair back and asked her to sit down. "I have to admit my theory sounds insane," he began, "but I need somebody to help me anyway."

"Good thing you have me, *mon Capitaine*," she replied.

After Blanc had told her all he knew, Fabienne took up Tonon's telephone and rang the Paris police to get Cohen's address and details of his next of kin. Meanwhile Blanc looked up on the Internet the number for the publisher of *L'Événement* and got put through to editorial. Nobody there was remotely aware of the journalist's death. Blanc got through to a man who introduced himself as Pierre DuPont. He sounded young and exhausted. Maybe the heat wave had struck the capital, too, Blanc thought to himself. For the tiniest of moments he didn't regret having been transferred. He gave his name but not his rank. As soon as he made it clear to a journalist that he was a cop, they would record the conversation. "I would like to speak to Monsieur Albert Cohen's supervisor," he said.

"AC doesn't have a supervisor."

"AC?" Blanc took a moment to understand. DuPont had pronounced the initials as "*assez*," meaning "enough already."

"Then put me through to whoever cooperated closely with Monsieur Cohen," Blanc said.

"The last colleague he flirted with left a year ago DuPont laughed with the tired resignation of someone who's known forever that nobody laughed with him. Blanc felt as if he was in a Samuel Beckett play.

"Somebody must have had something to do with him."

"I'll put you through to Jean-Claude Novoly. He takes care of the features pages when the editor in chief is on vacation."

The next voice Blanc heard sounded as if it had been through a hundred thousand Gitanes. "If you want to get AC interested in a story idea, I suggest you ring back in two months' time. He should be back from his research trip by then."

"He isn't going to be coming back." It was then that Blanc mentioned his rank and immediately thought he could hear a click on the line. He told Novoly about the accident but made no mention of the suspicion that somebody might have been involved in it. Nkoulou would have been happy with his cautious wording.

"*Merde*. Most reporters want to die with their boots on, but I doubt Albert would have imagined something like that." Novoly sounded reproachful, as if his colleague had made a mess of a story. He asked for a few more details, more about the bull than Cohen. "For the obituary," he explained. He didn't seem for a moment to imagine that it might have been anything but an accident.

"What was Monsieur Cohen doing in Provence?" Blanc asked finally.

"You seem very interested for a cop dealing with an accident."

"I just need to know if there's anybody here down south I need to inform."

"Our boss. I expect you'll have to go and see him. I'll call him in advance to warn him. Cohen was staying with Ernest Leroux."

"The publisher?"

"And editor in chief of this magazine. Or what remains of it after all the firings. In any case AC went to see him after . . ." Novoly hesitated briefly, "getting over a few health problems. Leroux had even given his old pal a nice story to do during his convalescence: 'On the Trail of Vincent van Gogh in Provence.' To accompany the big exhibition opening down there in the fall."

"What sort of thing was it supposed to be?"

Novoly laughed. "Pretty pictures of Provence alongside pretty paintings by the old ear mutilator, and accompanied by pretty words by AC and pretty quotes from anyone who doesn't run away the minute he switches his recorder on. Basically a convalescent vacation."

"And for that Leroux invited him to spend the summer in his vacation home in the Camargue?"

"Some journalists are luckier than others."

"Do you happen to have the address?"

"Give me your email address and I'll send you details of how to get there. You'll never find it otherwise."

Fabienne pushed a piece of paper across the desk to him when he put the phone down. "The address of Cohen's apartment," she explained.

Blanc whistled in recognition as he read the address. "Fifth arrondissement, Latin Quarter."

"That's going to make some real estate agent's day; the place will be available now. Cohen lived alone. No brothers or sisters, parents dead long ago, no close relations to the best of my knowledge."

"No wife?"

"There was one fourteen years ago. But she remarried long ago and now lives in Montreal."

"Is there a last will and testament?"

"Our colleagues in Paris are looking into that. No news so far."

"So no greedy nephew who might have let a bull out to get his hands on a smart apartment in Paris."

"And a few hundred thousand euros. Maybe more. Monsieur Cohen wasn't exactly poor, at least according to a friendly official on the other end of the line who did a bit of digging around on his computer."

"Which is completely against the rules. You flirted with him."

"Do you think that just because I prefer women it means I can't get my way with a man?"

Blanc closed his eyes and began thinking aloud. "Cohen is wealthy and successful. A few too many snorts of cocaine and he has a heart attack and ends up recovering in a discreet sanatorium. It changes his life and for the first time in ages he decides to do a real piece of reportage."

"Under luxurious conditions at a time when his colleagues are being fired."

"He was 'On the Trail of Vincent van Gogh,' whatever that's supposed to mean. Doesn't exactly sound like a story that gets you killed."

"No obvious scandal."

"No obvious motive for murder."

"Are you sure Marius isn't right?"

Blanc muttered something incomprehensible and opened a version of Outlook that anywhere else would have been displayed in a software museum. "I've got an e-mail from Paris with details on how to find a Camargue address. I'm sure Monsieur Leroux won't mind me paying him a visit."

"Should I give you a lift on my Ducati? We'll get there quicker."

"My brain hasn't been completely frazzled. We'll take the patrol car."

Fabienne just laughed and blew a farewell kiss to her helmet lying on a shelf on the coatrack.

They took a Mégane again. No air-conditioning. Blanc rolled down the windows and drove faster than the speed limit to get more air inside. There was so little going on that even the normal to-and-fro radio traffic had died off. In the quiet he picked up the melody that Fabienne was humming as she sat in the passenger seat with her eyes closed. Of course he didn't know the song. As he drove through the Camargue for the second time that day, the sky in the west was pale pink. It wouldn't be long before the sun would finally touch the horizon. The last breezes were dying down, and in the sunlight there was no sign of any motion on the lakes or among the plants. Blanc felt as if he were driving through one immense painting. By Van Gogh. He wondered if that was why Cohen had been cycling through this marshy plain, for inspiration?

Even though he had directions and was using his cell phone as a GPS, they twice missed the driveway to Leroux's place. Only on the third attempt did Blanc turn the patrol car off the road and onto a sandy dike that ran like a wall through a green ocean of what looked like thick, medium-sized clumps of grass.

"Rice," Fabienne told him lazily. "Tough stuff."

They trundled just over half a mile down the track, leaving a yellow dust cloud behind them, hanging in the leaden air like a fine mist with nervous mosquitoes dancing around it. Eventually the dike widened out into a sort of raised plateau surrounded by thick hedges nearly ten feet high. They drove through the only gap in the thicket and suddenly found themselves in front of a white-plastered one-story house with a straw roof. Blanc had no idea whether it was ancient and well restored or a new building designed to look that way. The ground around it was strewn with gray gravel and bloodred bougainvillea grew from pots hanging from an iron frame. To the left side of the house they could see a large curved pool, the other half hidden behind the house. In front of the entrance, which consisted of tailor-made weathered beams, stood an imposing white Volvo XC70 and a Toyota Auris Hybrid in the same color. Blanc thought of the light-colored car that Girel had seen rushing off.

He parked the Mégane next to the pair of polished modern vehicles. In comparison it looked like an aged peasant who had sat down unasked next to two supermodels at a table in a Paris bistro. Even as Blanc was unfolding his large frame from the driver's seat, the house door opened and a couple emerged on the threshold, the man with his arm around the woman.

Blanc and Fabienne walked across the gravel toward the house. Blanc recognized Ernest Leroux from his regular appearances on television. He was in his midfifties, with sparse gray hair, short and tubby and so bent over you might have thought he had a hunchback. But his dark brown eyes sparkled like those of a puma on the hunt. And when he spoke into a microphone, his smoky voice was more gripping than most Hollywood movies, even when he was simply answering a question about the absurdities of the French taxation system. He was wearing a bright pink polo shirt, white linen pants, and sailing shoes. Gold-frame reading glasses dangled from a little chain around his neck and on his left wrist a steel Rolex glistened in the sun, as did the wedding ring on his finger.

The woman on his arm had been gifted with the natural beauty denied her husband. Blanc assumed it was Marie-Claude Leroux, the publisher's wife, even though he couldn't remember having seen her in magazines or on television. She was about the same age as Leroux and was one of those women who look elegant enough to go to the opera dressed only in a T-shirt, jeans, and sandals and without any makeup. She had the body of someone who did yoga or swam regularly, or at any rate had found the balance needed to stay slim without looking haggard, supple but not muscle-bound. Her long glistening gray hair was tied back in a ponytail, and countless hours in the sun had given her skin a brown glow that made it shine like oil-polished wood.

For a minute she made Blanc think of Geneviève. He had never stood arm in arm with her outside their country house, because they had never had a country house. He cursed himself as an idiot and had to repress the impulse to be overwhelmed by this idyll. But there was something wrong with this picture. Rather than looking at Blanc and Fabienne Souillard, the woman's gaze was directed far away at some point in the sky. There was an attitude of rare sadness about her. She wore no jewelry, not even a wedding ring. On her left wrist was a strip of untanned skin. It gave the impression of being a bangle or a strap. Then Blanc spotted an old scar on her wrist, an incision at an angle across her artery. She put her arm around her husband's waist, hiding it from his sight.

"One of the editorial staff already called me," Leroux said. "Thank you for coming."

Blanc introduced Fabienne and himself. His colleague shook hands with Madame Leroux longer than was necessary. As their host led them around the house past the swimming pool, Blanc bent down and whispered in her ear, "It's unprofessional to flirt during an interview."

"My job is sacred and my relationship is tried and tested. But I admire beauty wherever I find it."

"You've never shaken my hand for that length of time."

"Exactly."

They reached the back of the house. Between it and the pool was a terrace of yellowish sandstone tiles shaded by an awning that was suspended by wires between the main building and an old pool house made of wooden beams. Leroux pulled up wicker chairs and fetched a tray with a jug of iced tea and chilled glasses from the pool house. As he poured for them, Blanc noted that his hand was shaking.

"I've known Albert more than thirty years," the publisher said, then corrected himself. "I had known him. We did the same philosophy course at the École Pratique des Hautes Études, Roland Barthes, Régis Debray. The usual suspects. I published a student magazine. Either revolutionary, critical, or deconstructionist articles that were always hard to understand, bashed out at night on an old manual typewriter until my fingers were sore. Accompanied by a bottle of cheap red wine, with Gauloises for breakfast. My magazine was comprised of hectograph copies on yellow paper, the sort you wouldn't even use to wipe your backside. Headlines in capital letters in a homemade font, copied graphics: hammer and sickle, red stars, Lenin, Marx, and Ché. Then we trailed around from café to café, trying to sell them. Nobody would buy them except for old ladies who took pity on us. And gay middle-aged professors. Does that ring a bell with you, were you also students?"

"Law," Blanc replied.

"IT," said Fabienne.

"Ah, in that case, it obviously wouldn't ring any bells at all," Leroux replied with a sympathetic click of his tongue. "Anyway, that's how I got to know Cohen: He began turning out pieces for us. He was the only one who could actually write. He was so good and so fast—and his typing was almost perfect—that before long he was filling half the magazine. The others felt insulted and gradually left so that there was basically only him and me. The magazine folded, but we never lost sight of each other."

"He was your employee."

Leroux cleared his throat. "I didn't inherit much from my parents except for ambition. I founded *L'Événement* at a time when it wasn't considered completely mad to rely on the printed word. For a long time it was a worthwhile investment, not just politically but economically, too."

"Cohen, on the other hand, inherited a lot from his parents," Fabienne interjected. She had clearly done her research on the Internet.

Leroux nodded. "A family of industrialists. Neuilly. Only child. Private school. He could have made a career in politics or in big business, which is more or less the same thing. But Albert was always on the left, and incorruptible, even if that wasn't exactly fashionable and earned him a lot of jokes at his expense. And he always wanted to be a reporter, a storyteller. He didn't just have the family silver, he also had talent and a certain hunger, if you know what I mean."

"Yes," Blanc said laconically. Hunger for the truth. Hunger for the whole story. Both had led his own career to a spectacular demise. It was possible that they had led Cohen to an even worse fate. "Your friend was working on a story about Van Gogh?"

"It was my idea," Marie-Claude Leroux intervened. She spoke gently and carefully, as if weighing up every word. Like a suspect under interrogation, Blanc found himself thinking, being careful over every untruth.

"He had had a mild heart attack," her husband resumed. "And a few other health problems. Nothing serious. After a few weeks in a rehabilitation clinic, he wanted to dive straight back into work. And he wanted to avoid some of his past mistakes. Stop smoking. Play more sports."

"He borrowed one of our mountain bikes and from the very first day became obsessed with riding around the Camargue," Madame Leroux finished for him.

"The same circuit every day?" Blanc pushed.

"I imagine so," Leroux said. "I went with him toward the end of the first week of the vacation. But Albert was far too fast for me. He always put one hundred and fifty percent into everything. So I didn't bother to do it again, but I imagine he always did the same circuit."

Blanc and Fabienne exchanged glances. "You invited Monsieur Cohen to stay with you?" Blanc's young colleague asked.

"Yes, part job, part rest. It was Marie-Claude's idea actually."

"I used to work in a little museum on the Côte d'Azur," she explained. "My first job after university."

"She's an art historian," her husband interjected, with what sounded to Blanc like an almost proprietorial tone.

"A little Van Gogh was our pride and joy. Maybe that's why I've always felt a special affinity for his paintings, though as a student he hadn't particularly interested me." She fell silent for a few moments, lost in her thoughts. "In any case, I suddenly remembered the upcoming exhibition in Arles. The Fondation Vincent van Gogh is getting paintings on loan from museums around the world. It will be the greatest-ever exhibition of the master in the South of France. I convinced my husband that we should have a special story dedicated to it. We live, after all, in Van Gogh Land. The painter lived in Arles, he visited Saintes-Maries-de-la-Mer, spent long months recovering in Saint-Rémy-de-Provence, after his crisis."

"After he cut his ear off," Blanc interjected.

She made a face. "That's about the only thing most people know about the painter," she complained.

"Cohen was just out of the clinic. He wanted to get back to doing reportage, not just opinion pieces and commentaries. On the other hand, he still wasn't at his best healthwise, a bit rusty, I should say, maybe. We could hardly send him off to Syria straightaway, could we? We suggested he come down here for the summer and write about Van Gogh. Whatever, we more or less gave him a free hand. Let's call it an extended rehabilitation therapy with the happy side effect that it would make a good cover story. Who could have imagined that the Camargue would be more dangerous than the Middle East?"

"Did you get your cover story?" Blanc asked.

"Not one single line. At least I haven't seen anything. Albert still had enough time."

"He didn't show you a draft? Didn't give you an idea, a structure, no chat about his research around the pool in the evening?"

"Albert was superstitious, like all good reporters. He only handed in his copy when it was perfect down to the last comma."

"So what was he up to when he wasn't racing around on his bike? Did he lock himself in the guest room and write?"

"He took one of our cars and drove around, going to see the places where the master painted. The beach at Saintes-Maries, even though there are no fishing boats fading in the sunlight there anymore, just German RVs. The yellow café in Arles, the old monastery in Saint-Rémy, cypress trees. The starry sky above the Rhône. The famous drawbridge in Arles."

"He was curious about everything, as enthusiastic as a child," murmured Madame Leroux. "He even got interested in the rice that grows in the Camargue."

Leroux turned his eyes away. "My wife's great passion. Now you're in for it. Nobody gets away from here without a lecture on rice production."

Blanc looked at him with incomprehension.

"Haven't you noticed? We're drowning in rice."

"Those are your fields?" Blanc asked skeptically.

His hostess gave her husband a brief reproachful blink, then nodded. "We harvest in September. This isn't just a summer-house, *mon Capitaine*. This is a farm. One of the two hundred *riziculteurs* in the Camargue. This is the biggest rice-growing area in France. Some of the farmers here harvest around three tons per acre. We manage about half that."

"And it's all organic," her husband added.

"No insecticides, no artificial fertilizers." Marie-Claude Leroux had indeed suddenly come to life. Her eyes beamed, her gestures became more lively; she seemed almost to have forgotten that she was talking to two gendarmes, as well as the reason they were there. From her jeans pocket she pulled out a crumpled pack of menthol cigarettes, fished a lighter out of the other pocket, lit a cigarette, inhaled greedily, and blew a cloud of perfumed smoke into the air.

"Without the rice, the Camargue would have been a salt-water wasteland ages ago," she explained, smoke still coming from her mouth. "The rice more or less keeps this marshland between the Rhône and the Mediterranean together. The plants regulate the water table and the quality of the water. Without rice, there'd be no flamingos, no white horses, no endless landscape."

"No fighting bulls," Blanc added. Fabienne gave him an inconspicuous kick to the shin.

"The rice keeps everything together," Madame Leroux continued as if she hadn't heard. "We grow red rice, typical of the

Camargue, a particular mutation. We dry it on frames exposed to the sun and the mistral."

"Marie-Claude insists you can taste the sun and the mistral."

"The rice is as much a part of Provence as wine and olives. A lot of people have no respect for that. Did you know that oil pipelines run through the Camargue? From the tanker harbors in Fos and the big refineries to the north. In the summer of 2009, one of the pipelines split open, spilling the shit out into the Camargue. Do you know how long it's going to take them to pump the oil out of the soil? Half a century."

"I played up the story quite a bit in *L'Événement* for her sake. It didn't exactly win me any friends in the Department of Commerce. Nor in the Department of Tourism," Leroux added.

Blanc pricked up his ears. "Was it Cohen who wrote the story about the pipeline?"

Leroux laughed. "That was at the time when he was writing nothing but commentary and fighting his way onto every talk show. He didn't mention a word about it. That would have meant him having to do research. It was only after his convalescence that he got a thirst for such things again. He missed out on the oil scandal completely because all he was interested in then was sounding off. Having to make the effort to do research into facts would only have been a nuisance."

Blanc leaned back. It would have been too easy: an environmental scandal, an incorruptible journalist, and unscrupulous, powerful opponents. "Do you know if Cohen had been researching any other scandal? Maybe as a new project? After he had exercised his fingers knocking out the piece on Van Gogh?"

Leroux shrugged. "It's possible. Like I said, he preferred not to talk about unfinished stories."

"Do you think his death might not have been an accident?" Marie-Claude Leroux asked.

Clever Madame, Blanc thought. She's caught on faster than her husband. Then he remembered Nkoulou's warning. "At the moment it looks as if it was an accident," he reassured her with a statement that was not one hundred percent true. "We just have to exclude all other possibilities. Might we take a look at the room where Monsieur Cohen was staying?"

Leroux, only now understanding, hesitated for a second and then raised his hands. "I'm sure you're only doing your job." He led them along a corridor to a room on the far side of the house from the pool. A small, clean room with a single bed, desk, cupboard, and chair, all apparently handmade. It looked a bit like a monastic cell.

Blanc took a look around. "Did Cohen take anything with him?" he asked, opening the cupboard with practiced movements. On clothes hangers inside were the famed jackets and shirts he recognized from television, as well as a few pairs of pants and shoes. The usual. No notebooks. No medicines. No drugs.

Leroux gave his wife a searching look. "I took the Volvo down to Port-Saint-Louis-du-Rhône before Albert left. That's where my yacht is. I'd bought a new GPS and wanted to install it. I only got back here just before the call from Paris. You were here."

His wife looked down at the floor in embarrassment. "I didn't notice anything. I don't even know what time Albert left the house," she admitted.

Maybe Monsieur Leroux had an alibi then, but his wife didn't, Blanc thought, making a mental note to check out the story about the yacht and the harbor. Fabienne pulled open a rickety drawer under the desk. In it was a MacBook. She picked up the computer as if it was the most natural thing in the world, making it quite clear that she intended to take it away with her. That was not allowed because there was no obvious suspicion and certainly no search warrant, but she did it so confidently that Leroux, who had come to himself again, just took a deep breath but said nothing. Clever girl.

"Monsieur Cohen must have had a cell phone?" Fabienne asked, having finished her search of the room.

Leroux gave her a look of surprise. "Of course, an iPhone, belonging to the magazine. He always had it on him. Wasn't it found at the scene of the accident?"

Blanc all of a sudden decided it was better to say nothing and squeezed out of the room.

When they were all back at the pool again, a new VW Polo roared into the courtyard, braking so fast it sent up a spray of gravel.

"My daughter, Nora," Leroux said with a sigh.

Yet another white car driven fast, Blanc noted.

Nora Leroux jumped out of the little car without even bothering to close the driver's door. She was so young that she could only have just gotten her driver's license. She was wearing provocatively tiny shorts and a Hollister T-shirt. She was swinging a packed Longchamp handbag and had a big Ice-Watch with cracked glass on her wrist. Her body was as slim as her mother's, and she had a pair of metallic orange sunglasses pushed back and glittering on her long blond hair. Her eyes were brown and attentive, just like her father's.

"Have the cops finally found your stash of coke, Dad?" she called out, jerking a thumb toward the patrol car. She kissed her father on both cheeks, ignored her mother, glanced at Blanc and Fabienne for a brief second but didn't bother to introduce herself. The boss's daughter, Blanc told himself. Glad I don't work at *L'Événement*.

"Nora is in her last year at the Lycée Henri-IV and will

probably be the first student there not to pass her *baccalauréat*," the publisher said, as if that would explain her behavior. He seemed to find it amusing.

Blanc, who had two children about the same age, would never have been so relaxed talking about his children doing badly at school. Quite the opposite: in fact, he hardly ever spoke about them at all, and even less with them. The only way he really got news about Eric and Astrid was via Facebook, and that was only because people he didn't even know posted stuff he didn't really understand.

"Did you know Monsieur Cohen, Mademoiselle?"

"That's enough, *mon Capitaine*," Marie-Claude Leroux called out, and placed herself between him and her daughter.

"Sorry, a professional reflex," Blanc reassured her. "I ask questions like that all the time, without thinking." A straightforward lie, because he was thinking again about the light-colored car. But he wasn't going to get any further here, at least not now.

Nora had listened to this exchange with a look of astonishment, all of a sudden transformed back into a scared and clueless teenager. Then she pulled the sunglasses down over her eyes and walked past them into the house.

Her mother followed her. Leroux watched after the two women until they had closed the door behind them. Then he accompanied the gendarmes to the patrol car. "Your question was rather impertinent, *mon Capitaine*," he commented, opening the passenger door gallantly for Fabienne. "What could my daughter have had to do with it? I know you're only doing your duty, but do it as discreetly as possible. My wife is very sensitive. And my daughter is at a difficult age. Sometimes, even over breakfast, I have to watch my words as carefully as if I were at a conference in the Middle East. And now Albert, an old friend of the family, is dead. I really don't need any more fuss on the domestic scene. Plus, I have friends in Paris, unlike yourself."

Blanc, who had been squeezing himself behind the steering wheel, stopped moving immediately and said, "What makes you assume I have no friends there?"

"I don't have to assume anything, I know it. You have something of a reputation in the capital as a corruption investigator, among my reporters at least. And here's this Paris supercop suddenly calling the news desk from the depths of the provinces? The minute you put the phone down, *mon Capitaine*, my people began making a few inquiries. A professional reflex." He gave a thin smile. "They couldn't immediately find out why you were transferred just a few weeks ago. But one of our political correspondents found out who it was that had you transferred. Perhaps I'll have a chat about you the next time I have lunch with Minister Vialaron-Allègre."

"My transfer isn't exciting enough to make a story for your magazine."

"You can make a story out of anything, count on it. Have a good trip back." Leroux smiled and rapped the car roof in farewell, rapped it a little too hard.

"Congratulations, you've made yourself yet another nonfriend in Paris," Fabienne said after they had driven clear of the courtyard.

"If there are three people in a city of eight million who can't stand me, that's not that bad a quota."

"Vialaron-Allègre. Leroux. Who's number three?"

"My wife."

"The most important minister in the government. The most influential publisher in the country. And your own wife. You're exactly the sort of cop they warned us about in training."

"In that case why did you come out with me to see Leroux? You could have stayed in the office."

"A ship in the harbor is safe, but ships aren't built for harbors."

They both laughed, and Fabienne bent down to find a station on the radio that didn't have hyperactive hosts moderating game shows. Mark Knopfler, "Get Lucky." Blanc nodded his approval. "You know he composed that one just for me." And started singing along.

"Sounds like something from the last century," Fabienne teased.

Blanc sang along for some time. The sun had half sunk beneath the horizon. Because they were traveling northeast, its red light in the rearview mirror was so intense that he had to turn it away. Dense clouds of thousands of mosquitoes danced over the patches of water, the low sun reflecting off their tiny wings like diamond dust in the air.

"Do you think there was anything behind Nora's joke?" Blanc asked finally.

"That her father snorts cocaine?" Fabienne shrugged. "His nose didn't look inflamed enough for him to be doing a line a day."

"Leroux acted as if he'd always been a publisher: first a student magazine, then *L'Événement*. But the press isn't his only passion. He's also into politics. Did you know that under Mitterrand he was a secretary of state in the Ministry of Culture? Very young, very ambitious. Then he suddenly disappeared from the world of politics and became a full-time publisher. All the other politicians who had reached that level smelled blood. None of them would give up of their own free will. So why did Leroux give up? Never interested me. Until now."

"Maybe there's something on the net." Fabienne pulled out her iPad and for the next thirty minutes she worked on the screen as they drove leisurely through the twilight. Blanc was in no hurry to get back to his dilapidated oil mill. His colleague gave the impression that she had lost track of time and space. She only looked up when they got back to the gendarmerie station in Gadet.

"Welcome home," Blanc announced, turning the engine off.

"Just hang on here for a moment," Fabienne said. "I'd rather tell you this here than in the office." She rapped her iPad. "There's always a million hits on the net about a publisher like Leroux. Most of them reputable, very unsuspicious, just what you'd expect."

"But even in the most beautiful rose garden there's a compost heap."

"You just have to be able to smell it. Here a tweet, there a Facebook post. You track from a few mischievous lines here to the next insider leak, and all of a sudden you end up at the profile of a young woman who works in Bercy."

"In the finance ministry."

"In the press department there. Mademoiselle is tied in with all the media women. She chats online with colleagues from other ministries, with company PR ladies, with freelance female journalists. And once upon a time she posted a film poster for *Jurassic Park* with Leroux's head photoshopped onto the body of a T. rex."

"Our flawless publisher depicted as a ravenous monster."

"It gets more interesting still when you see how many likes her post got. And the comments." Fabienne tapped the touch screen. "Media women warning one another against sitting next to Leroux at press conferences or going to a reception he's giving. Or even to get into an elevator with him."

"As bad as that?"

"As soon as Monsieur Leroux sees tits, his hands turn into tentacles."

"Borderline sexual harassment?"

"If you believe the posts, Monsieur Leroux goes a long way beyond that."

"And you can just find all this on Facebook?"

"The women concerned have all turned their privacy settings to very high and imagine they're just chatting among themselves."

"But you just hacked into them in a few minutes sitting in the passenger seat."

"People are so naive."

"But what you're doing is illegal."

"That's why we're talking about it in the car, not in the office."

Blanc clapped her on the shoulder in admiration. "Monsieur Leroux's promising political career ended abruptly while still on the launchpad back in Mitterrand's day. For reasons unknown."

"Maybe he groped Mitterrand's wife." Fabienne followed his train of thought. "Or maybe one of his concubines."

"From then on Leroux concentrates entirely on his magazine."

"But decades after his first political career, suddenly he's meeting regularly with Minister Vialaron-Allègre, the would-be new man in government."

"A comeback onto the political stage, after the grass has grown over the old affair, whatever it might have been? Something everybody has forgotten?"

"Everybody except perhaps his oldest friends like Albert Cohen."

"Cohen, who after his own crisis, returns to partly buried and totally old-fashioned values such as idealism, engagement, morality."

"And quality reportage."

"Cohen spends every day with Leroux in the Camargue and knows exactly what the publisher thinks and what he's planning."

"And Leroux knows what Cohen thinks and what he's planning."

"For example, he knows that Cohen rides his mountain bike every day past the field with the fighting bull in it. On one occasion he even goes with him, even if he's lagging behind."

"And Leroux drives his light-colored car through the Camargue every day, allegedly to work on his yacht in Port-Saint-Louis-du-Rhône."

"And a witness spots a light-colored car racing away from the scene of the accident." Blanc pulled the iPhone from his pocket. "While we're talking about the scene of the accident, that's Cohen's cell phone. I took it out of his pocket."

"You lied to Leroux?"

"Good thing we're in the car. You have the dead journalist's computer. Now you have his iPhone. Have fun with it. Discreetly. If you find something, then we can tell Nkoulou."

Fabienne dropped the cell phone along with her tablet into her leather bag. Then she leaned over and gave him a kiss on the cheek. "It's good to know you're not wedded to every paragraph in the book."

Wedded, thought Blanc, as he climbed into his old Espace and drove home. He had never formally proposed to Geneviève because he knew she didn't care for such old-fashioned things. Their wedding had been a sober mutual decision. If their divorce was to be the same, he only had to wait to receive the papers from her lawyer. After the summer vacation.

When he turned off the minivan's engine outside his old oil mill five minutes later, Blanc was surrounded by the bleating of goats and the smell of dung. He was astounded to find Serge Douchy driving a few black and brown billy goats off Blanc's land with a stick. His neighbor, who frequently swore loudly, had launched into such a tirade that he didn't even notice the car. Eventually he looked up and shrugged his shoulders apologetically.

"Sorry, the animals got out. Might have been a fox that damaged the fence last night. I'm having to get the herd back together from all over the place."

"It doesn't matter," said Blanc. "This isn't exactly a garden they can munch to the ground."

"Take a look at the oleander at the corner of your house. But it'll come back."

Blanc had been told by one of his colleagues that Serge had been refused permission by the prefecture to produce goats' milk cheese. His dilapidated farm on the opposite bank of the Touloubre had not met the examiners' hygiene standards. He had often asked himself why his neighbor still kept the herd and what he lived off of. Goat leather? Or was there someone who ate goat meat?

Serge lit up a Gitanes Maïs and pointed with the yellow cigarette at a sort of curved reddish cup of clay under a goat's hoof. "A '*tuile canal,*'" he muttered, "from your roof. If the mistral blows a tile down from your roof, you've got a bit of a problem, but when a gentle wind like we had today can blow one off, then you've got a big problem." Blanc thought of his climb up onto the roof the day before and picked up the tile. It was hard and porous and still hot from the sun, and in the sunset light it looked like burned ocher. One end was cracked and still bore the remains of gray mortar. The other, broader end bore a relief of a cicada. "Looks like an antique," he grumbled despairingly and tried in vain at the same time to work out how many similar *tuiles* he would need and how much replacing them would cost.

"They still fire them these days in Aubagne," Douchy muttered. "Not exactly practical, if you ask me." He pointed at the grayish roof on his own house, shimmering like a deserted bunker among the dense fig trees that grew from the reinforced bank of the Touloubre. "Put a few Eternit panels on it and you'll have no more worries."

Yes, Blanc thought, then I can put plastic window frames in the walls, too. But out loud he said genially, "Who can I get to fix the roof?" It was summer, it was hot, he had no family to feed anymore. If he was going to replace the roof, now was as good a time as any.

"Fuligni can do that."

"Don't joke." Pascal Fuligni had been a local master builder, but he'd been murdered during Blanc's investigation into his first case down here in Provence.

"His son has taken over the firm," Douchy explained. "He's a good lad, just needs to find his way in the business."

Blanc nodded. "I'll have a word with him."

Douchy forced his weathered face into a smile; it looked like a sea sponge being wrung out. "Then I'll get back to seeing to my herd," he told him. Blanc looked after his lean, big-boned frame until the farmer's mop of white hair disappeared into the twilight. Are you my friend or my enemy, he wondered.

A little later he was sitting on a wicker chair next to the oil mill's outside walls, still glowing with the heat, drinking a cool rosé. He pensively used one finger to push a thirty-year-old Matchbox car along the table he'd set next to him. It was a yellow Ford Mustang. It had once been one of his favorite cars. It had been left in the kitchen drawer alongside the corkscrew. Blanc had no idea how the toy had gotten there. All of a sudden his Nokia rang. He glanced matter-of-factly at the display. It was a 06 cell phone number he didn't recognize.

He knew the voice on the other end well enough, though. Minister Jean-Charles Vialaron-Allègre didn't usually bother to introduce himself. "We keep coming across each other so often, *mon Capitaine*, that we'll soon be on first-name terms." He laughed at his own joke, because there was no way that an insect like Blanc would ever be offered that level of familiarity by one of the planets orbiting the Élysée Palace.

Blanc had no idea how the minister had got hold of his private cell phone number. He decided there and then to change it. He managed a neutral "*Bonsoir*," trying to sound enthusiastic, even though the man on the other end had ruined his career and he didn't even want to think about his wife right now.

"I read on the *Figaro* website an extremely thorough, extremely flattering obituary," the minister went on as if he were just continuing a recently interrupted conversation.

Blanc replied in a neutral tone, "Monsieur Cohen was your friend."

"We often had lunch together." The minister hesitated for the tiniest of moments. "Is there anything in this . . ."—he was looking for the right word—"tragic incident that didn't appear in the *Figaro*?"

"I'm not sure what you mean," replied Blanc, who understood only too well.

"Monsieur Cohen was a prominent journalist," Vialaron-Allègre said, clearly impatient. "He was also considering a career in politics. I would just like to be sure that his unexpected demise isn't going to cause any waves and that his death doesn't have any unanticipated consequences for anyone in Paris. We all want to arrange a dignified funeral. As soon as possible, if you know what I mean, *mon Capitaine*?"

"There are just a few formalities to be gone through." It was astonishing how easily the lie came to him.

"Was that why you had to seize Monsieur Cohen's computer?"

So the publisher had already lodged a complaint, Blanc thought, not exactly surprised. "Monsieur Leroux needn't worry," he said reassuringly. "It's only routine."

"Don't treat me like a fool. If it had been a traffic accident, no matter how bizarre, you would never have found it necessary to seize a computer in a guest room. If you really think that somebody was involved in Cohen's death and if you find a clue on his computer, then I want to be informed immediately: name, details, motive. Everything."

What does he imagine might be hidden on Cohen's computer? Blanc wondered.

A Less Than Harmless Text

The next morning Blanc was woken by the brief chime of an incoming text message. He had slept badly in the heat, haunted by a dream in which he was careering in a white car through the Camargue like a lunatic under a monstrous sun. He couldn't remember any more details and was glad about that. Now he was staring at his cell phone display and it took a few seconds before the letters managed to join up into a message he could understand: *Negotiations collapsed, don't need to be in court until later. Come over. A.*

Blanc staggered to the shower and submitted himself to the shock of the ice-cold water. I really shouldn't do this, he thought, when his brain finally stumbled into life. Just don't reply to the text, but head off to the office like on any other morning. *Merde.* At the same time he knew he was just trying to talk himself out of it. Of course he was going to go.

Aveline was an investigative judge in Aix-en-Provence. The best in the Midi and the toughest. And the wife of Minister Vialaron-Allègre. How much time would the collapsed trial negotiations give them? An hour? Maybe two? At some stage today she would have to go to Aix and then . . . Friday. Her husband would come down from Paris as he usually did. She would pick him up at the TGV railway station and they would spend the weekend together, perhaps even Monday morning, too. It was now or never. He shaved particularly thoroughly and used more aftershave than necessary. He gave up the idea of breakfast. Every moment now was precious.

Just outside his oil mill, however, he had to stamp on the brakes because Paulette Ayhalen was coming toward him on the back of a Camargue horse, without a saddle or a blanket and with an old leather strap for a rein. He was in a hurry, but it would have been impolite and indeed might have attracted unwanted attention if he had not exchanged a few words with his neighbor. Also he thought about her more than was good for him.

"You're up and about early," he greeted her.

"It's the horse that's up and about, I'm just sitting on him," Paulette replied with a laugh. But she wasn't fooling him. Beneath her tan she was pale and her narrow, rather hard face showed the lines left by a sleepless night.

"Are you feeling okay?"

"Are you asking me as a neighbor or as a cop?"

"As a friend."

For a moment she looked flattered, then she gave Blanc an exhausted smile. "Are you an expert in divorce law?"

"I suspect I'm soon going to be an expert," he replied cautiously.

"You can't start learning soon enough, and you need to keep at it. Even though I got divorced two years ago already."

"Problems?"

"I got a letter from my ex yesterday. He wants to see Audrey and Agathe more often than the judge decreed. Agathe is twenty, he can't tell her what to do anymore. But Audrey is just seventeen. Do you think he can push something through? And if so, what tricks can I use to delay things until the kid is eighteen?"

Blanc decided there and then that when he got down to the station he would make sure a patrol car cruised through Sainte-Françoise-la-Vallée now and then over the next few weeks. "For tricks like that you need to ask a lawyer," he replied.

"A lawyer costs money. I only just have enough for my daughters, the horses, the farm, and myself. In that order. And in any case"—she bent down until she was nearly level with his car window—"the only good lawyer is a dead lawyer." She clearly enjoyed the expression on his face. "My ex is a lawyer," she said eventually.

"One more reason to beat him at his own game."

"I should be reining in his subordinate clauses rather than my horses?"

"We can bone up on the law together," he said, so spontaneously that he surprised himself.

Paulette sat up again and swept back the strands of her midnight-black hair that had fallen over her forehead. "I'm really pleased you've moved into this old shack down by the riverbank," she told him.

"I could have done worse," Blanc admitted.

Five minutes later he stopped at the edge of Caillouteaux. He had promised Aveline he would never park his car near her house. So he strolled obliquely through the town. Does anybody here ever go out on the streets? he wondered. Or are they all on vacation? The alleyways were already suffocatingly hot. His footsteps sounded unnaturally loud on the cobblestones. Perfectly restored façades, closed shutters. He went into Caillouteaux's only *boulangerie*, just a few yards from the church square but built into a house as inconspicuously as a cave in the side of a mountain. Blanc had spent several weeks in the Midi before he even realized the existence of this bakery. This morning he was its sole customer and the old proprietor gave him a weary, disinterested glance. He bought croissants. For later.

Rue du Passe-Temps, where the Vialaron-Allègres' house was located behind the church, was a tiny pedestrianized street that wound around the hill on which Caillouteaux sat. The rocks and the forests of *garrigue* scrub bushes in the broad valley down below were already fading into the bluish heat haze, while on the horizon the Étang de Berre reflected the sunlight like a massive sheet of glass. Somewhere in the distance lay the airport for the Salon-de-Provence flying school. He could see no aircraft but could hear the occasional accustomed rhythm, the rising and falling hum of propeller blades. In his mind's eye he pictured the two-seaters as giant flies forever flying around in the same circle.

One final, careful check all around. Nobody. He quickly went up to the front door, rang the bell, and looked into the lens of the little video surveillance camera on the porch. He heard the dull clicks of three heavy locks and then there was Aveline standing in front of him.

Blanc felt a wave of adrenaline rush through him as if he was a bungee jumper on the way down. She was nearly twelve inches shorter than he was, slim and with hair dyed dark brown. She was barefoot, in a bright red summer dress, smelled of Chanel No. 5 and Gauloises, and she didn't say a word, just routinely closed and locked the door behind them. Only then did she kiss him, passionately, hungrily. Her right hand reached behind his head and gripped him with her long, strong pianist's fingers. With a few deft movements of her left hand she turned off the cordless phone and the doorbell, without having to search for either.

She's done this more than a few times, Blanc thought. But strangely, rather than awakening any jealousy, it only spurred his passion.

"Nice of you to think of croissants," Aveline said casually, when she had finally released him from her embrace. She had never suggested that they address each other with the familiar "*tu*." It was absurd, but even that made Aveline all the more desirable in his eyes. She took the bag from him, set it on the kitchen table, and led him along the hallway and up a tiny staircase to the second floor. Japanese woodcuts on unplastered stone walls. A well-executed copy of a Cézanne view of Montagne Sainte-Victoire, not exactly postcard-sized. Gold frame. Maybe an original? It wouldn't surprise him.

The guest bedroom with the narrow bed. Their lovers' nest. She had already closed the shutters on the windows, against the sun and against the neighbors' view. Yellow strips of sunlight in the partial shade. Her short dark hair. Her long, narrow nose. Her dark eyes. Her fingers. Her lips.

Afterward they lay next to each other, skin touching skin. Aveline had fetched the croissants. While she was downstairs, he had heard the screeching of an electric grinder, then the house was filled with the aroma of freshly ground coffee. They had eaten the croissants and drunk from their steaming cups, no sugar, no milk, Aveline hadn't even asked. Now she was lying there next to him, a glowing cigarette in her hand, her beautiful body totally relaxed. This is complete madness, Blanc thought, even as he wished he would never have to leave the darkened room.

"Thank you for this hour," he whispered.

She just smiled.

"Can I ask you something?"

"The answer is: No, I'm not getting a divorce."

Blanc stared at her speechlessly for a moment, then raised his hand defensively. "It's not about us."

"If it's not about us, that means for you it's about work."

"We have a lot in common."

"Your question, *mon Capitaine*?"

"Will you take my case, *Madame le juge*, should it become a case?"

"I haven't seen a new dossier with your name on my desk."

"I'm still in the early stages. It's to do with the death of Albert Cohen."

"I heard about that, obviously." She sat up and gave him her full attention. Is she looking at me as a lover? Blanc asked himself. Or is she all of a sudden thinking only about the case? "My husband told me about it on the phone."

"Then we have one more thing in common: He called me about it, too."

He enjoyed the rare instance of having dealt Aveline Vialaron-Allègre a surprise. It didn't take long, however, for her to regain her composure. "Why did my husband do that? Was he trying to exert pressure on you?"

"*Oui*, *Madame*, and I've been asking myself why, too." He told her what he knew of the journalist's death so far. It didn't exactly take long.

"That is bizarre," she said when he had finished, more to herself than to him, and it sounded approving.

"I have neither a suspect nor a proper motive. But I just have a bad feeling about the business. Perhaps I'll know more when my colleague has examined Cohen's computer."

"Do me a favor. If Cohen had already written some of his article, then send it to me." Without another word, Aveline got to her feet and left the room. A few seconds later she came back with a big heavy art book in her hands. Blanc could see the cover—a yellow field beneath a volcanic sun, and above it the title and name of the author: Daniel Boré, *Vincent van Gogh and the Light of the South*.

"It's a standard work," she said, sitting down on the bed, opening the book, and flicking through the pages. "Very good reproductions. An intelligent selection from the oeuvre. Decent text, though perhaps"—she gave a teasing smile—"a little over-academic. I'd rather not think what Van Gogh in his famous letters to his brother would have said about these learned commentaries. Possibly Albert Cohen would have done the job more elegantly and maybe with greater originality. Something more surprising. In any case, I would like to read what he thought about Van Gogh, should you unearth it from the depths of his hard drive."

"Art is your great passion?"

"One passion." She leaned over and kissed him. "I actually did take part in a few history of art seminars at university, as a kind of relief from studying law. The law course was dreadful, not least because I had a horrible professor. Simultaneously a member of parliament and a professor of law. Terribly demanding, terribly dull, terribly comprehensive."

"Vialaron-Allègre," Blanc blurted out, suddenly seeing the light.

"I wasn't the first student to snag her professor."

Blanc wondered if it had been love or cool calculation or something unusual and in-between: a passion fired by career ambition.

"So you could be working in a museum, too?"

Aveline shook her head. "No, I didn't do the right exams. But exams in art are meaningless. Art and exams are a contradiction in themselves."

"But you know your stuff."

"I've remembered a few details." Aveline nodded toward the book.

"Could an article about Van Gogh in Provence be a motive for murder?"

"I can't think of any connection." Aveline laughed. "Back in those days a train journey from Paris to Arles took fifteen hours. Most of the time he spent in the Midi, that's where Van Gogh lived, was in the famous Yellow House on Place Lamartine. He wasn't here much over a year. From the end of February 1888 until the beginning of May 1889. In June 1888 he went down to Saintes-Maries-de-la-Mer, where he saw the Mediterranean for the first time. As a grown-up, can you imagine?"

"Very well. I discovered it myself just a few weeks ago. I was born on the channel. Later I always took my family on vacation to the Atlantic, when I managed to take a vacation."

Aveline kissed him again, this time as if she felt sorry for him. "In the fall of 1888 Gauguin moved down to Van Gogh in Arles. Vincent's brother had fixed it. But Gauguin was the exact opposite of poor Vincent in almost every way: big, strong, self-confident, a bit stupid. A real stockbroker type.

"On the day before Christmas Eve, they had a huge quarrel that ended up with Vincent slicing off part of his ear and Gauguin leaving Arles in a state."

"Sounds like good times all around."

"Don't joke about it. Vincent's pictures of the Mediterranean reflect a great harmony and tranquility that he had never experienced before and would never experience again. He wrote that to his brother. And in those few months he spent in Arles he produced more than two hundred paintings and innumerable sketches."

"Which put together would today be worth more than the yearly budget of this town."

"More than the annual budget of the gendarmerie, *mon*

Capitaine. Provence left deep marks on Van Gogh's work, and in his soul, too. Not a bad subject for a good journalist. That's why I'd like to take a good look at Cohen's text."

"Not such a good story for a cop. Where's the murder motive?"

"It's unlikely that it's hidden in a Van Gogh picture and a lot more likely that it's in an office in Paris. Albert Cohen was, as they say, well connected in the capital."

"He had a lot of enemies."

"When you've been in politics long enough, basically all you have is enemies."

"Cohen was a journalist, not a minister."

Aveline gave him an inscrutable look. "In recent years he had commented on every possible electoral campaign and got involved wherever he could."

"So who would have found Monsieur Cohen important enough to want to get him out of the way?"

"That's your job to find out, *mon Capitaine.*"

"In other words, if I find enough material to officially present you with a dossier, you will take the case? No matter who the investigations might involve?"

"Is there anything else I can do for you?"

"Put the book down and forget your next appointment in court."

A while later he was standing next to Aveline in the narrow hallway, watching as she opened the complex set of locks. Before she opened the latch, however, she dashed upstairs and came back a few seconds later with the book about Van Gogh.

"Get some inspiration of your own from the land of the south, *mon Capitaine.*"

"I'm afraid I can't accept the gift," Blanc said, somewhat embarrassed.

Aveline gave him a relaxed smile and said, "Nobody will know I gave it to you. I don't put any Ex Libris stickers in my books. And in any case we have another copy in our Paris apartment. The next time I'm there I'll bring it back down south. My husband isn't going to notice a gap in the bookshelves. He avoids art and artists whenever he can." Then she became serious. "It might give you some inspiration in the Cohen case. Forget Van Gogh. You'll deal with the Leroux family next." It wasn't a question.

"Monsieur Leroux was Cohen's boss," Blanc replied. "They were old acquaintances. Cohen seemed to be a friend of the family. And they were the last people to have seen him alive. And there are . . ." he hesitated, "a few unexplained episodes in Leroux's résumé."

Aveline nodded. "He snorts cocaine while having sex with underage Ukrainian girls in luxury hotels in Lyon. Friends from the telecommunications sector pay for both pleasures. That's something to think about the next time you're moaning about your cell phone bill. And don't write a reader's letter to *L'Événement* because you'll never see a single line criticizing France's big business."

"If you know all that, why don't you do something about it?" Blanc exclaimed. "Cocaine, illegal sex. That's a bit more than parking fines. I only found out anything about this just recently and via oblique means. No more than rumors at that."

"There's been no investigation. Not once have any of your colleagues compiled a dossier. No one has ever made an accusation. Monsieur Leroux has never been caught in flagrante. I only know about his peccadilloes by circuitous means. Or to put it another way, from my husband."

"A friend of Leroux's, and of Cohen's."

"My husband might define the word 'friendship' rather

differently than you do. But yes, he knows both of them well. Or rather knows one and knew the other. All Paris in any case has an idea one way or another about the publisher's little pleasures."

"I never heard anything about it when I was in Paris."

"I mean everybody who matters."

"So why does 'everybody who matters' not say anything about it?"

"Because half of those in the know joins in these orgies. And the other half doesn't want to end up the subject of a front-page story in *L'Événement*. Leroux is untouchable, even though his daughter gets wrecked at druggie parties and has to be smuggled out of some jail cell or other every second weekend. And because even his quiet wife has a certain dark spot in her past, so dark in fact that not even those in the know, know about it."

"A good family with a lot of friends."

Aveline gave him a searching look. "Everybody involved in politics in Paris is a pig. But a very elegant pig. Leroux, however, not only has no taste, he's also greedy and stupid. Fifteen-year-old hookers and cocaine by the pound in a hotel suite, all arranged by one of the richest managers in France? I would bet this house against a shack in Lorraine that the room was packed with cameras and microphones. Leroux knows no boundaries these days, neither decency nor common sense. He considers himself invulnerable. He's a megalomaniac. As a publisher he knows far too much. He's a tyrannosaurus, but a tyrannosaurus at the end of the Cretaceous Age. The great period of journalism is over, and magazines are about to go the way of stagecoaches. There have been a lot of people in Paris for a long time now who would like to blow Leroux out of the water. My husband is at the head of the line, even though he has dinner with him every other day so as to avoid being caught out in any unwelcome revelations. So far nobody has dared to fire the first shot. But it's just a question of time: more cocaine, more little girls, and an ever-falling magazine circulation. Sooner or later the paths will cross and the last tyrannosaurus will be shot."

Blanc remembered that the female workers in the ministry whose Facebook accounts Fabienne had hacked had depicted Leroux as a tyrannosaurus. Coincidence? Or was Aveline in the same social network as the woman from Bercy? "So maybe it will take some exiled cop from the provinces to open fire on the primordial monster," he said.

"The monster isn't going to expect to be hunted down from this direction." She kissed him and at the same time turned both the telephone and doorbell back on.

"Contact to Earth reestablished," Blanc muttered.

"We were never alone out in space. My husband wouldn't have used the doorbell. He has a key, obviously."

Blanc's heart skipped a beat. "I thought you would only be picking him up this evening in Aix."

"Usually I do that. But sometimes he takes the earlier TGV and comes straight here without telling me. He likes giving me surprises."

"You mean your husband could have burst in here while you and I were upstairs . . . ?" He didn't finish the sentence.

"Without an element of risk, life would be dull, *mon Capitaine*."

When Blanc finally turned up at the gendarmerie station in Gadet, nobody paid him any attention. The officer on duty in the entrance hall just glanced at him and then engrossed himself again in the sports section of *La Provence* without even saying hello. Most of the office doors were left open because their occupants were hoping for the hint of a draft. His colleagues were looking through documents, talking on the phone, or had positioned themselves behind their computer screens so they couldn't be seen.

"Olé, torero!" Tonon called out when he eventually got to the office they shared. He was in a better mood than the day before.

Blanc could imagine why. "I guess the case is already done and dusted for you?" he said. "What's happened?"

"This morning Ronchard called and . . . Where were you this morning, by the way?"

"The officer from the scene of the accident?" Blanc asked unnecessarily to avoid the other question. He shoved the art book Aveline had given him between two box files as if it was just another official document.

"I sent our big game hunter to Alleins. Ronchard was to ask around among the members of the Club Taurin about our bull breeder. *Et voilà.* Ferréol was there from ten in the morning until two forty-five P.M., just like he said."

"The electrician's call was timed at three twenty-five P.M."

"So Ferréol had no chance of getting from Alleins to this fucking field in a quarter of an hour. Not even in that racing chariot of his. Ferréol has a rock-solid alibi."

"Did Ronchard ask if there had been any threats? There might have been a few whispers going around in the club."

"According to Ronchard, Ferréol is a pillar of the club. Like the breeder told you, he has lots of friends. And all of his friends get threats from animal-rights activists, it seems to go with the job: mirrors on parked cars get smashed, they receive anonymous hate mail, but nobody tampers with the bulls in the fields. If you were to 'liberate' a bull from his field in the Camargue, he would sooner or later find his way back. He can't eat rice or flamingos. And nor can you just load them into the back of a truck like minks or caged turkeys and drive them away. All of the animal-rights gangs know that. It can't have been them. If you ask me, tourists are just more stupid than we thought. At least tourists from Paris, who make a living from journalism and spend their vacations fooling around on mountain bikes. Cohen himself opened the gate for his killer, either because he was curious or because he wanted to take a photo. End of story."

"So what about the watch buckle? Cohen was wearing a steel watch on his wrist, with a steel band, both of them in pristine condition. The ripped-off remnant of the leather band can't have been his. Which means somebody else was playing around with the gate."

"The damn buckle, if it really was a buckle, doesn't mean anything. Somebody lost it some time or another. Why would it have been around three P.M.? Maybe the breeder caught his watch, when he was there two days earlier. Maybe it was some clumsy tourist there to photograph the flamingos weeks ago? Or some idiot in his swimming shorts waving a red handkerchief? Someone so stupid that—"

"Have you ever ripped the band of your watch while waving a handkerchief or taking a photograph?"

"I don't take photographs and I don't wave handkerchiefs either. But if I did, I'm absolutely certain I'd be clumsy enough to catch and rip the band of my watch. Many years ago, when I was still wet behind the ears, I surprised my wife with a weekend in Cannes. Cost me a fortune. She was blown away and lay down on the hotel bed as soon as we arrived. I wanted to rip my clothes off and undo the belt . . ."

"You want to close the Cohen case, then?"

"Close, put it to one side, and forget all about it." Tonon looked as pleased as if he'd just woken up after that night in Cannes.

"Just wait a few seconds. I'm going to see Fabienne. She might by now have hacked Cohen's MacBook or cell phone and found something interesting. Do you want to come along?"

His colleague made a surly face. "Call me if you find some porn on the hard drive."

There were two baguettes lying on Fabienne's desk, still in the Gadet bakery's brown paper bags. Their aroma filled the room with a warmth that was far more pleasant than the heat of the sun outside.

"Break a piece off if you want," his colleague murmured, glancing up from her monitor.

"What made you think I wanted to?"

"I could see your reflection on the screen. I could see two hungry eyes and two shaking claws. Looked a bit like the giant octopus in *Tomb Raider*."

"I've had nicer things said about me," Blanc replied, biting thankfully into the warm bread. "Have you had a look at the contents of Cohen's hard drive?"

"I'm looking at the contents of a protest resolution."

"From Cohen."

"From the future best-selling author Fabienne Souillard. I'm going to complain to my mayor."

Blanc stood behind his colleague and looked over her shoulder at the beginning of the text and exclaimed, "*Merde*. Your mayor is with the Front National!"

"And the bastard won't marry us."

It took Blanc a few seconds to put it together. The government had recently legalized same-sex marriages. His colleague clearly wanted to marry her girlfriend. But equally clearly the mayor wouldn't give them a date. "Congratulations on the forthcoming celebration," he said, "and to hell with the fact that it doesn't suit the FN. The mayor has to marry you. It's part of his job."

She gave him a resigned smile. "He simply refuses."

"So? The law is the law. His refusal is illegal."

"So what are we to do? If we take the jerk to court, he will lose in the end—and he knows that. But he will make a real scandal out of it. And Roxane and I will be stuck in the spotlight. Two uppity lesbians from Vitrolles taking on the virtuous and duly elected mayor of the community. I can just imagine the emails we'd get."

"Not just emails," Blanc muttered, finally getting the drift. "Letters and packages, too, even more than the fighting bull breeders get."

"From different people, I suspect."

"But with the same unfriendly content. What are you planning to do?" He nodded toward the screen.

"I'm building a Facebook page around the resolution, or at least I'm still working on it. Some form of protest against this damn mayor. Maybe we can mobilize a couple of thousand people. If we get a thousand likes, *Monsieur le maire* might just lift his blockade."

"Don't let this distract you from work, though."

Fabienne laughed. "So says the expert. If I'm not wrong, I'm one of your three Facebook friends. And the other two are your children."

"Practically," Blanc replied, slightly insulted. "Astrid is twenty and an event manager. Yesterday she posted a link to a fashion chain she's running a campaign or something for. In the old days daughters never talked to their fathers about fashion."

"Which fashion chain?"

"That Aberfitch and Com."

Fabienne stared at him blankly.

Blanc stared back. One second. Five seconds. Ten seconds. "Go on then," he said eventually, "the name wasn't exactly right. Okay, I've forgotten. You can smile if you like. Go ahead."

"I might die laughing."

“Was it that far out?”

“Further.”

He raised his hands in resignation. “*Bon*, I’ll take another look at the Facebook page.”

“You’d do better just to look around you in the real world, see what people who haven’t reached their thirtieth birthday yet wear.” She prodded him encouragingly and nodded at the empty chair next to her. “My Facebook page isn’t going to be much of a help, that’s for sure,” she said good-naturedly. She closed the half-finished page she was working on and opened a MacBook lying on the table next to her desktop computer. “*Voilà*,” she declared. “Luckily I at least keep track of what’s going on. This is Albert Cohen’s Mac.”

“That was quick.”

“I don’t know what you were doing this morning, but I was working. It wasn’t that hard. The hard drive was locked with a password that was so simple even you might have worked it out.”

“Albert Cohen.”

“See. You could have hacked this hard drive without me. On the other hand”—she gave him a conspiratorial smile—“some of the files have got extra security.”

“Those are the ones I’d like to see first.”

“And that’s the problem. I’m still working on them. AC wasn’t as clueless as it seems at first glance. Things that were particularly important to him were also particularly well encrypted. Pretty clever all in all: any idiot could have gotten into his hard drive—but wouldn’t have found anything. End of story. But there are these especially encrypted files hidden away in subfolders . . . If you have a superencryption code on your computer at startup, then you just attract a hacker’s interest. And every code can be hacked. But if you keep the security low but hide the really important stuff, then the hacker might not notice that there's anything there. That was Cohen's strategy."

"Not enough to keep you out."

"Only because in this torturous heat I've got nothing better to do than work on pointless Facebook pages. I have time, lots of time. And if someone searching for something has enough time, then even the best attempt to hide it will fail."

"Then let's take a look at the files you've already hacked. Maybe there's something in the data that Cohen considered of lesser importance that will give us a lead."

"Where to?"

"To the gate of a field in the Camargue."

"Let's start with the pictures," Fabienne suggested, clicking on a folder entitled "Photos, private."

"Marius is keen to see some good-looking naked girls. Should I give him a call?"

"Let him snooze on. The stuff here is about as interesting as a bingo competition in an old folks' home. Vacation photos. You can see the dates. All of them taken in the last two weeks."

"While Cohen was staying with the Leroux family?"

"Exactly. I had imagined that the snaps taken by intellectuals," she hesitated, and then gave an embarrassed smile, "would be, well, intellectual. Or at least more intellectual than those Roxane and I take. But this stuff is well within our league."

Blanc recognized the publisher's *mas*, his country house. Lots of pictures of the Camargue. Lots of sunsets. Flamingos. Rice plants. Ernest Leroux by the pool, laughing. Marie-Claude Leroux, smiling. Albert Cohen between Ernest and Marie-Claude Leroux. The journalist with one hand on the publisher's shoulder, his other arm around the publisher's wife's slim waist. Ernest toasting the photographer with a glass of rosé. Marie-Claude

Leroux had her left arm around their guest's neck, so close that he must have been able to hear the ticking of her watch. Blanc wondered who had taken the photo. Leroux's daughter?

"That was taken on the evening before his death," Fabienne told him. "It seems Cohen downloaded his photos from his iPhone onto his laptop every evening. But I couldn't find any picture from his last day alive on the MacBook. If he did take any photos, they're still on his phone. And I still have to hack into that." She was about to click the photo closed when Blanc reached out with his hand and stopped her.

"Let's just go through the pictures again," he said.

"You can't take really good photos with an iPhone, the lighting isn't even right in a lot of them. What do you think you're going to find out from them?"

"That Cohen never took a photo of a bull. That Cohen never took a photo of his bike and never posed with his bike to be photographed by anybody. That Cohen never took a photo of Nora Leroux. That Cohen took two or three times as many photos of Marie-Claude Leroux than of her husband. That Marie-Claude was smiling in those photos." Blanc clicked back to the last photo, of Cohen in between his hosts. "His arm around her waist. Her arm around his neck. Marie-Claude is a woman who likes to keep her distance. She doesn't let anyone get past her defenses that quickly."

Fabienne made a contrite expression. "Lesson learned, *mon Capitaine.* So you think maybe Cohen was having a fling with his publisher's wife?"

"Maybe. You were the one who shoved it under my nose that Ernest Leroux would put his hand up any skirt he could. Marie-Claude, on the other hand, gives the appearance of being a gentle person. But everybody needs a bit of consolation from time to time."

"And Leroux finds out that his wife is having a vacation affair with Cohen? He sets out that very day in his light-colored car, allegedly heading for the yachting harbor in Port-Saint-Louis-du-Rhône, but in fact he's waiting next to a gate in the middle of the Camargue for Cohen to come by on his mountain bike, as he regularly does. Then he turns a black fighting bull into the murderer of his wife's lover. Kudos to you! There's a certain style in that."

Blanc made a face. "Nora Leroux didn't exchange a single word with her mother while we were there. And she clearly didn't like Cohen either. She didn't once pose for a photo for him. What about this. Nora Leroux gets wind of her mother's affair, roars off through the Camargue in her white car, and does what any dutiful daughter would do in the circumstances: sets the bull free."

"Jealousy on the part of the husband or disgust on the part of the daughter."

"There're two good motives."

"If you can brew up a murder accusation from a few vacation photos, then there's no way I'm ever sending you a link to my Flickr account."

"What else have you got?" Blanc asked. He hadn't a clue what Flickr was.

"A folder entitled 'Correspondence.'"

"On my computer it's called 'Letters' and contains two emails from my wife's lawyer."

"I can imagine they're about as cheerful as this." Fabienne opened a document addressed to Vent d'Ouest. It contained thank-you notes labeled "In recognition of your thoughtful care in difficult times." Blanc's colleague sighed. "I googled the name. It's the rehabilitation center in Brittany." She flicked through a few other letters, all of which had "Dr." in the address field. "The text is always the same, only the name changes. Cohen obviously wrote thank-you notes to all of the doctors and carers who looked after him. For somebody who earned his living by writing, he wasn't exactly creative. I'd like to know what all the doctors thought of him if they'd met up at a conference and compared their notes from the famous journalist."

"*Déja lu*, is that all?"

"There is one little treasure." Fabienne clicked on a Word file labeled only with the date, August 3. The day before his fatal bike ride. "Strangely enough, Cohen addressed it to a friend he could have spoken to every day by the pool: Ernest Leroux."

Blanc whistled through his teeth. He had forgotten the heat, the stench of mold from the air conditioner, and the oil-painted green walls. He was no longer thinking about Marius in the room next door, or even about Fabienne, or Geneviève and his children, or even Aveline and the room with the closed shutters. His world had been reduced to a seventeenth-inch monitor and a few characters on a white background.

> *Cher Ernest,*
> *As you know, we have come a long way down the same road. You have always been generous to me, above all in the last few difficult months. Rest assured of my gratitude for that.*
>
> *In recollection of our old political ideas, you will, I hope, excuse this letter I am addressing to you but also intend to be an open letter. It is an appeal, like so many appeals that you and I put together, but never had to formulate like this: Ernest Leroux, do not throw the people who make your money out onto the streets.*
>
> *The journalists and editorial staff are not just*

writing for you, they are writing for the republic, for democracy, for France!

I know that times are hard for the printed word. But when was that not the case? It is not right to fire journalists just because an accountant wants to have one decimal place fewer than in previous years. Ernest, remember our old revolutionary ideas. We risked more for them than just money. And you and I both know someone who once upon a time did a lot more than that. Therefore I appeal to you, no, I demand of you that . . .

And there the letter ended.

"Pretty pathetic," Fabienne said, when she was sure Blanc had read it all and she wouldn't disturb his concentration. "Not exactly an Internet-generation document."

"It's the language of the 1968 generation. Is there any way you can find out whether this is just an unfinished draft? Or whether Cohen finished it and sent it to Leroux and it's here somewhere under another file name? If I understand one sentence properly, he intended to publish it as an open letter."

"His 'sent' folder is empty. It seems he used his smartphone for all his electronic communication. I can't find any sign that it was ever printed out. This laptop hasn't been connected to any printer in recent weeks. And I can't find any longer version either—it seems that if there is one it must be in the files I haven't been able to hack into yet."

"But on the day before his death, he was working on the text."

"He opened the file but only changed the title and nothing else. Looking at what you see here, it would seem to have just been sitting there on the hard drive for two weeks."

"So Cohen wrote it as soon as he came out of the rehab clinic and arrived down at his friends' *mas*?"

"That's how it looks. Maybe it was some form of payback. His pal organizes a vacation and convalescence for him, and he kicks back with an appeal: 'You used to be a lefty and now you're a filthy capitalist.' And if we bring Marie-Claude into it . . ."

Blanc nodded in agreement. "It's certainly something the publisher wouldn't have been counting on."

"If he knew anything at all about it."

"I'm beginning to enjoy myself."

"Here is the last folder, with two subfolders," Fabienne said. "He called them 'projects' and separated them into 'texts' and 'sources.'" She clicked on the first subfolder, which contained a single Word document entitled VanGogh.doc. "His vacation project. The piece that his publisher hadn't seen yet. The superstitious reporter's hidden treasure."

"Have you already read it?"

"Just the first few lines."

"And? Gripping stuff?"

"If all of Cohen's articles were like this, it's not because of the Internet that *L'Événement* is going bust."

It only took Blanc a few seconds to realize what Fabienne meant. The article was little more than a stump revealing the ruin of a man who had taken on more than he could cope with. The text was just a few dozen paragraphs, but they were all only first paragraphs, new beginnings, all of them unfinished after just a few lines. A description of the sunset over Arles, as seen from the main road that cut through the old city like a wall. Cohen used a stinking Spanish diesel truck to make a link to Picasso and then an abrupt switch to Van Gogh. Here the paragraph ended. The next was a description of a restaurant filled with tourists and gypsy music in Saintes-Maries-de-la-Mer, compared with the peace and quiet the painter had discovered there. End. A quotation from a letter from Van Gogh to his brother, followed by a complaint by Cohen that modern email didn't permit the inclusion of hand-drawn sketches. End. The home in Saint-Rémy-de-Provence where Van Gogh was cared for after he had cut off his ear, described in semidelirious French, as if the painter had written it himself. End.

Blanc gave up and scrolled through the endless fragments. "This is almost as badly written as my reports," he muttered.

"Then you can become a journalist when you finally quit. There's a job now going at *L'Événement*. One thing's clear here: Cohen wasn't up to it anymore. Maybe he had been away from it for too long. Leroux hinted as much: the former star reporter's tools had gone rusty."

Blanc battled his way down to the last of Cohen's attempted openings. Suddenly he broke into a smile. The last had far more paragraphs than any of the previous. "Maybe AC just had to get warmed up. Read what he finally came up with."

Nowhere in the world can you see so many unimaginably beautiful, unimaginably big, and unimaginably expensive sailing yachts as during the Voiles de Saint-Tropez. Every October, the owners of these shimmering bronze and teak Oldtimers, with one, two, three, or even four masts, gather together for regattas on the Côte d'Azur. The narrow streets of the once idyllic town are crowded with the smartly clad sailors of these luxury toys, along with tourists, tradesmen, part-time sailors, and women with exaggeratedly blond hair. Everyone stares at the yachts moored to the piers or at the women with their exaggeratedly blond hair.

If there was ever an ideal opportunity for a thief, this is it.

During the 1990 Voiles a thief opened the emergency exit

of the Musée Maly in Saint-Tropez. This museum is an institution created out of the fortune of a rich Englishman: an Empire-style castle on the slopes above the town, with a little park, a view of the Mediterranean, and ten rooms with respectable but by no means spectacular paintings from the nineteenth century. Very few leave the streets to stroll through these dusty rooms. Most of those who do, come to see one painting only: the pride of the Musée Maly and its greatest treasure.

A genuine Van Gogh.

The picture is no larger than a page from a calendar. Surrounded by a gilded frame that is far too big for it, which would not at all have pleased the Dutch painter with his troubled soul. But what a picture! The subject, as Van Gogh described it in a letter to his brother, is "Fishing boats on the beach at Saintes-Maries." Anyone who has ever heard the name Van Gogh is familiar with his sunflowers, his Langlois Bridge—and these fishing boats. The master captured them during a visit toward the end of June 1888, sketched them in hasty strokes, painted them in watercolors and in oil on canvas. "I'm enclosing the drawing from Saintes-Maries," he wrote to Theo. "I sketched the boats early in the morning, just before I left, and I am now working on a painting on a size-30 canvas with more sea and sky to the right."

Peace. Harmony. And just a touch of nostalgia for his Dutch home and its own fishing boats.

The painting in the Musée Maly is just one of a whole series of similar motifs, for Van Gogh did not rest with just the one enclosed in the aforementioned letter. But it is probably—the art historians are not certain (but when have art historians ever been certain?)—but very probably the very first of that famous series. The prototype for all the Saintes-Maries pictures.

What an irony, therefore, that this picture of a few boats would have been stolen during a boating festival . . .

For that unknown but clearly very well informed thief, too, the Voiles provided the opportunity to break into the extremely poorly secure-alarmed, as it would turn out—Musée Maly. And once in, he took just a single picture, the Van Gogh. It probably took him less than two minutes. More than two decades have passed since then, but this famous picture has never resurfaced. Nobody has ever seen it, and nobody has ever solved the crime.

But that might just be about to change.

Fabienne shook her head in amazement. It looked as if she was finding it difficult to accord Cohen any respect as a journalist. "That's definitely a bit better," she eventually admitted hesitantly.

"It's as if he suddenly felt at home again," Blanc stated. "Cohen wanted to make a new start after his breakdown. No more coke. No affairs. Good stories. Back to his roots. Leroux was giving him a chance. 'On the Trail of Vincent Van Gogh' was supposed to be just playing with words. Decorative writing to accompany a few pretty photos and paintings to fill the publisher's pages. Not real reportage. Cohen tried to find a way into it repeatedly, but he just couldn't bring himself to write something so flimsy."

"And in the course of his research, the reporter comes across the story of an old theft." She smiled. "For the first time I'm beginning to regret not having met AC."

"Indeed. He probably only came across the old story by chance. But it triggered his enthusiasm—an enthusiasm that had been battered over the years and was just waiting to be rekindled."

“He tells himself: To hell with the assignment. I’m going to write what I want to write. Every bit the star reporter.”

“Leroux had no idea that instead of some harmless cover-page story Cohen was going to give him a crime story that had been totally forgotten. Imagine how stupefied he would have been when he found out.”

“Maybe he already had?”

“Is Cohen’s story true? Is the theft of the Van Gogh from the Maly Museum still a mystery?”

Fabienne started hammering on her keyboard, humming the melody Blanc had heard on the radio but still couldn’t place. Something from the charts? Or maybe an advertising jingle? She probably didn’t even realize she was doing it. He watched Fabienne, her slender fingers flying rapidly over the keyboard. She was staring as if into the distance, through a telescope. A Diana of the net, the goddess of hunting. Blanc had always prided himself, at least since the early years of the new millennium, as being competent online rather than a dinosaur from the analog age. All the same he was still pleased to have his colleague by his side. He was an immigrant on the digital continent, she was a native.

Her humming ended in a little cry that might have been of astonishment or surprise. “Cohen’s story is genuine,” she announced. “The Van Gogh from the Maly Museum disappeared in 1990 and has never been seen again. Apparently that’s not rare.” She tapped the screen. “The Interpol database of stolen artworks lists forty thousand objects taken from public and private collections. So far only two thousand have been recovered.”

“Just five percent. That’s pretty poor.”

“It gets even more depressing.” She opened another tab in her browser. “The Art Loss Register is a database of stolen objects for collectors, art historians, and insurers. It lists more than three hundred thousand stolen works, of which only six thousand have been found again. And we're just talking about those cases that have been reported. There's a piece here about 'artnapping': thieves steal a painting and then announce they will return it for a finder's fee. The museums are too embarrassed to involve the police. Thefts are bad for their reputation. Who would lend a valuable object for a special exhibition to an institute from which things had been stolen? And it's also bad for insurance premiums, which shoot up if you've been lax with security."

"What's the situation down here in the south? Provence and the Côte d'Azur are full of museums and villas of rich collectors."

"Less than twenty percent of solved cases. There isn't a single art expert in any of the gendarmerie brigades in the Midi. Only in Paris."

"Idiots, those Parisians."

She gave him a weary smile. "Last year in Avignon two criminals threw a few paintings into the back of a station wagon and roared off. Our colleagues found the vehicle soon enough, parked on a highway. But there were no other traces to be found: the crooks had sprayed the entire interior with a fire extinguisher."

"Would that really be enough to get rid of all forensic clues?" Blanc asked disbelievingly.

"You're not in the champions league anymore, *mon Capitaine*. This is the second division."

"What did our colleagues do after the break-in at the Musée Maly?"

"They looked for clues. But they could find no fingerprints. No alarm had gone off, no locks had been broken."

"Inside job."

"Maybe. They quickly agreed on a prime suspect: Olivier Guillaume. No longer in the flush of youth, the caretaker of the museum, and the obvious ideal man for an inside job. They even detained him for a night, but then let him go again. And that was the end of it. Nobody was convicted, nobody was accused, and there weren't even any more interrogations. Guillaume was never found guilty of anything, either then or since."

"He didn't suddenly become rich at any time after the theft?"

"According to reports here, the man still lives with his aged mother."

"It would look as if the investigations hit a dead end."

"And that's where they still are, buried and forgotten. The case has been dormant for years. You can still see the case listed in the databases of Interpol and the Art Loss Register. And the Musée Maly still has a blank space on its walls, and a lot fewer visitors."

Blanc scratched his forehead. "Cohen gets an assignment to write about Van Gogh. Boring rubbish. He can't even get beyond the first paragraph. But he travels around Provence on his researches. And in the process stumbles on this old unsolved theft. A story about Van Gogh that none of his readers will know about. So he sets himself down to writing it up. And in the last sentence he wrote before his death he hints, more or less openly, that he has found an interesting clue. And that he is going to solve the case."

"Which would mean he knew where the picture was."

"Or who the thief was."

"There's a folder entitled 'Sources.' I found it confusing first time around. But now we might find some connections."

Fabienne clicked on a few photos. Badly photographed images of newspapers clearly taken from some library or archive. When they zoomed in, they realized that Cohen had taken photographs of newspapers from the fall of 1990 that had carried reports of the art theft from the Maly Museum. There weren't many and they read the blurred letters on the blurred pages until their eyes watered. Nothing new.

One piece had no headline. The first words were a name: Daniel Boré.

"The author of *Vincent van Gogh and the Light of the South.* It's a standard work," Blanc said matter-of-factly.

Fabienne stared at him in amazement. "You don't know Abercrombie and Fitch, but you do know art books like that? What were you doing in Paris the last few years?"

"I've only been interested in art since I came down south," Blanc said, trying to make his face as inscrutable as possible. "What did Cohen write about him?"

"An address in Provence. The Van Gogh expert whom apparently everybody in the world has heard of, except for a lesbian second lieutenant in the gendarmerie, lives just around the corner. Cohen wrote a few notes below the address."

Blanc wrote down the address and the comments about Boré in his notebook, causing his colleague to give a sympathetic sigh. "I can just send it to your phone," she told him.

He just smiled in return. He felt the thrill of the chase. "It seems Cohen met Boré in the week before his death."

"He's writing a reportage about Van Gogh in the south. The greatest Van Gogh expert lives down here in the south. It seems logical that he'd want to meet him."

"But look at this," Blanc murmured. "If I understand what he's noted down here, Cohen had done some research into Boré's past. In 1990 he was a junior curator in a museum. Guess which one."

Fabienne whistled beneath her breath. "Musée Maly . . ." She opened the next folder. The file was entitled "Olivier Guillaume." "He must have gotten the name from an old newspaper article," she guessed.

"But Cohen didn't stop there." Blanc read the notes aloud: *"Saint-Gilles—wall—Salon-de-Provence: Mother's house—rue*

Bel Air—father, father, father!—meeting 8/5 10:00, bar in Gadet."

Below was a copy of a photo of a man in his late fifties: lean, faded jeans, sandals, a shirt bleached by a thousand hours in the sun, tousled gray hair, a suspicious look on his face. "Cohen took this in front of a bar in Gadet," Blanc said, pointing to a sign on a house wall at the edge of the photo. "I recognize it. It's just around the corner: Le National."

"It looks as if Cohen took the picture covertly, a cell-phone snap taken from the waist." She clicked on the files of the old investigation and compared Cohen's photo with the police photo back then. "He's gotten older, but that is unquestionably Guillaume," she declared.

"Cohen tracked him down and photographed him!" Blanc slapped his hand down on the desk. "I have no idea what the cryptic reference to Saint-Gilles is all about. But that's where the breeder of our murderous fighting bull lives. Could that have anything to do with our case? And why does Cohen write down the word 'father' three times? A hint to the motive? But one thing is quite clear: The journalist found a clue of some sort."

"Are you thinking the same as me?"

He smiled at his colleague. "Cohen met the famous art historian Boré, who had been a junior curator in the Musée Maly at the time of the theft. And he was keeping tabs on Guillaume, the former caretaker at the Musée Maly and chief suspect for the theft."

"And that last note might mean that he was going to meet Guillaume on the morning of the fifth of August, in a bar in Gadet. Only he didn't turn up for the meeting."

"Because a fighting bull had impaled him on its horns on the fourth of August."

Inside Job

The next morning Blanc dashed out of the house early. It hadn't reached 90 degrees yet. This was the moment in an investigation that Blanc enjoyed the most. He knew there was a beast of prey lurking in the undergrowth, but he didn't have a concrete clue or a clear suspicion where. His mind and senses were acutely aware of everything. He was a hunter who could feel the beast's eyes on him, even if he couldn't yet see it himself.

He climbed into the Espace and turned the key in the ignition. Nothing. He tried again. Nothing. A third time. Blanc hit the steering wheel. He was so full of nervous energy that he could have burst. And here he was sitting immobile in this wreck of a car. He tried the ignition another five times, but there wasn't even the ghost of a rattle from the engine. He glanced at his watch: 8:00 A.M. He would call his neighbor.

Jean-François Riou was an engineer with Airbus Helicopters in Marignane. But it was on weekends that he lived the life God had made him for. He rooted around in the guts of rusty old cars until they were worthy of a place in a vintage car museum. He had saved Blanc's Espace more than once. The last time he had done it he had suggested they use the familiar "*tu*" form of address from then on. At this hour of the morning Riou would be out of bed. His children were at boarding school but hardly ever came home on weekends. Blanc had never met Riou's wife and from the few words his friend said about her, he reckoned that was not a bad thing. He tapped Riou's cell phone number into his Nokia.

"Your old crate's broken down," Riou said happily as soon as he picked up the phone. "Why else would you be calling me on a Saturday morning?"

"Are your hands covered in oil?"

"I'm already climbing into my Alpine."

"Then you can get here soon."

"Is there something I should be worrying about? Your Espace giving off more smoke than normal? Engine oil dribbling into the Touloubre?"

"When I turn the key in the ignition, the speedometer shoots up to 150 mph and the rev counter shoots up to the maximum. But nothing happens. Not a sound. No warning light, the starter doesn't make any noise."

"*Putain.*" Riou sounded even happier. "I'll leave the Alpine in the garage and take the Frontera."

"Sounds like some sort of mule."

"It's an old SUV. Four-wheel drive is better if I have to tow it."

"Welcome to the weekend," Blanc muttered.

"Don't rush off." He heard Riou laughing as he ended the conversation.

Ten minutes later Riou trundled up to the front of Blanc's house in an old, box-shaped red Opel. "Sure you don't want to sell this crate?" he asked after glancing under the hood. "Your kids are grown up and your wife . . . well, whatever. You don't need this old family bus anymore. Buy yourself a pickup and you'll always have friends. Or a convertible and you'll always have girlfriends." He took a tow rope out of the trunk.

Geneviève had hated driving through Paris in the big Espace. When his children were older, they were so embarrassed by the old car that they asked him to let them off a hundred yards away from the school gates so their friends wouldn't see it. Blanc didn't exactly have any sentimental feelings toward the vehicle. "How much would I get for it?"

"I know someone who ships old crates like that over to Algeria. He might give you a hundred euros for it."

"What if I tried to sell it here?"

"Do you really want to hear the jokes? At your own expense?"

"Where are you going to tow me to?"

"Saint-César. There's a mechanic there crazy enough to patch up an old Espace."

"And it'll cost me more than the car's worth."

"I told you: pickup or convertible."

Blanc thought of his old oil mill and its rickety roof, then his police salary, and sighed. "Let's get it repaired. How many hours will it take your friend in Saint-César?"

Riou gave him a sympathetic smile. "Days, you mean? Weeks? The ways of God are as unfathomable as is the Renault spare-parts supply service."

"*Merde.* What am I going to do in the meantime? I need a car."

"I'll lend you one of mine."

"Out of the question. I can't race around the place in an expensive vintage car."

"I didn't say I was going to lend you my Alpine. I was thinking of something more comfortable, a real classic." Blanc didn't at all like the grin on Riou's face.

After handing over a check for four hundred euros as a "down payment" to the smirking mechanic in Saint-César, Blanc let himself be driven to the old barn near the *route départementale* 70, where Riou kept his collection of cars. His neighbor opened the heavy wooden door and sunlight illuminated his blue Alpine as if it had been picked out by a searchlight, then an old green-painted jeep from the Second World War, a fifty-year-old Opel Rekord, and a Mercedes at least as old, with its left fender unscrewed. And then right at the back against the wall, where the sun hardly reached, a sky-blue 2CV.

"A 1990 model, just before they stopped making them, 600 cc engine, 29 horsepower, can get up to 60 mph, if you've got the mistral at your back to push you along," Riou told him.

"And what if you're driving into the mistral?"

"Then you can fold the window down and pick flowers as you're going along. The gears are on the steering wheel. Can you cope with that?"

"I've driven a 'steam horse' before. Like every real student."

It had been with Geneviève, in their second semester. The "steam horse" had belonged to a friend of hers and was the red of a washed-out T-shirt. They had driven through the Vendée. When they were going along one country road, part of the roof canvas had blown away. The rollback canvas was in any case so thin that whenever they ran into a summer storm, they might as well have been sitting on seats in a shower. And sometimes in the evening they would stop at a deserted parking place, so greedy for each other's bodies that they didn't even bother to put the tent up, but did it in the car . . .

"Everything okay?" Riou asked.

"It's just that it's been a long time since I last took the reins of a 2CV."

"Don't worry, it's like riding a bike: you never forget."

"It doesn't look as if I have a choice. Where's the key?"

Blanc drove carefully for the first hundred yards, but his

neighbor had been right: it was just the way it used to be. Except that he didn't have a woman sitting next to him. The wind was warm so he stopped at the side of the road and rolled the roof down. It was a convertible, wasn't it? When he turned back onto the *route départementale*, he could hear the engine chattering like an industrial sewing machine. Somewhere there was a piece of metal rattling. The tires swooshed along the tarmac. Every little bump in the road made the bodywork move like a boat riding a swell. On straight stretches of road he got the car almost up to 45 mph. The last cicadas were singing their songs in the *garrigue* scrub. A hornet the size of his finger was blown by the wind in through the open roof; it buzzed around his head three times and then vanished before he could be frightened by it. The aroma of pine and rosemary was all around him. All of a sudden Blanc felt wonderful.

On a Saturday morning only those gendarmes on the duty roster were actually at the station—and those with no families. In Gadet that meant only the duty officer, Nkoulou, and Marius. His boss was just getting out of a patrol car as Blanc trundled into the parking lot. The 2CV was about as far removed from the boss's Dyson Ventilator as Canned Heat's "On the Road Again" was from free jazz. Blanc didn't need to be a psychologist to grasp the meaning of the chief's expression. He pulled the roof across and closed the door gently for fear of denting the metal.

"I would lock it," Nkoulou advised him. "The singer Renaud Séchan recently had a 2CV stolen from outside his house in L'Isle-sur-la-Sorgue."

"Must have been a pretty desperate car thief."

"There are more desperate people down here in Provence than you might imagine."

Blanc followed his boss into the building and watched him pensively until the man disappeared into his office. Then he pushed open the door to his own office.

"I'm just filing away the case notes," said Marius, who didn't seem particularly surprised to see him. There was an open bottle of rosé and a plastic cup next to his ancient computer. There was only enough wine left in the bottle to reach the label.

"Since when have you been coming in on the weekend to do paperwork?"

"Ever since someone told me I ought to open a case file for a dead would-be *torero*."

"Well, the file is about to get thicker, and I wouldn't bet even a single euro that at the end of the day it'll read 'accident.' "

"Can't you just be a normal guy and spend the weekend sitting in a bar or lying on top of a woman?"

"You are my brilliant role model. Stop messing around with your computer. We're going on an educational excursion."

"Sounds like something I should say thanks but no thanks to."

"We're going to visit an art historian."

"Bound to be more exciting than the Olympique de Marseille home game this afternoon, for which I just happen to have gotten hold of tickets."

As they walked out of the station, Marius stared speechlessly at the 2CV.

"My new convertible," Blanc told him.

"Let's take the patrol car. I'd like to get back today. Where are we going by the way?"

Marius, who didn't drive if he could avoid it, crammed himself into the passenger seat of the Mégane. It was hot as a sauna inside and had the faint stench of vomit. That morning two of their colleagues had dragged a drunk out of the woods; he'd been wandering around with a gas lighter trying to light a cigarette.

Blanc wound the window down and told Marius what he had discovered about Boré the previous evening.

"Never heard of him. He lives down here in the south?"

"Boré used to work in Saint-Tropez. But for more than ten years now he's been living in Paris. He's famous in his own circles and not just for the book about Van Gogh. He organizes big exhibitions: well-known painters, famous museums, throngs of people. He's supposed to be curating a Van Gogh anniversary event in Arles for the Ministry of Culture. That's why he's been down in Provence over the past few weeks. He's living in the summer home of a friend, between Salon and Arles."

"And our bicycle bullfighter talked to him?"

"That's why we're going to talk to him."

Twenty minutes later they were driving through Eyguières. Blanc had given Marius the address he had written down in his notebook and his colleague was directing him through the little town center. The road's lanes went on either side of a war memorial with a bronze statue of a World War I soldier staring into the distance. They passed a bar, a restaurant, an art gallery, and an organic food store; there was hardly any traffic, with nobody on the street except for an old man dozing on a bench outside the local tax office.

"It's busier here in the evenings," Marius muttered. "Nice place." They parked outside a rather dilapidated house next to the gallery. There was a bakery on the ground floor, but it was closed. There was a grayish gleam to its poorly plastered façade. The entry door next to the bakery and the rectangular windows with wooden crossbars looked old. It was only when he pressed the doorbell that Blanc realized the wood was actually new. At the same time he noticed that the lock was modern and that there was an alarm system set into the entranceway.

The man who opened the door to them looked older and more

wearied than in the author's photo Aveline had shown him in the art history book. Daniel Boré was nearly six feet tall and had a barrel chest and belly to go with it, although they weren't immediately obvious beneath his brightly colored clothing: grass green linen pants, a bright pink shirt, and snakeskin moccasins that tapered to a sharp point and were last fashionable around the time of the Renaissance. His pale, watery eyes and jowly cheeks were partly concealed by steel-framed glasses from the 1970s. His long blond hair was so thin in front that the sunburned skin of his head gleamed through. On his left wrist he wore an old Jaeger-LeCoultre Reverso, a watch with a complicated mechanism that allowed you to turn the face and its glass cover inside and the rear side outward. That was how Boré wore it: a useless timepiece that looked like an armband made of crocodile leather with a rectangular steel inset. On his right hand he wore a gleaming signet ring made of lapis lazuli.

"Are you from the advertising agency?" the art historian said by way of greeting. His speech was slightly slurred as if his teeth didn't properly fit his jawbone. "I thought there was another two hours before we were due to go through the proofs of the exhibition brochure."

"Do I look like some ad agency jerk?" Marius replied, pulling out his police ID.

Blanc would have liked to have begun the conversation a little more politely. He gave a forced smile. "We have a few questions, Monsieur Boré. It relates to an accident. It won't take long."

"If it's to do with the Renault parked on the street, it belongs to my friend who lent me this house. He's always racing around. I hardly ever move the car. If you want to speak to my friend, however, you'll have to come back in eight weeks' time. He's on a diving vacation in Mauritius." He was about to close the door on them, but Blanc held it open, still with the frozen smile on his face. The car Boré had nodded toward was a yellow Laguna. Another light-colored car. One more reason to ask the man a few questions.

"It's about the accident in which Albert Cohen died."

"I heard about that on the radio." Boré suddenly seemed surprised and nervous. "Come in."

He led them up a staircase with worn stone steps to a tiny second-floor living room with framed movie posters from the fifties hanging on the white plastered walls. The floor had square terra-cotta tiles protected by a glistening layer of wax. The ceiling was supported by two round woodwormed beams that made the room so low that Blanc had to duck underneath the first before sitting down on a fabric-covered stool. Marius gave a satisfied sigh as he settled into an old rocking chair, while Boré sat on the sofa. He sat so upright that he didn't even touch the sofa back. In the middle of the room stood a low table, the surface of which had been made from an old oak door. On it lay an open black plastic case with an electrical gadget plugged into it that reminded Blanc of some old measuring apparatus. Next to it were a few tiny needles. Boré noticed the gendarme's glance and quickly closed the cover.

"Did you know Monsieur Cohen?" Blanc asked him.

"Why do you want to know? They said on the news it was an accident. Wasn't it?"

"Please answer my question."

"*Eh bien*, of course I saw Cohen now and again on talk shows. Not that I watch that sort of thing regularly. I never read any of his articles; he didn't exactly write much about culture. He didn't turn up to exhibitions either, as far as I know." Boré hesitated for a moment as if to catch his breath before continuing. "I only met him in person for the first time last week. He called me up and asked if we could arrange a meeting because he wanted to talk to me about Van Gogh."

"About what in particular?" Blanc persisted.

"About everything!" Boré raised his chubby hands and let them fall again, a gesture that suggested resignation at such naïveté.

"When did you meet?" Marius interjected.

The art historian took his smartphone out of his shirt pocket. "Let me look at my calendar," he said. "Thursday of last week, July 28, three P.M. Cohen was punctual. Not something I'm used to with artists and curators." He gave a nervous laugh. Blanc and Marius exchanged looks: one week before the accident.

"When did Cohen call you to arrange the meeting?" Blanc asked.

"That same day, sometime in the morning. He said he was writing something for his magazine, something to do with Van Gogh. 'Something,' I asked him, groaning to myself. The usual journalistic rubbish, I supposed, clueless hacks looking for me to give them a quote because they're too lazy to plow through my book themselves."

"In that case, why did you even agree to see Monsieur Cohen?" Blanc pressed him.

"Because he was Monsieur Cohen, a man on television. I make a living organizing art exhibitions that bring in hordes of people. *Mon Dieu*, I'm one who turns exhibitions of paintings into events that draw crowds as big as those that turn up for soccer games! I did the big Renoir exhibition in Paris back in the day. And in the same way as soccer wouldn't be what it was without television, art exhibitions wouldn't work anymore without cameras. That's why I agreed, though I have to say I was quite surprised."

Marius gave the art historian a knowing look. "Because Cohen was even more clueless than you had imagined?"

"Because Cohen had read my book cover to cover, and it

wasn't just my book. He had already seen with his own eyes the most important places in Provence where Van Gogh had painted, even though he'd only been down in the Midi for a week. You know," he said with a sigh, "most people think Van Gogh never sold a single painting in his lifetime. The stereotype of an unsuccessful painter. Most people are *connards*."

The way he said it made Blanc think the art historian was including him and Marius in this group. Which in his own case, at least in this respect, was true. "But Cohen knew Van Gogh had sold paintings?" he asked.

"Indeed. In 1882, right at the beginning of his career, the artist had sold a few drawings, even if not for much money. But by 1890, just six months before his suicide, a Belgian woman collector paid him four hundred francs, a considerable sum in those days, for his *Red Vineyard*. There was a hugely positive review in a reputable newspaper, and an exhibition. Van Gogh had just about made it; he didn't kill himself because he had lost all hope. And Cohen knew all that. He even knew how much the *Red Vineyard* had cost. He was very well informed, for a journalist."

"In that case what did he want to ask you about?"

"He wanted to know the real reasons behind Van Gogh's insanity and his self-destructive drive."

"That cost him his ear?"

"And eventually his life. My theory, which I put forward vehemently in my book and has attracted a lot of comment, not all of it complimentary, is that the artist was always unstable, but the extravagance of light and color down here in the south was more than he could cope with. Van Gogh lived through his eyes, more than anyone else in the nineteenth century. Now imagine this child, who lives through his eyes, growing up in the damp gray north and then turning up as an adult in the Midi. The sky during the mistral! The sun! Cypress trees! Stars! The sea! And the light that unveils colors as if peeling them raw! It was Provence that more or less killed Van Gogh."

Marius gave Blanc a look. It was obvious he considered Boré an old windbag. "And that was all you spoke to Cohen about?" Blanc asked dubiously.

"I gave him a few nice quotes, even better than the ones in my book. I explained the 'Van Gogh myth' to him. You see, I write a book about every artist I organize an exhibition in respect of. It's a sort of homage. But I don't have any illusions: six months later you'll find my art books in the remainder section of every bargain bookstore, a great Christmas present for somebody who doesn't want to spend too much money. It's only *Vincent van Gogh and the Light of the South* that gets regularly reprinted. The self-mutilating artist exerts a fascination over us. If he had had success after success from 1890 onward, he would today be one of those worthy artists whose works fill our museums. Nothing more. It was the insanity that was at the same time destructive and creative that makes him one of the modern saints in our world lacking saints."

Marius cleared his throat. "Let me get this straight: If Van Gogh hadn't sawn off his ear, he would never have become a pop star?"

Boré gave him an irritated look. "I think Monsieur Cohen would have found a more elegant way of putting it."

"Was the mythical status of Van Gogh's insanity all he wanted to talk to you about?" Blanc asked.

The art historian hesitated again for a few moments. "He also asked me about photos of Van Gogh," he eventually admitted in a quiet voice.

"Photos?" Blanc queried skeptically.

Boré got up without a word and disappeared into the next room, coming back with a copy of his own book. He flicked through the first few pages and then handed it across. "There are some forty self-portraits of Van Gogh extant. He had used himself as a model, in a manner of speaking, again and again."

"I know the picture of him with the pipe and the bandage on his mutilated ear," Marius declared.

Boré ignored him and tapped the open page. "Here are two photos. The only ones. The artist may have kept painting himself manically, but he had only two photos taken of him, one as a kid of thirteen and once again as a nineteen-year-old apprentice art dealer. It's the light, you see? As if Van Gogh was afraid of the incorruptible, the clinical eye of the camera. There is no photo of him as a mature artist, but . . ." He fell silent.

"But Monsieur Cohen showed you one?" Blanc suggested.

"No, no, no. I mean, yes, he paid so much attention to asking me about photos of Van Gogh that I came to believe—even though he denied it—that he had in the course of his research seen a photo. A photo of Van Gogh that nobody knows about." He looked at them as if he expected the two gendarmes to gasp with incredulity.

Blanc's heart rate was, however, unaffected by the number of existing photos of Van Gogh. "Did Cohen also ask you about the time you worked at the Musée Maly?" he asked in a congenial tone but allowing just the slightest touch of suspicion to creep in.

Boré stared long and hard at him before clearing his throat and answering, "I was obliged to promise Monsieur Cohen that that part of our conversation would remain confidential. He had done some research and didn't want anything to slip out prematurely. I had to promise him I wouldn't say a word to anyone about it."

"I'm quite certain Cohen won't be angry with you if you no longer keep your promise," Blanc replied drily.

"*Eh bien*," Boré began resignedly, opening a cupboard and taking out a glass, a carafe of water, and a bottle of Ricard. "I'd offer you a glass, too, if you weren't on duty," he said apologetically, pouring himself a good two fingers' worth of the pastis. Blanc waited until the art historian had knocked it back.

"Cohen was here for a good half hour," Boré said at last. "Up until then we had had a really interesting discussion about Van Gogh. And then he suddenly mentioned the theft from the Musée Maly." He shook his head, filling his glass again. "I was rather taken aback. I don't exactly think back to those days on a regular basis. I started working there back in 1988, my first job as a curator. What a commotion there was when the Van Gogh was stolen!"

"And Cohen was researching this old cold case," Blanc interjected.

"Yes, and he wanted to go over all the details with me."

"I would be very grateful if you could go over all the same details with me."

Boré sighed. "I couldn't tell Cohen anything more than I'd told the police at the time. And I can't tell you any more now. I had taken a vacation that week to go and look at the big yachts that had all come down to Saint-Tropez for the regatta. Me and a colleague," he hesitated a moment, "I was very close to at the time. Anyway, we only heard about the theft the morning after, on the radio. We rushed to the museum, but the cops had already closed off the whole area."

"Were you interrogated?"

"Of course."

"Inside job," Marius murmured.

"In my opinion they let the caretaker off the hook far too fast."

"Olivier Guillaume?"

"If you already know it all, why bother asking me? It was

just the same with Cohen. He already knew what I was going to tell him."

"I enjoy watching reruns on television," Marius said honestly. "Go on, tell it all to me again. It's just as interesting the second time around."

Boré gave him an irritated glance and downed the contents of his second glass. "For someone who loves art—really loves art, if you know what I mean—a theft like that hurts as much as . . ."—he looked out of the window—"a blow to the head. It really hurts, more than any layman can understand. Most thieves aren't the clever criminals you see in the movies."

"Our experience with criminals doesn't just come from the movies," Marius interjected. He was really in a bad mood now.

"Art thieves are either weirdos, for whom a painting is a bit like a little boy to a pedophile, or else they're *connards*, who only realize later that the work they've stolen is practically unsellable. Then they rip the painting out of the frame, sometimes even fold it up, damaging the canvas, rubbing off the colors. Sometimes priceless ancient artworks are hidden away in damp cellars or in lofts exposed to the sun and heat. When they're eventually found—*if* they're found—they look as if they've been in a street riot."

"Why did you suspect Guillaume? Which category did you place him in? The *connards* or the weirdos?"

"The weirdos. He was no idiot. He understood something about art. His father was an important collector. Olivier Guillaume practically grew up with art. He was cleverer than the rest of us put together, but"—Boré searched for the right word—"just somehow, weird. I'm sorry I can't find a better way of putting it. Strange. He had never graduated, never taken a course or anything, despite his brilliance. He never went out, never drank a glass of wine. He was the museum factotum. He knew all about the security system, how to turn off the alarm systems; he had the keys to every door. If there was one man who could rob the Musée Maly without setting off an alarm, then he was that man. But your colleagues just let him walk free almost immediately. The directors fired him straightaway, because nobody trusted him anymore. But that was his only punishment, if you look at it like that. And the Van Gogh has not been seen since."

"When did you leave the Musée Maly?"

"Not long after Guillaume. Of my own accord," Boré added quickly. He glanced briefly at the Ricard bottle, as if he was tempted to pour himself a third pastis, but decided against it. "My female colleague and I left for Paris because that's the only place you can really make a career in our business. I soon got to launch my first major exhibition. And my colleague got to know somebody else. We lost sight of each other. I had too much else going on in my head. I simply didn't think about the Musée Maly and the theft anymore."

"Until Monsieur Cohen came knocking at your door. Do you think the journalist might really have had a lead on the case?"

"He made hints, nothing more." Boré looked as if he was struggling with himself, then gave a sigh. "Look," he started. "I am responsible for the most successful art exhibitions in the country. But amid art historians I'm nonetheless—no, precisely because of that—considered to be a fraud. A lightweight. Do you have any idea what it's like when people at conferences roll their eyes whenever your name is mentioned? The way they snort snobbishly? With a single one of my exhibitions I introduce more people to art than *les messieurs professeurs* do with all the seminars in their entire dreary lives! But they despise me because I have a popular following. And then all of a sudden somebody bursts into my house telling me he can explain the case of a stolen Van Gogh. The first painting of the Saintes-Maries fishing boats series that disappeared two decades ago is rediscovered. And I'm part of it! Name any of *les messieurs professeurs* who've ever found a missing Van Gogh."

"Do you think Cohen also suspected Guillaume?"

"He didn't show his cards. Didn't say anything that clearly. But I am sure that Cohen had his suspicions. He told me he wanted to talk to Guillaume. But he didn't say anything more than that."

Blanc remembered the note in Cohen's file that mentioned Guillaume by name. "What did the town of Saint-Gilles have to do with Van Gogh?" he asked.

Boré gave him a surprised look. "Nothing. The painter never went there. There is no museum there with any of his works. All Saint-Gilles has is its famous church with the medieval entrance. Why do you ask?"

Blanc ignored his question. "Does Guillaume work there now?"

"I don't know. I haven't heard anything about the guy for the past twenty years."

"You didn't meet Cohen a second time?" Blanc asked.

"No. Cohen was going to call me. As far as I understood, he wanted to see me again this week. When I heard on the radio about his terrible accident I almost swerved into an oncoming car."

"You were in the car when you heard the news?" Blanc asked. "On the day of the accident?" He was thinking of Boré's absent friend's yellow Renault Laguna parked outside the house.

"Yes. I'd been in Marseille where I'd finally gotten to see the Museum of European and Mediterranean Civilizations, the so-called MuCEM. It was evening before I got back. I was just outside Eyguières when I turned on the eight o'clock news. You don't think Cohen's investigations had anything to do with his gruesome death, do you?"

"So far it just looks like an accident," Blanc lied, and gave a reassuring smile. "But as a cop, when you hear a story about an old, unsolved theft, then obviously you get a bit suspicious."

"Keep me in the loop," Boré requested. "Like I said, it would mean a lot to me to rediscover the disappeared Van Gogh."

The two gendarmes got to their feet and the art historian accompanied them to the door. He placed his feet carefully like someone frightened of stumbling. When they stepped out into the harsh sunlight, Blanc turned back to him and said, "Could it be that the female colleague you used to be so close to and who went with you to Paris, went on to marry Monsieur Leroux?"

Boré made a gesture that simultaneously suggested regret and a relaxed resignation. He reminded Blanc of a tennis player who considered his sport to be only a hobby and had just lost an irrelevant game. "Marie-Claude Elbaz was the prettiest and cleverest colleague in the museum, but she was somehow untouchable. Even though I spent more than a year with her virtually day and night, I somehow never had the feeling of getting to know her. When she went in another direction shortly after we arrived in Paris together, I never really felt it as a loss. There were so many women in Paris . . ." For a moment or two he lost himself in his memories. "To this very day I have not met the woman of my life, never married, but of all the women I've had relationships with over the years there was never one I knew as little as Marie-Claude."

"Did Cohen ask you about Marie-Claude?"

The art historian looked astonished by the question. "No. I haven't seen Marie-Claude for years. Cohen worked for Leroux. It can only have been Marie-Claude who set him on the scent of this old theft. I imagine she told him personally everything she knew about it."

"*Bon après-midi*, Monsieur Boré," Blanc said as they left. "You've been a great help."

"Do you think that's true?" Blanc wondered as they reached the Mégane. They opened all the doors to let the hot air out before eventually sighing and getting in.

"Madame Leroux admitted it was her idea to give Cohen the inconsequential Van Gogh in Provence story," the captain went on. "A story about the painter and his life down here in the south to accompany the exhibition in Arles, organized by her former lover."

"Madame Leroux neglected to mention that detail?"

"Her husband was standing next to her at the time. In any case she made not the slightest reference to the theft twenty years ago."

"But she knew what kind of a reporter Cohen was. There was every possibility that as soon as he started doing research about Van Gogh in the south he would find out about the theft. Was Madame Leroux so naive as to think Cohen would overlook something like that? Or was she putting him onto this harmless-sounding little story in the hope that he would stumble upon the old scandal? Maybe she even thought Cohen might come up with a lead?" Marius speculated.

"If that was the case, then her husband knew nothing about her plan. It seemed to me that the publisher believed Cohen was going to deliver the story they'd agreed on, not a smoking gun."

Marius laughed. "If the potential for a job in journalism wasn't even worse than that for a cop, I'd be asking Leroux for a job! After all we heard talking to Boré, I could write the story for *L'Événement* myself. How much do you think they'd pay?"

"Right now, not very much," Blanc guessed. "Are you short of money?"

"For the vet."

Blanc gave his colleague a puzzled glance. "Dog? Cat? Parrot? Or do you have a herd of goats at home?"

"A tomcat. Don't look at me like that. Everybody needs someone to look pleased when you open the door in the evening. You'll end up with a four-legged friend, too."

"A cat's only pleased because it can't manage the can opener on its own."

"My cat can't even find his own food bowl. Brain tumor."

"You're joking? About the brain tumor, I mean?"

Marius looked out of the passenger window as they drove past a field of olive trees, the leaves of which reflected the sunlight like tiny shards of glass. "When the cat began wandering around the living room for half an hour solid, banging its head into the same table leg every time, I had him looked at. The thing in his skull is as big as a marble. Really, I need to put him down out of kindness, but I can't bring myself to pull the trigger."

Blanc thought about the fact that Marius hadn't been promoted since he had accidentally fired at a colleague in a nighttime operation years ago. But then there were other rumors that went around the Gadet gendarmerie station, too, rumors among the old-timers who shut up whenever they saw Blanc, Marius's partner, the new guy, the Parisian, the cop whose career had also been dumped in the trash. Still at the wheel, he managed to pull out a fifty-euro note from his wallet and handed it to Marius, who gave him a nod of thanks.

"I'll drop you off at Le Soleil. But you'll have to have lunch on your own. I have another engagement."

"Where?"

"Salon hospital. I need to talk to the pathologist."

"Maybe Dr. Thezan will roll you a joint. I'm told that reduces hunger."

"Not true, I'm afraid."

It was a good hour later when Blanc met up with the doctor in the Institut Médico-Légal and she only had a steaming cup of green tea in her hand. He shook his head when she offered him one. "If I were to drink something hot in this weather, I'd melt."

"Have you cut open Monsieur Cohen yet?" he asked.

"The bull did that for me. I've sewn him up again, after taking a look around in his insides." She tapped a sheaf of papers on her desk. "I was just about to send you the report. It's not going to surprise you: serious internal and external injuries. Monsieur Cohen both bled out and suffocated: his lungs collapsed. The murder weapon was the animal's left horn according to blood and tissue samples on it. Zero alcohol in his blood and no traces of drugs or medication in his urine. The roots of his hair contained old traces of cocaine. But then that's not something we didn't know about."

"But at least you can confirm that at the time of his death Cohen was stone-cold sober. That means it's unlikely he would have opened the gate himself. The man was in full control of his senses."

Just then someone opened the door of Thezan's office without knocking. The young man who came in was the same one Blanc had seen sitting in the passenger seat of the Jeep. He nodded to the doctor, glanced disinterestedly at the gendarme, but held the door open.

Fontaine Thezan pulled her sunglasses down from her hair and put them on. "Would you excuse us please, *mon Capitaine*?"

Blanc accompanied the two of them out into the parking lot, wondering if the doctor and her taciturn companion were a couple. He was also wondering how somebody who daily used a scalpel and an electric saw to cut up human bodies could bring herself to caress a warm, living body. But he imagined Dr. Thezan would laugh out loud at him if he even gave a hint that he thought about things like that.

As it happened, she laughed out loud at him anyway when she saw the blue 2CV. “Is the public purse so stretched that we have to send the cops out in 2CVs?”

“We spend all our money on autopsies.”

“If you crash this tin can into a modern car, you’ll be next on my autopsy table.”

Her companion smiled for a second, but Blanc couldn’t decide if it was out of sympathy or irony.

On the way back to Sainte-Françoise-la-Vallée, he took the doctor’s words to heart and drove so slowly that even delivery trucks riskily overtook him. As the flow of wind through the folded-up side windows tousled his hair, he found himself thinking of Cohen and Marie-Claude Leroux. Maybe she hadn’t been responsible for setting him on the trail of the old theft, either deliberately or by accident. Maybe Cohen, as an old friend of the Leroux family, had known that she had been working at the Musée Maly at the time the Van Gogh disappeared? In which case, far from being the one who had put him onto a lead, she might have been the one who was prepared to do anything to get him off it. If a theft from a museum is an inside job, then everybody is a suspect, including a young female curator with an interest in yachts. Along with the young male curator . . .

Boré. Blanc tried to imagine the somewhat eccentric, somewhat overweight, far from healthy exhibition promoter with his snakeskin shoes standing by the edge of a field with a bull in it and pulling open the gate behind which the beast was already snorting. It was an absurd image. And what would his motive have been? The same as Marie-Claude Leroux's? Marie-Claude and Boré had left for Paris together, just after the theft. Was it really a career move that just happened to coincide? Or was it a well-disguised escape? Then many years later Marie-Claude Leroux puts her husband's most famous reporter onto a story linked to an exhibition in Arles being organized by her former lover. Maybe she was trying to put pressure on Boré? Maybe she wanted Cohen to dig something up? For a brief moment Blanc imagined himself going back to Paris, entering the art historian's apartment, and finding in one of the rooms a little picture of fishing boats on a beach . . .

Then he told himself to stop being ridiculous. There had been a chief suspect back at the time of the theft. A man Cohen had been keeping tabs on, as the blurred photo proved. A man Cohen wanted to meet but hadn't yet spoken to because death had caught up with him first. It would be interesting to ask Olivier Guillaume a few questions, Blanc thought.

An Old Suspect

On Monday morning Blanc was woken up by Douchy's rooster crowing on the other side of the river as if trying to scare Napoleon's army. Mist rising from the Touloubre was drifting between the tops of the plane trees. At least three dozen jackdaws, little dark ghosts of the dead, fluttered upward in the foliage squawking angrily as he emerged from the oil mill. The sun hadn't quite risen yet, but the sky in the east was as white and clear as soft chalk. It seemed to Blanc that every breath was drawing warm air into his lungs. It was good that Sunday was over, he thought to himself.

The day off had felt like twenty-four hours in jail. He had forced himself not to go to the gendarmerie station so as not to make it even more apparent to his colleagues that he had nothing else to do. But he *had* nothing else to do: he had paced up and down outside his old house like a tiger in a cage. He had thought so long and hard about Cohen's death and imagined so many ways in which it might have happened that it seemed ludicrous in the end. The guy just died in a stupid accident, he told himself, and I'm every bit as stupid for hunting a nonexistent murderer. No, it *wasn't* an accident, *merde*, it was a cleverly thought-out attack. Back in Paris he had known he was a tenacious investigator. Not always on the right track, not always successful, and often enough disliked by his bosses and his colleagues. But tenacious. Down here he was no longer so sure: what was it that was driving him on? Was it still tenacity? Or was it blindness?

He longed for Aveline. But her husband had come down from Paris, and he had no interest in finding out how she spent her Sundays. He longed for Geneviève, but she had long been living a life in which he no longer played a role. He longed to see his children. He'd called Astrid and Eric, but in both cases he had only gotten their voice mail. He'd found himself stupidly not knowing what to say. He'd just stammered a few sentences and hung up, fully realizing that he must sound like an idiot to his children, if they ever even heard it. Eric didn't reply. That evening on Facebook he'd found a message from Astrid.

Good to hear you're well. I'm fine. Since when did you start being interested in my well-being?

Blanc had closed the message. How could he answer it? His children blamed him for the breakup of the marriage: Papa was never home. Papa had missed the piano recitals, the basketball games, and sometimes even birthdays. Papa was more interested in criminals than us.

It was good that Sunday was over.

Blanc had arranged an early Monday morning meeting with Fuligni Junior, the son of the dead building contractor. He had been a bit apprehensive about the meeting, but when a battered white truck pulled up outside the oil mill, the driver gave him a friendly wave from behind the wheel.

Matthieu Fuligni was in his late twenties, had his black hair shaved almost to his skull, and was wearing torn jeans and worker's shoes spattered with mortar. His upper body was bare and more tanned than any sunbed could achieve. He shook Blanc's hand and introduced himself. Either he didn't know that the captain had investigated the murder case in which his father had been the victim or he didn't think any ill of him for it.

Blanc was relieved. He showed him the tile and told him he wanted his house reroofed with the same.

"Good choice. Even the Greeks and the Romans used *tuiles canals* to roof their houses. The clay is Provençal and the tiles are still made by hand today," Fuligni told him. He pointed to the relief on the fired clay. "A cicada, the firm's trademark. You put the cicada facing upward when you lay the tile on the roof. Perfect protection. Turn the tile over and put a load of them together and *voilà* you have a perfect clay water chute. Clever, isn't it? I'll fix the tiles onto the roof beams with mortar and then the wind won't blow them off."

"Not even the mistral?" Blanc pushed him, hoping the tiles would be nailed on or fixed with screws or glue or in some other less traditional manner.

"*Pas de souci*," Fuligni said. "No worries."

Blanc was of the opinion that when a doctor told you "*Pas de souci*," it was time to start writing your will. He was beginning to wonder if his oil mill was a hopeless case.

Fuligni was now talking about quantities and price and something called Manitou. It took Blanc a while to realize that he was talking about a type of crane he would need to get up onto the roof. He did a mental accounting of his financial problems and nodded reluctantly when he heard Fuligni's initial estimate. *Pas de souci.*

When the builder was just about to head off, Blanc heard footsteps and saw his neighbor approaching. Paulette Aybalen waved to Fuligni, who had climbed into his truck, and kissed Blanc on both cheeks.

"I have some loose tiles on the roof," he told her, showing her the one he was holding.

"Matthieu will soon fix that."

"It sounds as if it's going to be expensive."

"He'll charge you the proper price. It looks as if he could have a few more jobs to do for you here." She nodded smilingly at the old oil mill.

"It's going to burn up all my money. Nothing left for my kids to inherit."

"I didn't know you had kids."

"Two," Blanc told her, embarrassed all of a sudden. "They already go . . ."—he searched for the right way of putting it—". . . their own ways," he ended up saying, somewhat lamely.

Paulette looked as if she had been about to contradict him, then thought better of it and changed the subject. "Yesterday I saw the battered Renault of the village policeman from Caillouteaux going through Sainte-Françoise-la-Vallée. I've never seen him here before and certainly not on a Sunday. Do you know why that was?"

Blanc had called his colleague and asked him to. For a moment he considered lying to his neighbor so as not to worry her. *Pas de souci.* But he realized she would see through him. "To watch out for aggressive lawyers," he said.

She shook her head, leaving him uncertain as to whether she was pleased or annoyed. Paulette took the *tuile canal* from his hand. "I could never again live with a man under the same roof," she muttered.

"Take the tile as a gift," Blanc said.

"For my damaged roof." She laughed. A loud neighing sound

came from across the road. "I'd better go and deal with my horses in the field," she told him. She took the *tuile canal* with her.

By the time Blanc got into his 2CV, he was in a substantially better mood than he had been an hour earlier. He picked up Marius from Gadet in the patrol car, Fabienne jumping into the backseat at the last moment: "I want to see the troll," she explained.

Her two colleagues stared at her uncomprehendingly. She rolled her eyes theatrically. "I've never seen a silver-haired mommy's boy face-to-face."

"I hope he doesn't disappoint you," Marius said. "What if the mommy's boy turns out to be J. R. Ewing?"

It was Fabienne's turn to stare at him in puzzlement, then she laughed. "Sometimes I think you've come into the century through a time warp from the 1980s."

"I'm a very conservative person deep down," Marius grumbled. "In any case, I know Guillaume," he told them. "At least slightly. I saw the photo you printed out, Fabienne, and somehow the guy looked familiar. It took me an hour before I realized he's a server at the bar in Le National."

"The bar in Gadet where Cohen took the picture of him?" Blanc asked, surprised.

"Yes. Although to say he serves there isn't quite right. I don't go into Le National that often. I've just heard that he's worked there as a waiter. But I managed to overhear the boss and a few of the regulars at the next table making jokes about him. Apparently he turned out to be a bit too odd to be allowed to have regular contact with human beings. Since then he just stands behind the bar, far away from all the customers, and spends the whole of his day opening wine bottles and washing dishes. I've never exchanged a word with him."

"Sounds just like *Dallas*," Fabienne said.

They took a detour around the center of Salon and drove through Bel Air, a suburb of faceless big houses and dead-straight avenues. It wasn't just the name that made Blanc think it resembled an unfortunate mixture of Provence and California. The district had been thrown up without planning over the past few decades on the flat plain of the Crau. Marius made a sign to him at a traffic light and they turned into a narrow tarmac road running toward a horizon already shimmering in the heat. Blanc was driving alongside a drainage ditch that was giving off brackish clouds of steam from the pale brown water in it. Rice fields. A horse paddock. Hedges of cypress trees some sixty feet high. Countless numbers of frogs croaking so monotonously loud that they drowned out the noise of the patrol car's engine. There were fewer and fewer houses and those were looking shabby with dirty plaster. In the middle of the plain stood a dilapidated barn that had been turned into a garage. With his newly acquired connoisseur's eye, Blanc noted a few partially eviscerated 2CVs, but there was no sign of a mechanic. In fact, there was nobody at all to be seen along the road, no pedestrians, no cyclists. Only in his rearview mirror did he spot the silhouette of a car, one that had been following them for some time at the same distance.

"This is where the guy lives," Marius said suddenly, recognizing a house number from his notebook: a building that had once had white plaster but was now mottled with glistening gray as if it had been touched all over by children with sticky hands. The roof was of an indistinguishable color and so flat it looked as if it had ducked down in fright. There was a sort of front yard with a broken asphalt surface where the gaps were filled in with gravel or black soil. A wooden door that looked as if it had seen its last lick of green paint some thirty years ago. As the Mégane's engine came to a halt, the car that Blanc had seen following them in his rearview mirror rolled into the yard. It was a battered Peugeot

Partner, with tin panels instead of a glass window set into its padded rear chassis. Yet another white car, Blanc realized. It was like a curse.

They sat there silently in the patrol car for a moment, giving the driver of the Peugeot time to get out before they did. They took a close look at him: late fifties, thin, pale hair of an indistinguishable color, a gaunt face that looked somehow uncoordinated—his forehead and cheeks were almost free from lines, but his small eyes seemed stuck together at the corners and his narrow, pressed-together lips could have been those of an old man. He was wearing light linen pants, but despite the heat a long-sleeved shirt, tennis socks, and sandals. A gold crucifix hung from a fine chain around his neck. He limped clearly on his right leg.

"Olivier Guillaume," Fabienne announced triumphantly. "I recognize him from his photos. A perfect troll."

"Take a look at his right wrist," Blanc replied with a smile. "The guy is wearing a heavy old diver's watch, the way macho guys used to. Except that he's wearing it on the wrong arm. It doesn't exactly fit with your troll image."

"Maybe he bought it with the money he got for the stolen Van Gogh?" Fabienne replied, tapping on the car window. "Let's get out and go troll hunting."

Guillaume was standing next to his car waiting for them. He looked suspicious, which wasn't exactly surprising for a man who had spent a night in a cell awaiting interrogation, Blanc thought. At that very moment the door of the house opened and a tiny bent-over woman with a pale yellow ribbon around her thick snow-white hair, bound up into a long ponytail like a young girl's, emerged. Even though she must have been at least ninety years old and moved with tiny footsteps, she came over to them quickly, a lot more quickly than her son, who seemed reluctant to move away from his vehicle. She took a long look at the new arrivals with unpleasantly dark eyes.

"You!" she shouted, pointing at Fabienne with her gout-afflicted right hand. Her voice was high but remarkably strong. "What are you doing here?" She was looking only at the young policewoman, aggressively and challengingly. Blanc was beginning to understand why Olivier Guillaume had never married.

"We're investigating an accident," the captain said. "We just want to ask Monsieur Guillaume a few questions. As a witness," he quickly added as the hot glare of an old lady spoiling for a fight was turned on him.

"It will only take a few minutes of your precious time, Madame," Marius added.

Blanc gave his colleague a look, surprised to hear him so formal all of a sudden. Whether it was his well-put words, his deep voice, or just Marius's rather shabby appearance that was in no way threatening, one way or the other Guillaume's mother suddenly seemed to relax and gave Marius a toothless grimace that might just have been a smile: "Very well then," she croaked. "As long as it's brief." She didn't invite them into the house. The gendarmes, Guillaume, and his mother had been standing between the parked cars and the building, in a sort of no-man's-land. The asphalt surface was like a giant hot plate beneath their feet and the torturous concert the frogs made from the drainage ditch next to the road was so loud that Blanc had to raise his voice to be heard. "We're investigating Monsieur Cohen's accident."

"So that's why the guy didn't turn up," Guillaume interrupted him. "Did he crash into a tree?"

The gendarmes exchanged brief glances. Guillaume didn't watch television or listen to the radio. Nor did he surf the Internet.

Not that sort of "troll," Blanc thought. Either that or he's lying to us. "You've heard nothing about it?" he asked, to be sure.

"We're not interested in other people's business," the old lady shouted, looking at him defiantly. "We're not cops!"

"Unfortunately, Monsieur Cohen is dead," Marius told her, explaining the circumstances of the accident in the Camargue in a few sentences. Once again his words seemed to have a calming influence on Guillaume's mother despite the strangeness of the story.

"So what are you doing here?" Guillaume asked. He didn't seem at all calm.

"Because Monsieur Cohen wanted to talk to you." Blanc's vision dimmed. It seemed to him the cacophony made by the frogs was getting louder by the second. It felt as if the frogs were laughing at him. Pull yourself together. "In our investigation of this tragic accident, we by chance came across Cohen's papers," he said, being somewhat economical with the truth. "And among them was his research into an old criminal case. The theft of the Van Gogh in the Musée Maly."

"That didn't have anything to do with his accident," Guillaume blurted out.

"Probably not. But a criminal case is a criminal case. We're gendarmes and can't just ignore something like that, even if it's only an unusual chain of circumstance that brought it to our attention. Regulations are regulations," Blanc said, looking regretful. "It would appear that Monsieur Cohen had come across some new lead in this old business. And we're following up on it."

"And so, of course, you come up with me. You're no wiser than your colleagues all those years ago."

"It was Monsieur Cohen who came up with you," Blanc replied drily.

"He called me. I have no idea where he got my number from.

We aren't in the phone book. I didn't want to meet him. Journalists are almost worse than cops. But I let myself be talked into it because . . ." Guillaume gave his mother a look like a dog wanting a pat on the head, but she was staring at Fabienne again. "Because, for some reason or other, I believed he considered me to be innocent," he said, finishing the sentence a bit more dejectedly.

"Is that what he said?" Blanc asked.

Guillaume changed his weight from one foot to the other. Standing around on this parking lot must be even worse for someone who limps than it is for us, Blanc thought. "Not in so many words. But for one reason or another, I had the impression that Cohen suspected somebody else. On the phone he was so . . ."—Guillaume sought for a word—"sympathetic," he finally blurted out. "I would genuinely have been glad to meet him. I might have been able to tell him something or other."

"You also had a suspicion of your own back then?" Fabienne interjected. Her voice sounded higher than normal, nervous because of the old lady fixing her constantly with a hostile glare.

Guillaume rubbed his right temple. He wasn't sweating despite his socks and long-sleeved shirt. "They just suspected me back then because I was the janitor. A doormat. They could pin it on me, they thought. But I defended myself!"

"We're talking to you as a witness, not a suspect," Marius reminded him.

"Your colleagues should have interrogated that Boré! And his girlfriend!"

"Marie-Claude Elbaz?" Blanc asked, to be sure. He was wishing people in Bel Air ate more frogs' legs so that they could have had an easier conversation.

"They were a fine pair, I can tell you! Boré always presented himself as a tough guy, ran around like pop star Johnny Hallyday, and wanted to paint like Picasso. But nobody would have taken him for either of them." Guillaume gave a short, bitter, ironic laugh. "He was a phony, a loser. He was always going to the doctor's with his diabetes." Blanc recalled the little machine he had spotted in the art historian's house—a test set, for measuring blood sugar levels. Were diabetics allowed to drink that much pastis?

"Real artists," Guillaume went on, "are tough and good. Boré was weak and hated all artists because he was jealous of them. In the Musée Maly he set up the spotlights so as to create shadows or reflections on the canvases. On one occasion I caught him deliberately turning a light the wrong way. I was the one who had to rectify it all. He didn't write any explanatory texts to go with the pictures. There was all the correct information about the artist, about the year the work was done. But even that always sounded somehow . . . patronizing, condescending. As if the artists didn't really deserve to be shown in the museum, know what I mean? He couldn't do that with Van Gogh, he was too famous. And the drawing was really, undoubtedly sublime. And then one night it was gone. Odd, eh?"

"You think Boré stole it?"

"He insisted he had gone to see the yachts down at the Voiles. But he couldn't have told the difference between a schooner and a punt. He probably can't even swim. And could you imagine Marie-Claude on a millionaire's yacht?"

Blanc thought of her natural elegance—and the fact that she was married to a rich and influential publisher. "Yes," he said calmly.

"Then you have more imagination than me," Guillaume replied irritatedly. "Marie-Claude wasn't as harmless as she looks. She has a past, you should be interviewing her! I wondered back then why the cops didn't dig deeper. She would have had no scruples about stealing a picture. She already had someone on her conscience."

Blanc glanced at Marius. His answer was to turn his bleary eyes up to the sky. *Connard*, that meant. A few minutes before Fabienne had gotten out her iPad and googled Marie-Claude Elbaz. She shook her head: no entry

"Did you mention your allegations when you were being interviewed?" Blanc asked.

"I mentioned it, and a young woman typed it up in the minutes of the interview, but the cops looked at me as if the moment I left the room they would throw it in the trash."

"Are you still in touch with Monsieur Boré and Mademoiselle Elbaz?"

"After the stolen Van Gogh business they fired me. The pair of them scurried off to Paris. Every now and then you hear something about Boré. But wild horses couldn't drag me to an exhibition organized by that guy. I've had nothing to do with that pretty pair for ages."

Fabienne quickly typed something into her iPad and turned it as inconspicuously as possible so that Blanc could read it: *G doesn't know that B and M-C split up long ago.* And he probably doesn't know either that both of them are currently down here in the south, Blanc filled in mentally, nodding.

"Monsieur Guillaume," he said aloud, "in his notes Cohen also refers to a place on the edge of the Camargue, not too far from your house: Saint-Gilles. Have you any idea whether that could have anything to do with the theft?"

Guillaume automatically grasped the golden cross hanging on his chest, then noticed that the gendarmes had noticed and immediately let it go again. "That's a long way from the Côte d'Azur," he mumbled, as if that had some significance. Then he stood up straight. "I have no idea why Cohen made some note about Saint-Gilles," he declared. It sounded honest but at the same time as if he was concealing something.

"You had arranged to meet Monsieur Cohen on the morning of Friday, August the fifth. When did he call you to arrange the meeting?"

Guillaume shrugged. "Tuesday? Wednesday? Down here one day's much the same as the next. Hard to say for sure. Wednesday, I think."

"Could it have been Thursday?"

"No, I don't think so."

"Because you weren't at home on Thursday?" Blanc pressed him, trying hard to sound indifferent.

"My son is at home every day. It's only in the evening he goes out to work in Gadet," Guillaume's mother interjected, staring at Blanc to challenge him. The old woman had worked out why I was asking, the captain realized. Clever old witch. She's just given him an alibi for the day of Cohen's death. He was at home with *Maman*.

"*Merci beaucoup et bonne journée*," Blanc said, concluding the interview and holding out his right hand.

Guillaume hesitated fleetingly and then shook his hand.

"Nice watch," the captain commented in passing.

"It's a memento from my father," Guillaume replied, somewhat embarrassed. His mother glared at Blanc with open hatred and snorted. "Time for lunch," she announced, and began to lead her son off. Marius just nodded in farewell, but Fabienne took a quick step forward and shook Guillaume's hand.

"Why did you do that?" Blanc asked when they were back in the hot patrol car. "And don't tell me again that you were admiring beauty."

"I just thought that for once at least Guillaume might feel the touch of a woman," Fabienne explained.

"A troll!" Marius exclaimed, slapping the dashboard with his hand. "I'm thirsty, let's get out of here."

"Do either of you believe a word Guillaume said?" Blanc asked when they had finally turned back onto the main road and the frog chorus from the drainage ditch was behind them. "Boré a would-be Johnny Hallyday? Marie-Claude a sinister murderer? And Guillaume himself an innocent doormat?"

"If I had a mother like that I'd be crazy in the head, too," Marius observed.

"One thing is clear," Fabienne said. "He knows next to nothing about Boré or the woman who is today Madame Leroux. He doesn't even know who Cohen was. He's a hermit crab."

"Or maybe the stolen Van Gogh is hanging on a wall somewhere in that shabby little house," suggested Blanc. "Maybe that's why the old woman wouldn't let us in."

"And why did Guillaume react so strangely to the reference to Saint-Gilles?" Fabienne asked. "There was some reason why Cohen made a note of the name. It had something to do with the case. And then there was that outsize watch . . ."

"That might be irrelevant," Marius said. "He maintained it was something he'd inherited. His father was a respected lawyer in Gadet, everybody knew him. If a farmer wanted to argue about a public right-of-way over his land, or a baker wanted to fire one of his hired hands, or somebody wanted a quickie divorce, then *voilà* there was Guillaume Senior. I would have used him in my divorce case, but he was no longer with us. He was a cultured man, respected, and apart from that chairman of the local arts council. He was said to have had quite a collection."

"Boré said the same thing," Blanc continued.

"One day the old man was simply gone," Marius said. "To Paris, or Nice, nobody knew exactly. There were a few rumors about a younger woman doing the rounds in Gadet. One way or another there was another quickie divorce for his colleagues, this time one of their own. And that was that."

"Leaving behind an embittered wife, a disturbed son, and a decrepit house," Blanc suggested.

"Guillaume was just a kid back then?" Fabienne asked.

"Yes, not even ten years old, if I remember correctly. No surprise that he's not quite right in the head. And no surprise that ever since his mother has had no love for young, good-looking X-chromosome carriers."

After work Blanc invited his two colleagues to dinner. "We could try somewhere a bit grander than the restaurant in Gadet," he told them. "I dragged you both into this crazy case, so I ought to treat you."

"I'm glad you've realized that, better late than never," Marius replied, rubbing his hands together. "Let's go to Le Villon!"

"You're really going to make Roger pay up!" Fabienne laughed. But she didn't say no.

They took the 2CV to Saint-César, where Blanc recognized that the steam horse didn't really fit in with the restaurant. Le Villon stood on the bend of a narrow ill-lit street on the edge of the town, with a few houses from the seventeenth and eighteenth centuries. It had previously been either a mews for coaches or perhaps an artisan factory: a wall of unplastered stone separated the courtyard from the street. An LED spotlight in a niche illuminated the glass-covered menu and the Michelin star underneath the restaurant's name. They walked through a wrought-iron gate into the cobblestoned courtyard, where wooden chairs and tables stood in the shadow of a mimosa, the ten-foot-high crown of which acted as a sunshade. Its flimsy leaves fluttered in the breeze, and there was the scent of herbs and roasted meat in the air. As the young waitress led them to the only free table, Blanc was trying in vain to remember the figures on his last bank statement.

"What is the house specialty?" he asked Marius.

"They change the menu here every six weeks. Let's wait and be surprised." Marius sat up straight and began studying the menu with more attention than he'd ever applied to a case file.

Eventually he ordered the foie gras on apricots and then the liver ragout. Fabienne and Blanc both decided on the tomato carpaccio with crayfish as a starter. To follow, Blanc's colleague ordered the monkfish medallion, while he himself, thinking of Madame Leroux's enthusiasm, ordered the filet of veal with Camargue rice. As an accompaniment, they began with a local white wine, which Fabienne stayed with, while the men switched to a Châteauneuf-du-Pape. Altogether it was going to cost Blanc as much as the repairs to his Renault Espace. *Merde*, it would probably last as long, too.

Blanc didn't want to talk shop all evening, so he asked Fabienne, "How's your petition against the Front National mayor going?"

"If you hung out on Facebook a bit more often you would already have given it a like," she replied with a sigh. "I could do with a few. You wouldn't believe the comments you get when you come out as a lesbian. We're living in the Middle Ages."

"Trolls live in the Middle Ages," Marius said sympathetically.

"Well, it seems that half of France has been colonized by trolls. They get so worked up about our wedding plans you'd think we'd thrown Molotov cocktails into the Berre oil refinery. I thought the public would be on our side."

"The Front National is the biggest party around here. What did you expect?" Marius asked. "The medal of the Légion d'Honneur?"

"The hatred of others will only strengthen your relationship," Blanc added, trying to cheer her up.

"There's the experienced marriage guidance counselor talking." Fabienne laughed and held up her wineglass for a toast. "To women!" she shouted.

"Well, at least one of us is successful with women," Marius muttered, once again knocking his wine back in one.

"You'll both find beauties who'll give you a chance. You, Roger, have definitely got a chance with our marijuana-smoking body slicer. Or you could start an affair with the chilled investigating judge."

Blanc's wine went down the wrong way, leaving him coughing and spluttering until his eyes watered.

"I was joking!" Fabienne said hastily, embarrassed. "*Pardon*, I'd forgotten who she was married to."

Blanc smiled and wiped his face. "It was just that the joke was out of the blue," he apologized. He was going to have to be extra-careful. Once a rumor about him and Aveline got out in the little world of Gadet, he could kiss his job good-bye.

"Let's talk about the case," Marius suggested, to the surprise of the others. He held up his hands when he saw them look at him in astonishment. "What? At least the dead guy by the field is less depressing than having to listen to you two going on about women. And when we've finished discussing it, we can all agree over coffee that we should close the file."

"Ah, that's where you're coming from," Blanc said, shaking his head. "But I'm only just starting to enjoy the whole business."

"Me, too," Fabienne said. "At first I was with Marius and reckoned that Cohen had been stupid enough to open the gate to the field. But after what I found on his computer, I'm dead set on continuing the investigation."

"You and your computer," Marius declared theatrically.

"Not Fabienne's computer, Cohen's," Blanc corrected him calmly. "So, we have Cohen the journalist who enters the happy hunting grounds in a bizarre fashion, and we have Leroux the publisher, who may or may not know that his star reporter had gotten himself involved with a story that had nothing to do with the one they had agreed on. A man who fires his journalists to the extent that Cohen complains about it. A man who feels up so many women that *tout* Paris would like to see the end of him sooner rather than later, but nobody dares. We have the publisher's wife, Marie-Claude, who had previously had an affair with an ambitious art historian and was maybe having one with Cohen. A woman who grows Camargue rice and may have a dubious past." He reflected that it was not just Guillaume but Aveline, too, who had hinted at that. But he could hardly mention that here. "We have her former lover Boré, who just happens to be in Provence at the same time. A star in his field, but scorned by all his colleagues. Someone who spoke with Cohen shortly before he died, someone who desperately wanted to know more about Cohen's research. And we have a cranky guy living with an old witch of a mother, who's accused Boré and Marie-Claude Leroux of theft, among other things, and who had been persuaded to talk to Cohen about an old theft. Except that it never got that far."

"At the precise moment when the bull was exposing Cohen's guts to the light of day, Ernest Leroux was supposedly on his yacht at the edge of the Camargue. Marie-Claude Leroux was in their house in the Camargue, but with no witnesses. Their daughter, Nora, was somewhere or other, we have no idea where. Boré was allegedly in a museum in Marseille. And Guillaume was at home with *Maman*. Shaky alibis, every one of them," Fabienne summed up.

"*Putain*," Marius exclaimed. "What alibi do you have? We can't suspect everybody who was out and about in Provence last

Thursday afternoon! Can you imagine ladies' man Leroux standing by the gate of a fighting bull? Can you imagine his elegant wife planning to kill her lover in such a gruesome manner? Do you think a spoiled teenager like Nora was up to it? Or a pastis-guzzling diabetic wet blanket like Boré? A mommy's boy like Guillaume, who can't even make a decent job out of working as a waiter in a bar in Gadet? Please, I ask you, you want to go to Nkoulou on the basis of this?"

"I'd put it like this," Blanc went on, unfazed by Marius's outburst. "Cohen's curious death accidentally led us onto a lead in an old, unsolved case: the 1990 theft of a Van Gogh. That's not the febrile imagination of a forcibly relocated captain with sunstroke, it's an unsolved crime. *D'accord?*"

"Yes," Marius reluctantly admitted.

"As long as we're still investigating Cohen's death, we can also stay on the trail of the old theft. If we close the Cohen file, we have to give back his computer and his phone. Leroux will make sure of that. We would find it hard to convince Nkoulou why we might want to interview Boré or Guillaume again or follow up on links that involve them. Not to mention the fact that Marie-Claude Leroux would become virtually inaccessible. So let's officially keep up our investigation into Cohen's death for a few more days at least. Meanwhile we can be secretly hunting down the Van Gogh."

"The goddamn bull should have just kept grazing in its field," Marius muttered. But he raised his glass to them. Fabienne and Blanc did the same and they clinked glasses and laughed, and Blanc got the impression that his invitation to dinner might have been an expensive idea but it had also been a good one.

Later, Blanc was sitting alone in his office. He perversely loved neon-lit nighttime offices, where the only trace of his absent colleagues was a whiff of cold cigarette smoke and unwashed clothing. He wallowed simultaneously in a deep sadness and a diffuse sensation of well-being to know that everyone was out there somewhere in the night and he alone sat in here in the bright light. He had driven Fabienne and Marius back to Gadet, where the young computer specialist had leaped onto her Ducati and his partner had climbed into his old Fiat Marea. They had both roared off into the night and Blanc hoped that they had neither crashed into an olive tree nor come across any of their colleagues testing for DUI.

It was already almost midnight and the thermometer still showed the temperature stuck at 77 degrees. But in comparison with the heat of the afternoon, it was relatively cool. Blanc would have liked to throw open the windows, but then half the mosquitoes in Provence would have swarmed in and sucked his blood dry. Stale air was the price you paid for working at night.

He wrote up a report on his interviews with Boré and Guillaume, printed out the pages, and put them into the Cohen file. He flipped blankly through the gray-black file, glancing at his own report, Dr. Fontaine Thezan's autopsy report, the photos of the Camargue road with its gruesome traces of blood. Page by page, almost unnoticeably, but increasingly clearly, the file was metamorphosing from that of an extraordinary fatal accident into a collection of leads on a half-forgotten art theft, from a routine summer incident into a journey into the past. The past . . .

There had to be an officer of the Police Nationale in Arles right now also sitting under a neon light with next to nothing to do. It was a good time to ask such a colleague to do something unusual, so unusual that on a normal working day, at a normal time of the day, on a normal hectic shift, it would have been dismissed with a shake of the head. A request like the one Blanc was thinking of would only be heeded in the long night hours and considered as normal as a request for a new lunchroom card.

"*Sous-brigadier* Accoce."

A smoker's voice, Blanc thought, introducing himself. A *sous-brigadier* in the Police Nationale was a rank it took at least twelve years to reach. This man would have seen it all. "I'm investigating an art theft case and would like to take a look at an old Arles police file."

"No problem."

"It's a very old file."

"No problem."

"December 24, 1888."

"No problem."

"On the morning of that day the police were called to the house of the painter Vincent van Gogh. They found the artist there bleeding from a head wound and . . ."

". . . a whore waving a part of his ear that the crazy Dutchman had given her a bit earlier as a sort of present. I know all about it. It's a sort of legend for us cops here in Arles. Every couple of years somebody asks to see the file. Would it be okay if I scan the stuff and email it to you? That way you'll have it within the hour. There's nothing going on here."

"It's the damn heat."

"You can say that again. Gives people the craziest ideas."

Blanc hung up with a smile. Cohen had done some research in Arles. Maybe they'd find something that had interested the journalist in the old files. The photo on Cohen's hard drive made it clear that he had taken pictures of the old police files. Blanc had no idea if that had had anything to do with Cohen's death or the old theft, but it hardly mattered. There was another reason to ask for the file, even if he wasn't exactly going to wave it under anybody's nose. He would surprise Aveline with it. She might be an art connoisseur, but had she ever held a Van Gogh document in her hand? He would make a present of it to her at their next meeting. Whenever that might be.

He was shocked out of his reverie by the telephone. It was nearly one in the morning. As soon as he lifted the receiver he realized it wasn't a call from Arles: a booming bass, two or three men talking in the background, the clinking of glasses.

"Hello?" Blanc said, but nobody answered. He thought that above the noise he could hear someone breathing. He glanced down at the number on the display: 04. It was local. Then he realized that the call had not been meant for him, but for another extension at the office, an extension that after hours was automatically relayed. The number that had been called was Nkoulou's.

"Hello?" Blanc called out again into the party noise.

"Nic?" It was a woman's voice. "Shut up!" she called out, not talking to him.

Blanc took a second to put it together. Commandant Nicolas Nkoulou. Nic. A young woman. Her words were stressed too heavily, but lazily, as if her lower jaw was too heavy for the muscles that moved it. Drugs. A few weeks earlier he'd had the unknown woman on the phone when he rang Nkoulou at home. His boss had given him a drubbing the following day.

"Gendarmerie station Gadet, *bonsoir*," he replied, trying to sound as official as possible. He reckoned it was a good idea not to give his name.

The woman cursed obscenely. "You're the cop who called me a while back! You sound like some hick from up north. *Merde*, I wanted to talk to Nic, not some run-of-the-mill cop!"

"Commandant Nkoulou has left his office." Then, with just the slightest trace of furtiveness, "Can I take a message?"

"He should go fuck himself." She ended the call.

Blanc put the receiver down. Marius was right, he told himself, our female colleague is the only one who has a normal relationship with women. The guys were all damaged. Or maybe it was just that Fabienne needed a few more years of service with long nights and chaotic investigations. Maybe there would come a time when no woman would put up with her either.

When the phone unexpectedly rang again, Blanc thought for a second that the unknown woman was going to launch a few swearwords at him again. But this time the number on the display was that of Arles.

"Sorry, pal. Can't manage the Van Gogh files tonight."

"Something come up?" Blanc asked in astonishment.

It seemed for a minute or two that Accoce was about to laugh out loud, but had to draw breath instead. "Arles is as quiet as the tomb," he said. "It's just that . . ." Blanc could hear the click of a cigarette lighter and a deep intake of breath. "*Eh bien*, I hope you won't consider us complete idiots, but the file has disappeared."

Blanc knew there and then that he wasn't going to get a wink of sleep that night. "What do you mean 'disappeared'?"

"Vanished, gone, into thin air, whatever you like. The box file in the archive is on the same shelf as always, but the box is empty. Not one goddamn piece of paper left in it. No report of it being out on loan, no comment, simply nothing. *Merde*, it would appear that the Arles police force has been robbed."

A Woman with a Past

Blanc spent the few remaining hours of the night at the old kitchen table in his oil mill watching the dim reflections of a clear 25-watt light bulb in his wineglass. A moth was flapping around the light and the thought occurred to him that his brain was acting the same way as the insect. It flew in one circle after the other without ever getting anywhere. Cohen had seen the Van Gogh file and photographed it with his phone, Blanc thought. And, seeing that Cohen, according to Fabienne, had downloaded all the photos that evening to his computer, it had to have been the morning before his death. And, a few hours after the reporter had seen the files and photographed them he had had his guts ripped open. And did that mean Cohen himself had stolen the files? In which case, where were they? Neither Fabienne nor he had found them in his room, but then they hadn't searched the whole of the Leroux house. And there was no way Blanc was going to get a search warrant to search the house of the most influential publisher in France for a police file from Arles that was more than a century old. Not even Aveline would grant him that.

Aveline. Yet one more reason he couldn't sleep.

He forced himself to go over the case in his head again. If Cohen had stolen the file, was his death the result of an attack so that the murderer could get his or her hands on it? Or was it punishment for stealing it? But who could have considered the file so valuable that he or she would take such dreadful revenge on the person who had stolen it? Or maybe Cohen had only seen the file at the police station in Arles and photographed its contents there but hadn't stolen it? Had somebody else made off with it—and then killed the reporter? But why? None of it made sense. Somehow the rosé had disappeared from his glass, the morning light had made the light bulb irrelevant, and Blanc knew no more than he had before.

He wasn't exactly in the best of moods as he forced himself to take a shower. And his mood certainly didn't improve when just as the water got going he heard a crashing sound from outside. He ran out with only a hand towel to cover his loins, fearing that one of the walls of the old house had collapsed. Instead he found himself facing a huge green machine with MANITOU painted on its flanks. It was a sort of combination forklift truck and digger that with its shovel and two enormous steel claws looked like a diesel-driven Tyrannosaurus rex. From up in the driver's cabin, some ten feet above him, Matthieu Fuligni waved down at him.

"It's Tuesday, Monsieur Blanc," he called out. "We have a date."

Behind the Manitou a dented white truck piled high with glowing red tiles drove into the yard. Two builders sitting in the cabin gave him a bored glance. None of the three men who had just arrived seemed to think it in the slightest unusual to be met by a bewildered customer outside his house wearing nothing more than a hand towel. Blanc gave them an embarrassed wave.

"I hadn't forgotten," he lied.

"We're going to go up on the Manitou platform and take down all the damaged *tuiles*," Fuligni explained. "That'll only take a couple of hours. We might even have time enough to lay a few of the new ones."

"What if it rains?"

"*Pas de souci*," Fuligni called back. "Then your shower water will come from an even greater height."

Back at the station later, Blanc told his two colleagues about the disappearance of the file in Arles. He didn't mention the call for Nkoulou he had intercepted. "I'm going to see Leroux again," he told them. "I'm going to give him the results of Dr. Thezan's autopsy, including the traces of cocaine in Cohen's hair roots. Leroux will think I've come to see him personally rather than call him because of his reporter's drug abuse history. He'll even be grateful to me for doing so. But what I really want is to get into his house again, to see if I can spot the goddamn file. It might even still be in Cohen's room or somewhere else in the *mas*."

"Sounds like a crazy idea to me," Marius replied in a jovial mood. "If the two of us were to turn up at Leroux's place with a story like that, it would be even less credible. So it's better you go down to the Camargue on your own."

"I'd come with you," Fabienne said, "but I've got an appointment with my lawyer."

"About the wedding?" Blanc asked.

She nodded. "Sometimes even Facebook isn't enough. Roxane and I are taking legal advice. It may be that we will have to start proceedings against our own mayor."

Marius groaned. "If you do that, the Front National will give you both honorary membership—that's just the sort of publicity those bastards want."

"I don't know how the Front does it. Either you kowtow to them or you fight them, in which case you end up looking like a *connard.* But, *merde*, I'm a cop. If I can't enforce the law, who can?"

"When you get back from the legal eagle, grab Cohen's laptop and phone, you need to crack the access code," Blanc told her.

Fabienne forced a smile. "At least that'll relieve me from the stress. I should be thankful to Cohen's killer."

"You can pay your thanks down at the meat counter in the supermarket," Marius muttered. "His murderer's already chopped up in the freezer."

"Just forget the bull, will you?" Blanc sighed.

As neither of his companions were accompanying him, Blanc didn't take the patrol car. Instead he rolled back the roof of the 2CV and trundled at up to 40 mph through the Camargue. It was like being on a vacation while working. Tell that to his colleagues in Paris. His ex-colleagues. On his right he spotted a dozen dark shapes some fifty yards from the road. What was it the bull breeder Ferréol had called a herd? *Manade.* The dark-colored cattle were trotting slowly through the marsh. Bulls or cows? The grass was so tall that Blanc couldn't see the lower parts of their bodies and didn't know enough to be able to tell their gender from the shape of their heads and backs. The animals looked pretty big to him. The horns curved inward in the shape of a lyre. There was no fence between them and the road, and not a *gardian* to be seen. He wondered briefly how long his steam horse would withstand an attack by a bull. The cattle strolled across the plain as majestically as water buffaloes in Africa. They didn't even glance at him, even when his old car screeched as he turned to take the track up to the Leroux house.

The white Toyota hybrid and the VW Polo were parked outside the house. Madame Leroux was at home with her daughter, Nora, Blanc reckoned. Maybe that was for the best. He would be able not just to look for an old file but also to discreetly put a few questions to the lady of the house about a museum in Saint-Tropez and a Van Gogh that had gone missing.

Before he could use the bronze door knocker, the door opened. Marie-Claude greeted him with an open smile, only for it to fade the moment she realized who it was standing in front of her. "*Pardon*," she muttered, "I thought that . . ." She pushed her hair back from her face. She was wearing a summer skirt and an old, plain light green blouse that made her look as if she had just stepped out of an Italian film from the 1950s.

"I'm sorry you're disappointed to see me," Blanc replied.

She laughed and waved her left hand around as if chasing some insect away. Blanc tried to ignore the scar on her wrist. "I saw your car approaching from the kitchen window," she explained, somewhat embarrassedly. "And for a moment I thought someone was coming to visit my daughter. Maybe a young man who might be," she hesitated briefly, "different from the friends she's had so far. A student maybe, an intellectual or an artist. For a moment I could see myself, in my last year at the *lycée* with the friends I had back then. I ran to the door before I could see who was in it. But come in nonetheless."

Marie-Claude led him into an elegantly laid-out living room that was pleasantly cool. Nora was nowhere to be seen, but from somewhere in the building the heavy bass thumping of house music could be felt rather than heard. Blanc tried to look around as nonchalantly as possible to see if he could glimpse the old file while rattling off the story he had prepared about the autopsy report, the cocaine traces in Cohen's hair roots, his own discretion.

"Would you like a glass of iced tea?" his hostess asked calmly.

"You aren't surprised by the pathologist's report?"

"Albert took coke? So what? Everybody knew that. If you were to lay out all the cocaine that Parisian politicians and journalists take, you could make a line the length of the Champs-Élysées. My iced tea is homemade, not that awful stuff you get from Géant Casino supermarket."

"In that case I'd welcome a glass," Blanc replied. He didn't like iced tea whether it came from a supermarket or not, but his hostess disappeared into the kitchen for a moment, giving him the chance to take a better look around: a white sofa, as thin and hard as a folded futon bed, ten different issues of *L'Événement* on a little white-lacquered table, an iPad with its touch screen dark, a closed notebook and next to it a pencil the end of which had been chewed. A wobbly old desk with three drawers that he quickly flicked through. Nothing. On an old wooden trunk, black as oil, stood glasses and a few bottles of pastis and whiskey, behind some family photos and a shining bronze seated Buddha. Hanging on the wall was a large, framed black-and-white photo of some Asian-looking men in round straw hats. Blanc took a closer look: the Asians were standing up to their ankles in water, one of them holding a plant in his fist and smiling. China, Blanc thought to himself, then in the background of the photo he spotted a dark object: a Camargue bull.

"It was taken back in 1942," said Marie-Claude, who had crept back in so silently that Blanc hadn't heard her. She was holding in her hands two glasses containing an orange-colored liquid. "Your iced tea, *mon Capitaine*. I found the photo at a flea market and had it framed."

"Chinese in the Camargue?"

"Vietnamese."

"In the middle of the war? How did they get here? Did the Germans allow it?"

She laughed. "They were here before the Germans, if only by a few weeks. Bad luck for the Vietnamese, good luck for us. They brought the rice back."

Her passion, Blanc thought. Let her talk. That'll make her more relaxed and less suspicious. For when you ask the questions to come.

"They were already planting rice in the Camargue back in the Middle Ages. Under Henri VI it was practically a legal obligation," she continued. "But by the nineteenth century nobody was interested anymore and the fields went to seed. When the Second World War broke out, the government brought in twenty thousand workers from the colonies in Indochina, many of them against their will. They arrived in Marseille in 1940 and were supposed to be sent to work in arms factories. But the Wehrmacht got there faster than the government could have dreamed. What was to be done with the Vietnamese? They couldn't send them back as no French ship would have made it to Indochina. Then a few farmers in the Camargue had the idea to put those workers who had grown rice in Indochina to work on their fields, which had lain fallow for years. The Vietnamese spent two years digging water ditches, hard graft with their bare hands. They brought in their first harvest in 1942. This photo documented the event."

"Well done for rescuing it from the flea market."

She lit a cigarette and succeeded in making this routine act into a gesture of scorn. "Nobody wants to know anymore," she said. "I was the only one interested. In 1945 the farmers kicked the Vietnamese out and sent them back home, as if they were coolies. And then continued to harvest the Camargue rice with the clearest conscience in the world."

"I assume your rice fields, too, were fertilized by the sweat of the Vietnamese, Madame," Blanc answered calmly.

"Of course. That's precisely why my husband and I bought our place here. I heard about this forgotten chapter of imperialism when I was a student. We were big opponents of imperialism back in those days. We went out onto the streets in protest."

"My older colleagues in Paris still tell stories about the demonstrations," Blanc confided in her.

She gave him a derogatory look for a second or two, then shrugged. "*Eh bien*, I was on the left. I was an idealist, I was horrified. I never forgot the story of those Vietnamese, even though in those days I had no more to do with rice than I had with bananas or yams. My family was from Lorraine, not exactly farming country. It was a lot later when I learned that this piece of farmland was for sale. I heard about it accidentally and my husband and I restored the land before it could turn back into a swamp. Ever since, we've been growing rice, the way we ought to, and I collect everything I can about the Vietnamese forced laborers. It's a sort of way of paying tribute to them in hindsight. Keeping the memory alive is the least we can do."

"Speaking of memory," Blanc mumbled. "There wasn't any sort of memento among Monsieur Cohen's bits and pieces, even if not something that goes back as far as the story of the Vietnamese rice farmers. A story from 1990."

Marie-Claude looked at him with mild curiosity. She didn't appear to be in the slightest concerned—until Blanc continued and told her about Cohen's research into the art theft from the Musée Maly.

"Oh," said Marie-Claude Leroux, suddenly nervous, "*that* old story. That must be why Albert gave me such strange looks in those last few days."

"His last few days. You knew nothing about it, Madame?"

She just shook her head.

"But you were the one, more or less, who put Monsieur Cohen onto the Van Gogh story! Were you not aware that Monsieur Boré was organizing an exhibition? Van Gogh, Boré. Did it not occur to you that a reporter like Cohen might make the connection?"

"I'm an art historian, not a journalist! That old story was forgotten long ago. I have admired Van Gogh ever since I had the opportunity back then in the Musée Maly to study one of his masterpieces whenever I wanted to, undisturbed. The artist has had a grip on me ever since. That was why I would have been pleased if *L'Événement* had brought out an issue with a Van Gogh cover story. Whether it was Boré or someone else organizing the exhibition was completely irrelevant." She lit up another cigarette.

The scent of menthol mingled with the sweet aroma of the iced tea. Blanc suddenly felt the need for fresh air and a glass of cool rosé. He pulled himself together. "Monsieur Cohen had dug up witnesses from back then, did you know that? Not just Boré but Guillaume as well."

"If you know that name, then you know everything to do with the case."

"I don't know who the culprit is," Blanc said with a friendly smile.

"Nor do I," Marie-Claude answered, shaking her head. "Did Albert find out?"

"Possibly. On his computer hard drive there are certain . . ."—Blanc searched for the right word—". . . clues," he decided. "I'm amazed he never talked to you about the theft, Madame. Especially as you were his host and friend."

"It's certainly odd," she concurred. "I can't remember ever having mentioned the theft to Albert. It was all so long ago, I didn't exactly think about it on a daily basis. And back then when it happened I didn't know Albert. I didn't even know my husband back then, and it was only through Ernest that I got to know Albert and all the major players on the stage of Paris politics."

"But back then," Blanc tried to use the most neutral form of words he could find, "you were a close friend of Monsieur Boré's."

Marie-Claude Leroux gave an ironic laugh that left Blanc uncertain if it was at his awkward way of putting it or at the memory of Boré. "Daniel's world was art, Ernest's is politics. Daniel and I left for Paris together after the police investigation had more or less run into the sand and nobody had any more questions for us. In those days it was easy to find a job. Although I have to admit that I never thought Daniel would go so far. The shy, rather eccentric curator from Saint-Tropez has become Europe's most successful exhibition organizer. He and I have lost touch since then."

"You never met again?"

"Not for years. I'd have to work out how long it's been."

"You didn't even call Monsieur Boré? Never sent him an email? Not even when you knew your magazine was going to do a big piece about his next exhibition?"

"If it had been necessary, then Albert would have done that. He was the one writing it. I really didn't see any reason for me to get in touch with Daniel. We remember some people kindly, but there are others we'd rather not be reminded of, if you understand what I mean, *mon Capitaine.*"

"In which case I regret all the more that I must test your memory a bit more. On the night of the theft you were with Monsieur Boré at the Voiles de Saint-Tropez, were you not?"

She nodded with a suddenly nostalgic smile. "Daniel always had a weakness for the chic world. He was as overwhelmed as a little child by the yachts, the elegant people, their riches. So overwhelmed in fact that he forgot to take his insulin injections. When he suddenly took a bad turn, he had to lean on a giant anchor that had been erected on one of the quays as a sort of monument while he fished out his utensils from his pockets with shaking hands. Then he was nearly beaten up by two sailors who took him for a junkie taking a fix right outside their glittering palace. They came running down a gangplank, cursing and waving their fists and . . ." Marie-Claude shrugged her shoulders.

"We cleared it all up. The pair of them were embarrassed at nearly having beaten up a sick man. They invited us on board their yacht—the owner wasn't there—and gave us a drink, the only drink I've ever had on the deck of a ship like that. Very romantic."

And very easy to check, Blanc thought. If you had told our colleagues back then what had happened in Saint-Tropez, they would have easily found out where the anchor on the quay was and which yacht had been moored there. If it had been a lie, they would have found out inside half an hour. The fact that there was no mention of it in the file meant that Boré and Marie-Claude Leroux had an alibi for the night of the crime. Or at least for several hours that night.

"Cohen wanted to talk to Monsieur Guillaume," Blanc let her know. "He lives nearby here."

She gave him a surprised and rather nervous look. "I didn't know that. Olivier isn't exactly the sort of man you want for a neighbor."

"Is he aggressive?"

"More of a loose cannon. At least he used to be. I haven't heard from him since 1990."

"He was the chief suspect back then."

"He only got the job in the Musée Maly because his father was such a famous art collector and had contacts all over the south. Olivier Guillaume was a weird character. He should never have been given a job in any public institution, not even as a janitor. He couldn't even get along with people he knew. And certainly not with visitors to the museum who thought their entrance ticket also entitled them to expect the staff to be friendly."

"Guillaume would have been fired at some stage even if the theft hadn't happened?" Blanc asked.

"Absolutely. He was just too unfriendly toward people."

"Did Guillaume have any idea he might be about to lose his job?"

"I couldn't say. Nobody had a clue what was going on in his head."

"Was he fanatical about religion?" Blanc asked, remembering the cross around his neck and Cohen's cryptic note. "Did the church in Saint-Gilles have any particular importance for him?"

Marie-Claude Leroux blew a cloud of menthol smoke toward the window. "You'd have to ask him that yourself. I'm not exactly a churchgoer." She paused. "Strange," she murmured. "There was only one time I had anything like a sensible conversation with Guillaume. And now that you mention it, I have to say yes, it was about a church. Although not exactly to do with religion."

"About what then?"

"Art theft."

Blanc leaned back as far as he could on the hard futon sofa. "Tell me more."

"I don't know exactly how we got onto the topic. It was at the end of a long working day. Anyway, to my surprise one summer evening I got into a conversation with Guillaume at the entrance to Musée Maly. He told me in detail about the theft of the Ghent altar."

"I have no idea what you're talking about," Blanc said.

"Because you're not an art historian. The Ghent altarpiece is a masterpiece of Jan van Eyck assembled from several paintings on wood, fifteenth century, absolutely unique. It stood in Ghent cathedral—until one day in 1934 two of the pictures disappeared. Stolen. One of them was soon returned by the thief. It had been placed in a safe deposit box and the thief revealed the number in an anonymous letter. The other, however, has never been seen again, as if it vanished from the face of the earth."

"And the thief was never found?"

"That's the crux of the story. A man on his deathbed confessed to the theft—and claimed that he had hidden the picture in a place visited by lots of people. But he never said exactly where. Ever since, dozens of experts have suspected that the picture is still hidden somewhere in Ghent cathedral. They've turned the 'House of God' upside down time and again but never found a trace of it. So, were we just dealing with some old fraudster who with his last breath decided to play the world for a fool by telling a crazy story? Or was it really the thief on his deathbed and he told the truth? If the latter is the case, then all the experts have failed to solve the riddle he left us with. Guillaume was fascinated by the story of the thief who'd flipped the bird to all the acknowledged authorities, who was cleverer than all the art historians, police, and priests. He went on and on about it."

"Do you think it's possible that Guillaume knew that he was going to be fired soon and stole the Van Gogh in revenge? And that he hid it somewhere in the Musée Maly in the same way as the thief who hid the Van Eyck back in the place he had stolen it from?"

"Hiding the picture in a museum that hardly anyone visits isn't exactly a masterstroke," Marie-Claude replied.

"So could he have hidden it in a church that's as well known as a cathedral?"

"You're the gendarme," Marie-Claude Leroux replied thoughtfully. "I suspected Guillaume, as did all my colleagues and the cops. But I never connected the theft with the conversation about the Ghent altarpiece. It would have been absurd. But now that you've done it, it doesn't seem absurd at all."

The church of Saint-Gilles, thought Blanc.

"*Merci beaucoup*, Madame," he said, getting to his feet.

"Now that sounds like a really interesting story for

L'Événement," she whispered thoughtfully, pulling another cigarette out of the pack.

Blanc walked alone over to his 2CV. He had left the top rolled down and the windows folded up. Now he noticed that someone had been at the car. There was a yellow Post-it note on the steering wheel. Blanc got behind the wheel but didn't touch the sticky in case Marie-Claude Leroux was watching from the window, the way she had been when he had driven up. He didn't want her to notice anything unusual. He drove down the driveway until he turned onto the *route départementale.* A mile or so along the road there was a spot by the side of the road firm enough for him to pull off the tarmac and stop.

He took the sticky from the steering wheel and read it. *I was eavesdropping. Mama and that tub of lard Boré are still in a relationship.*

Blanc drove back to Gadet with his head full of thoughts. The air above the pools of water shimmered. He could make out the shapes of flamingos, pink blotches in a distorted mirror. Two Camargue horses were tied up by the side of the road, staring miserably at the tarmac. Later he arrived in the town, where all the guests at all the shady seats under the plane trees by the bars looked as jaded as the horses.

The station was deserted, as if the state had withdrawn from this corner of France. The air-conditioning was no longer functioning. Blanc sat down at his computer and began searching for whatever the police, gendarmerie, or just rumor had about the publisher's wife. It didn't take long.

Marie-Claude Leroux brought up not a single hit.

Marie-Claude Elbaz: just one. Back in 1983 she had been arrested in Paris at a demonstration against "capitalist exploitation," though she had been released after only a few hours. Her father had picked her up from the police station.

Perfectly normal, Blanc thought to himself. Young people were allowed to be left wing and get picked up by the police once or twice. At least that was the way it used to be. Astrid and Eric would see things differently in their Facebook world. Shame. But thinking about his own kids inevitably turned his mind to Nora Leroux. What was the relevance of the information she had given him to his investigation? And, *merde*, what was a daughter doing denouncing her mother to a cop she hardly knew?

Missing Years

Blanc was on his feet at daybreak. He pulled on just a pair of sneakers and shorts and ran out bare-chested into the woods behind the oil mill. The temperature before 6:00 A.M. was still tolerable and he wanted to be back before Fuligni and his men arrived to remove the second half of the roof. He took a deep breath of the spicy scent of thyme and rosemary. The dew had collected on the spiderwebs that spread like gauze curtains between the bushes. A dead snake no longer than his index finger lay on the path. The tracks on the ground suggested some fat, tired cyclist on a mountain bike had broken its back. The animal doesn't always win, Blanc reflected. The ocher-colored sand absorbed the sound of his footsteps and with the birds still asleep and the cicadas silent it was as still as on the third day of creation.

Until he got over a mile deep into the woods.

Even before he could see it, he heard the rattling clanking of a diesel motor in idle mode. There was a buzz of voices above the engine noise. He made out Douchy's rough bass. He couldn't make out a word he was saying but he didn't sound friendly.

Blanc walked across a path where slabs of gray stone shimmered in the morning light between the sand. Douchy was sitting on a dented green tractor.

One of its rear tires had dragged one of the stones a way out of the ground. In front of the tractor stood the Michelettis—Blanc's neighbors and the owners of the Domaine du Bernard winery. Bruno and Sylvie were wearing lightweight walking shoes, T-shirts, and Bermuda shorts that looked as if they'd been patched together from old cloth bags. They each had a pair of modern aluminum walking poles in their hands. Bruno was swinging his back and forth like samurai swords while Sylvie had pushed the points of hers into the ground and was leaning on them. She was the first of the quarreling threesome to notice Blanc and greeted him with an apologetic smile. Blanc felt like some half-naked anthropologist who'd stumbled on a native quarrel.

"This guy and his tractor are destroying an ancient Roman road," Bruno Micheletti called out when he, too, finally noticed Blanc.

"To hell with the Romans! The woods belong to the *commune*, not you!" Douchy grumbled.

"There's a Roman road that runs over the top of the hill," Bruno explained, looking to Blanc for support. "That stone has been lying here for two thousand years. And now look at it!" The weight of the tractor had either pushed some stones out of position or broken them.

Blanc wished he could disappear into thin air and to hell with both ancient roads and tractors. But as a captain in the gendarmerie he was here and now more or less the personification of state authority, even if his naked belly was on display. Douchy, who hated everything and anything that stank of authority, was staring at him viciously. *Merde*, Blanc thought to himself, let's get this over with. "I'll phone the town hall," he said, trying to sound as neutral as possible. "If tractors are allowed here, then Monsieur Douchy has every right to drive along this path. If not, then he will have to pay for the repairs."

Douchy's bright red face went white, when he realized money might be involved. "I'm not paying a penny for a few ancient stones." But at the same time he put the tractor into a rattling first gear and turned it around, breaking yet another old stone as he did so. He put his foot down and roared off down the path he had just come along without a single look behind him.

"Serge is a coarse peasant. He'll make you suffer for that, Roger," Sylvie Micheletti said when the noise of the diesel had faded away.

"He's forever making all his neighbors suffer," her husband added offhandedly. "We've got nothing to worry about until the fall."

"What happens in the fall?" Blanc asked, somewhat disquieted.

"That's when the hunting season starts. Serge doesn't even have a *permis de chasser*, but who checks on things like that? He'll be out there in the woods with his shotgun every day. Not someone you want to run across by accident."

"I think I'll find a new jogging route from September on," Blanc said resignedly. His pulse had settled down again. He took a look at the Michelettis. Bruno had an SLR camera in a case attached to his belt.

"We came out to take photos," he explained, noticing Blanc glancing at it. "In the dawn light, when the dew is still shining. We won't give up; we'll try again tomorrow."

"I'd better go back," Blanc said, "or I'll be late for work."

"Evil never rests," Sylvie Micheletti replied, and turned in the opposite direction. For a moment or two it seemed as if she was going to use her walking poles as crutches.

Blanc took a rushed shower, had a quick breakfast, and glanced at Fuligni and his men, who were once again attacking his roof with an anarchistic joy, then drove as fast as the 2CV would allow him in the direction of Salon-de-Provence. The car swerved into the big roundabout at the entrance to the town and someone honked at him, whether in annoyance or in congratulation for his rally-style driving, Blanc couldn't tell. He wanted to get to the hospital early, before Dr. Fontaine Thezan was already at the autopsy table in her smock and rubber gloves.

When he got there, he turned his cell phone off, pulled out his ID card, and asked until someone finally pointed him in the direction of the staff canteen. The pathologist was sitting alone at a table eating a croissant. "Got a new corpse for me?" she asked in greeting, indicating the seat opposite.

Blanc sat down, hesitating a moment before he opened his mouth. He looked at the doctor with her narrow face framed by long hair and her intelligent eyes, which were examining him coolly. He hardly knew her, certainly not well enough to place his trust in her. *Merde*, what was life worth without the occasional risk?

"I need to ask you to do something you're not supposed to."

"You want me to fetch you drugs from the hospital pharmacy?"

Blanc stared at her for a moment in silence, not sure whether she was serious or not. "I was thinking more about a few discreet inquiries."

"I see, to breach the medical code of privacy." Fontaine Thezan's smile was so small it was hard to say if it implied conspiratorial agreement or sarcastic refusal.

"Possibly," Blanc admitted. "Look, Doctor, I know medical staff talk to one another: gossip, rumors, anecdotes about patients, interesting cases, things like that. It's just the way people are. We cops gossip about our criminals, too, more than the law allows. Perhaps your colleagues occasionally mention . . ."

He took a deep breath. "Well, Madame Leroux or maybe Nora Leroux."

"The wife and daughter of the famous Paris publisher? What white-coat stories do you want to hear about them? Off the top of my head I couldn't tell you any about either of them."

"I'm not interested in appendix operations, but maybe drugs. Breakdowns. What do I know? Has either of them ever been in therapy? Had treatment? Maybe after an attempted suicide?" His mind went back to the scars on Marie-Claude Leroux's wrist.

"*Mon Capitaine*, I get all the successful suicides. I don't see the failed attempts. Why are you asking a pathologist to sniff around in psychiatric cases? Don't you think that's a bit cheeky?"

"You're the only doctor I know down here in the south," Blanc admitted. "And apart from that"—he sought the right words—"I think you know when it makes sense to stick strictly to the rules. And when it doesn't."

"You're dangerous," she replied thoughtfully. "Dangerous to me, and even more dangerous to yourself."

"So you won't do it?" Blanc asked, disappointed.

"Of course I'll do it." For a couple of seconds Fontaine Thezan gave him a warm conspiratorial smile, then she covered the traces with a look of cool irony, a mask as impenetrable as a surgeon's. "It's time for me to deal with the day's first customer," she declared, dusting off the croissant crumbs from her fingers and getting to her feet. "I'll let you know if I hear anything."

"There was a call for you," Corporal Baressi told him when Blanc turned up at the station. "From Paris," he added in a tone that suggested it wasn't something that happened every day, and nor was it welcome.

"Who was it?" Blanc asked, half guessing the answer.

Baressi looked at the note, taking ages to read his own

writing. "Monsieur Vialaron-Allègre. He wanted to know if the funeral was going to be on the agreed date. A relative of yours? Should I be expressing my condolences?"

"Feel free to pity me."

The minister wanted to know if Cohen's computer had provided the ammunition he needed to take a potshot at the publisher Leroux, Blanc assumed. He hurried into his office and wrote a very polite, very formal, very noncommittal email to the interior minister. As long as he kept Vialaron-Allègre at a distance, he could continue to investigate the case of the stolen Van Gogh, because the minister wasn't going to call him off as long as he believed Blanc might find out something about Cohen. I never thought Vialaron-Allègre would turn out to be an ally, Blanc mused.

He had to find out more about the people who had anything to do with the vanished picture. He went to find Fabienne, but she was on the phone with her girlfriend, Roxane, and it didn't exactly sound like a pleasant conversation. So he just waved to her, exaggeratedly mouthed the word "Later," and crept out again. The other seat in his office was empty: Marius had disappeared without leaving a note.

Blanc planted himself in front of his computer. He decided to start his Internet search with Boré, because he was more prominent than Marie-Claude Leroux or Olivier Guillaume. The more hits on the net, the more dirt on Boré's clean white jacket, at least that was what he hoped.

An hour later, however, Blanc wasn't sure whether he had made any progress or not. Boré hadn't been kidding about the opinion his learned colleagues had of him, quite the contrary. In several online publications by art historians, Boré was dismissed as a phony and a parvenu, and there were comments on blogs and forums that Boré could have taken libel action over. It would appear that he didn't consider his detractors all that important because there was no evidence that he had ever launched legal action against any of them. And even though Boré tirelessly turned out catalogs, made speeches, and wrote art stories for *Figaro*, he never once took the opportunity to take revenge on his critics. No matter what the topic, he wrote about it as if he was the only expert in the world on the subject and it would be a waste of time to even mention any other name.

Eventually Blanc turned to studying Boré's own website, which was primarily dedicated to the exhibitions he had organized. In his résumé he referred to the topic of his dissertation, which had gotten him noticed in Paris before he went to the Musée Maly. It was about a letter written by Vincent van Gogh to his brother Theo, which Boré had edited and commented on. Blanc didn't understand, and didn't really care about, precisely what it was the art historian had actually written. But he noted that Boré was already an expert on Van Gogh before he even set foot over the doorstep of the provincial museum in Saint-Tropez. That could mean everything or nothing. Could it just be a coincidence? And yet . . . Just one year after an ambitious Van Gogh expert starts work at the museum, an important work by the artist goes missing. In what other museum in the world could a thief have so easily stolen such a valuable work? And wouldn't you have to be a Van Gogh expert to even know that a poorly guarded picture was hanging in an almost unknown museum above the bay of Saint-Tropez?

More out of duty than with any real hope of finding a lead, Blanc clicked on a seemingly endless photo gallery of hundreds of pictures showing Boré at the opening of his exhibitions surrounded by celebrities: film directors and actresses standing in front of a Renoir; Boré with industrialists and bankers in front of a Matisse; Boré with the culture minister in front of a Picasso, the culture minister who in turn was surrounded by a huge entourage, as was always the way in Paris—his personal advisers, publicists, bodyguards, journalists, and more journalists. Behind the culture minister in this three-year-old photo Blanc could clearly make out Ernest Leroux. He seemed to be talking to an elegant woman and was paying no attention at all to Boré, the culture minister, or the photographer. And Boré, at least as far as it appeared in the photo, was paying no attention to the crowd but was focused firmly on the minister and holding out both hands toward the Picasso.

Blanc enlarged the photo, but there was no sign of Marie-Claude Leroux. Had she been there or not? Had Boré and Monsieur Leroux exchanged a word or two that evening? Boré might or might not have known his former lover's husband. Marie-Claude Leroux might have seen Boré in Paris on evenings like that, then again she might not have. It was possible that Boré and Marie-Claude Leroux really had lost track of each other in the cosmos that was Paris. But it was also possible that their lives had crossed a lot more often than they admitted.

He tried again to search for traces of Marie-Claude Leroux and also as Marie-Claude Elbaz. He checked on the police computer system. He put her name into Google. Nothing that he hadn't already come across the first time. Nothing.

"*Merde*," he muttered. "That's just it: nothing."

Blanc jumped at the sound of the telephone. The number that came up on the display was vaguely familiar, but he only recognized it when he heard the voice on the other end of the line: that of a very young woman, sober this time, even a little shy. "Please don't give me away," she began without giving her name. "About the night before last, I mean. It was the night before last, wasn't it? Or last night? And it was you who picked up the phone, wasn't it?"

"The hick from up north, that's right," Blanc confirmed.

"Did you tell Nic . . . Monsieur Nkoulou? That I called, I mean?"

"No."

"Good." Heavy intake of breath. Maybe she's gasping with relief, Blanc mused, or she's sighing heavily, or she's trying to stop herself from laughing. "He doesn't like me to call him at the police station."

"I'm not surprised."

"He's so terribly stuffy." The unknown woman was speaking faster now, more fluently, as if she was desperate to explain something. "You see, his parents were illegal immigrants to France. That's why he hates everything that isn't one thousand percent according to the rules. It's a father complex, know what I mean?"

"Absolutely, Mademoiselle," Blanc assured her, without understanding any of it.

"So you won't say anything to Monsieur Nkoulou?" she asked him again.

"I won't say a word about your call. In any case, it was the night before last."

"Ah . . . *bien.* The night before last. Then it's time I got out of here. Time I ate something. You're a treasure."

Blanc stared at the display, cleared now. He could hear the dial tone coming from the receiver. He tried in vain to imagine a face to match the voice. A party girl? A junkie? Rich? Poor? White? Black? It was all the harder for him to imagine Commandant Nkoulou with this faceless woman. A wife? Lover? Relative?

"Was the phone sex good?"

He whipped around. Fabienne was standing in the door frame giving him a sarcastic look. "You're holding the receiver in your hand as if it's a phallic symbol."

"I'm holding it in my hand as if I'm about to strangle it."

"Thirty seconds ago I wanted to strangle the telephone receiver, too."

"Quarrel with Roxane?"

"Close enough. I'm getting angry with our lawyer, but Roxane wants to give her another chance. I'm slowly beginning to wonder if it's worth battling our way through a court to get our right to marry. . . . But in the end we more or less agreed. How was your phone call?"

"Bad phone sex," Blanc replied, carefully replacing the receiver. "I've got a job for you."

"When you don't get anywhere with Google, I'm your next call." She nodded toward the computer monitor.

"I'm glad to have you." He pointed at the list of hits for Marie-Claude Leroux/Marie-Claude Elbaz. "I haven't just googled her, I've been through the usual police databases, too, and all the other official databases I could get into: the Foreign Ministry, she might have traveled to some non-European country and needed a visa. The Education and Culture Ministry, she had been a student, otherwise she'd never have gotten the job as a curator at the Musée Maly. The prefectures, the town hall records of her home in Lorraine, Paris, where she allegedly studied, and Saint-Tropez, where she got her job at the museum. Take a look through all that and see if there's something I've missed," he said in encouragement.

She clicked through the results, Blanc sitting patiently next to her. "Marie-Claude is a fine citizen," she noted.

"That's what I thought at first."

"There's nothing to worry about here."

"That's just it!" Blanc exclaimed triumphantly. "Nothing! There are hundreds of entries, just like you might find for most fine citizens. But when you look through all of it you'll see that there is *not one single entry* for the years between 1983, when

Marie-Claude Elbaz was briefly arrested at a left-wing demonstration, and 1989, when she took up her job at the Musée Maly. Which high school did she graduate from and at what university did she study? Social Security has no record of her paying any contribution during this period and there is no trace of any address. No employer to be found. She didn't get married, didn't have a child, didn't attract the attention of a cop, didn't make any application to public services, was never treated in a hospital."

"Maybe she was in jail?" Fabienne suggested.

"She was never sentenced. No record of any time in jail. No accusations against her, no summons as a witness."

"She was abroad. Maybe she just went backpacking round the world? That was the thing to do back in the eighties. Or maybe she met a foreigner and went to live in his country?"

Blanc shook his head. "Marie-Claude Elbaz never applied for a passport, never paid a visit to any embassy or consulate. Back in 1983 even within the European Union you needed a residence permit or a work permit. She could never have lived abroad somewhere without leaving a trace, at least not legally."

"Hmmm." Fabienne seemed to have completely forgotten her phone call with Roxane and was staring at the screen as she spoke.

Blanc smiled. "So what I want to know is if there really is no digital trace of Marie-Claude Elbaz in those years. Or if I've just been too dim to find it."

"You're too dim," Fabienne replied and got up. "I'm going to lock myself away in my office. I'll call you when I find something. There's always a trace."

A short while later there was a knock on Blanc's door. For a second he hoped that Fabienne had already found something, but the hope vanished when he told himself she wouldn't knock on the door: she would just charge in. Instead of Fabienne it was the slightly overweight Marlboro-smoking colleague whose name he could never quite remember.

"Barressi called me," she announced with more than a touch of schadenfreude. "He's on duty downstairs. He says Tonon is with him, but he's in no condition to even get up the steps."

Blanc swallowed a curse, ran past the woman, and headed downstairs. Marius had dropped onto the hard wooden bench for visitors next to Barressi's counter. He was wearing a rumpled shirt and a pair of jeans that were dirty down the front.

He was snoring and a line of dribble hung from the right corner of his mouth. Close up to him it was not a good idea to breathe through the nose. "Into my office!" Blanc ordered. "Before Commandant Nkoulou opens his door."

"The boss already knows," his female colleague answered indifferently. "Ever since the incident, Marius has just let himself go. You might think he was trying to get fired. And that not long before he's due to take his pension. The guy's nuts. He should get a sick note." She grabbed Marius with a practiced, surprisingly strong grip so that Blanc, taking his arm on the other side, found it not as hard as he had expected to haul him up the stairs. On the way up he wondered what she had meant by "the incident." Everybody in the Gadet gendarmerie station seemed to know, everybody except him. For a long time Blanc had believed his colleagues were referring to the time many years ago when during an arrest Marius had fired his service pistol too hastily and wounded another officer. But from the various hints he had since gathered that it had to be something else—something Marius had done shortly before Blanc had been transferred to Gadet from Paris. But even Fabienne refused to say a word.

They dragged Marius's massive frame along the hallway,

squeezed him into his chair, and left him there, slumped and unconscious.

"*Merci beaucoup*," Blanc muttered.

"I'll be interested to see how long you put up with him. Should I leave the door open on the way out?" When she saw Blanc's face, his colleague gave a throaty smoker's laugh. "Just a joke," she reassured him, and pulled the door shut.

Blanc opened the neck of Marius's shirt and felt for the pulse in his neck. He's just drunk, he told himself. He hasn't had a stroke or heart attack. Would he be able to get him out of the station later? Or would it be better if Marius slept it off here? He was still debating the pros and cons of either alternative when the phone rang. It was an internal call. Fabienne.

"I've found something about your girlfriend." Blanc was amazed to hear her whispering. "I think you'd better come to my office."

Action Directe

Blanc threw a last glance at his unconscious colleague, checking that he wasn't about to slide out of his chair, before hurrying into the young second lieutenant's office. Fabienne tapped the screen of her laptop. "There's always a trace," she said.

He had expected that she would be triumphant in giving him the news, but instead she was looking at him seriously. "I found something on the DST server."

Blanc sat down. The domestic intelligence agency. No cop was allowed onto their server without special permission. "We're both going to end up in Lorraine," he whispered.

"Or in court. I opened a back door into the DST computers and had a quick look around. Then I got the hell out of there before an alarm bell went off. I hope I haven't left any traces."

"There's always a digital trace. Always."

Fabienne made a face. "I want to marry Roxane, and you know what I'm having to go through. Trouble at work is the absolute last thing I need right now."

Blanc raised his hands reassuringly. "You're too clever to get caught."

"We'll see," she muttered gloomily. Then she nodded at the screen. "I was no more than sixty seconds on the DST server. But that was long enough to copy an entry on Marie-Claude Elbaz. One single reference. But I would be amazed if it is the only one. Read that."

It was a scan of an old document that had been written on a typewriter, a single page under the DST logo, apparently the summary of a long-term investigation. Blanc zoomed in on the scan and read the date: January 5, 1987. There was no title and no details of the sender. It was a pulled-together table of dates in the life of Marie-Claude Elbaz from her birth in 1964 until 1983. There was nothing that Blanc didn't already know, nothing unusual, until the abrupt last line of her résumé.

At the bottom of this list of harmless entries he found one reference: "ELBAZ, Marie-Claude, urgently sought on suspicion of attempted murder for Action Directe, January 3, 1987, in Saint-Gilles. Current whereabouts unknown." Then came a file name that somebody had rendered illegible with a black marker.

"Action Directe, that was back in your days."

"I wasn't a cop. I was in high school and they were just background noise at the *lycée*."

Action Directe. He tried to remember what he had learned about them in the gendarmerie training college: a collection of extreme left-wing activists—anarchists, autonomists, allegedly also Spanish refugees from Franco. The group just suddenly popped up in 1980: arson attacks on the DST's head office, on the ministry for development, letters claiming responsibility marked with a star. But no bloodshed. Not like the Red Army Faction in West Germany and not at all like the Red Brigades in Italy. Mitterrand had just been elected. The first Socialist president anyone could remember, he brought Communists into his government, an idealist with a vision. It was a period in which Mitterrand secretly offered asylum to extreme left-wingers from Italy, to keep them safe from persecution. The gang with the white star on a black background were treated almost like a legal youth club. *Le tout Paris* was enraptured by these angry, impetuous revolutionaries. That was until Action Directe began shooting people, especially people from the tiny circle that considered itself *le tout Paris*.

The first killings were either in 1983 or 1984, Blanc couldn't remember precisely. But he could remember the uproar when Georges Besse, the chairman of Renault, was murdered in November 1986. It was only when the elite found themselves in the radicals' firing line that the Mitterrand regime took Action Directe seriously enough to put their faces on wanted posters. A few months after the attack on Besse the cops encountered their leaders at a farm they were using as a hiding place. He told Fabienne about it.

"Marie-Claude Elbaz wasn't arrested at that farmhouse near Orléans," she replied. "You can google the terrorists who were. Most of them are now free or dead. It would appear that Elbaz was never arrested."

"She disappears from the radar screen in 1983 and doesn't show up again until 1989," Blanc mused. And all of a sudden the fragments of the story fell together in his mind, like two pieces of a jigsaw puzzle that, once put together, made it obvious where all the other pieces should go. "She's left wing, radical. Back in 1983 she's a young girl and after her first arrest at a demonstration she disappears into the underground and links up with Action Directe. It was almost a fashion thing back then, nobody got upset about it and nobody was after her, nobody cared," he began, expanding his theory, becoming ever more certain of it with every word. "But then she gets her hands dirty—our colleagues from the DST suspect her of involvement in an Action Directe murder. After that, they're no longer complacent. She's a wanted woman."

"But Marie-Claude Elbaz escapes the arrest of the terror group's leadership in 1987," Fabienne added.

"She's still an outlaw, but she keeps her head down until the whole business is all but forgotten. Somebody must have helped her during all that time, must have furnished her with clothes, money, and a roof over her head. Two years after Action Directe is wiped out, all of a sudden she pops up on the Côte d'Azur, as a curator in a provincial museum."

"Where would she have gotten the credentials and papers? Did she really attend a university somewhere? Nothing is more harmless than that. And then a few years later she returns to Paris."

"By which time nobody remembers Action Directe anymore. Where nobody is willing to admit that once upon a time they had idealized a group of murderers and more or less publicly tolerated their existence. Where nobody says a word about left-wing terrorism, at least not officially. Where Marie-Claude Elbaz from the provinces becomes Marie-Claude Leroux from Paris, the wife of the most influential publisher in the capital. Even though her husband is a celebrity, she avoids the spotlight. She's never seen on TV, never turns up at receptions, but prefers to concentrate on rice in the Camargue. And nobody in the little circle of power in Paris knows anything about her past?" Blanc asked in conclusion, looking at Fabienne for a response.

She smiled and shook her head. Her eyes sparkled as if ready for a battle. "Nonsense. I bet they all know about it—the ministers, the managers, the journalists—they all have an idea about Marie-Claude's involvement with Action Directe. Her husband knows. Cohen knew. Think about that draft letter on the reporter's computer where he says he and Leroux know somebody with a secret. But nobody wants to be reminded of Action Directe. Her former lover Boré more or less knows about it. Even a creature like Guillaume somehow found out, maybe through the gossip at the museum. He told us to our faces that Marie-Claude Elbaz had somebody's life on her conscience. But nobody except for this troll takes it seriously, nobody talks about it, nobody has published a single line accusing her, nobody has tried to take her to court. That's why you can't find anything online. Even the DST has buried its files so deep that you can only get to them via a risky hack. And even then there's only a single document that doesn't give us that much information. It's as if Marie-Claude Elbaz had a child when she was a teenager and gave it away to an orphanage: everybody knows about it but out of politeness acts as if the child had never existed."

"Except that it's not an unwanted child they're covering up, it's another murder."

"A murder that took place in Saint-Gilles. Strange, isn't it? Is it just a coincidence that Guillaume was drawn there? And that Cohen noted down the place name? We need to find out who it was that Action Directe killed there. I'll look into it."

"Show me Cohen's laptop again," Blanc said.

Fabienne pulled the computer out of a desk drawer and held it up. Blanc opened Cohen's draft letter to his publisher. "There," he mumbled. "*We've risked more for her than just money. And you and I both know someone who back then took on a lot more.* Do you think that could be a hint that Cohen was remembering something from the past that everybody else in Paris wanted to forget? What do you think a reporter means when he refers to something like that?"

"That he's intending to do a story on it," Fabienne replied thoughtfully.

"A story that Leroux with his newly rekindled political ambitions would find extremely inopportune."

"And a story that could put his wife in jail for the rest of her life. No statute of limitation applies to murder."

"A story that would also be an embarrassment to *le tout Paris* because they'd all of a sudden have to deal with their own past. All of a sudden they'd have to ask themselves why they'd raved about a few guys running around with bombs and guns as if they were resistance fighters."

"Perhaps that old ear slicer Van Gogh had nothing at all to do with somebody setting a fighting bull onto Cohen," Fabienne said.

"I'm enjoying this more and more," Blanc told her.

"I'm not," Fabienne said in a whisper. "It's hot as hell out there, but suddenly I've got a chill running down my back."

The phone was ringing in Blanc's office as he walked back in. Marius didn't stir; Blanc lifted the receiver. It took him a moment to recognize the voice. Paulette Aybalen. His neighbor had never called him before and he was simultaneously flattered and alarmed.

"*Pardon* for bothering you," she began rather embarrassedly. "Can you get off a bit earlier than usual today?"

"Why?" Blanc felt absurdly like a fourteen-year-old being smiled at by a girl of the same age at school. But only for a second.

"Because Fuligni and his men are turning your house into a convertible."

"*Pas de souci*," he muttered, after putting down the receiver. He had been looking forward to contemplating Marie-Claude Elbaz's past, working out what it meant for his case, thinking up new strategies and lines of investigation. But to do that he needed a clear head, and there was no way he could be reflective when less than a couple of miles away his house was being turned into an uninhabitable ruin.

Blanc checked Marius's pulse once more and then hurried

out of the office, past Baressi, out of the station, and into his steam horse. He would happily have given a few euros for a faster car, a helicopter even! He hammered the 2CV around the bends in the road until the shock absorbers groaned. By the time he reached his old oil mill he was imagining himself as the lead character in a hilarious family comedy. Hilarious for the audience because the lead character was stumbling from one catastrophe to the next.

The Manitou was jacked up outside the house and Fuligni's workers were loading the last *tuiles* from his roof down on a pallet. The oak beams of the roof looked like the ribs of a prehistoric animal skeleton against the blue sky. Lots of new ocher-colored *tuiles* were piled up in layers in the dust next to the huge machine. None of them were on the roof. Matthieu Fuligni was directing the work from the cabin of the Manitou, talking at the same time to Paulette Aybalen, who had climbed up to him and was waving her cell phone. Sylvie and Bruno Micheletti were leaning against their old Peugeot 504, parked in the shade of a plane tree. In the back sat three children Blanc had never come across before. They were staring at the displays on their iPods and didn't see him coming. On the other bank of the Touloubre, Serge Douchy was sitting on his tractor cursing. But above the noise of his diesel engine and the roar of the building machine, nobody could hear anything and nobody paid him any attention.

"*Pas de souci*," Fuligni called out when he noticed Blanc coming toward him.

"What's going on here?" Blanc asked. It was straight from a TV script. Any minute now the next catastrophe would hit him.

"You've got woodworm in the beams," Fuligni replied happily.

Blanc went pale.

"We'll deal with it," the builder replied. "We just need to get a few buckets of Xylophene. We paint the beams with it and *voilà*, for the next ten years not a single one of the little beasts will even think of sinking its teeth into your roof."

"Sounds as if it's seriously poisonous."

"You could commit genocide with it. But within twenty-four hours all of it that hasn't sunk deep into the wood will have vaporized. Then we can put the new *tuiles* on."

"My house is going to have to go topless for a day."

"Just twenty-four hours, Monsieur Blanc. Or forty-eight. It's not going to rain. *Pas de souci.*"

Paulette had climbed down from the Manitou and laid a hand calmingly on his arm. "He's right," she reassured Blanc. "You can't have woodworm in the roof beams. It'll all be over in a day or two. It'll be sunny for at least the next week. We're not in the north, you know."

"And when I'm out at work, anybody passing by can just climb over the walls and empty the place."

"The cops come by more regularly now in Sainte-Françoise-la-Vallée," she replied with a smile.

The Michelettis came up. They had dragged the kids from the backseat of the car, more or less by force. Two teenagers and a girl of elementary-school age stood staring at the bare roof beams once they realized what was going on.

"Léo, Julie, and Anouk." Sylvie Micheletti introduced them. "Our kids. They could lend you one of their tents. Or you can come and stay with us at the winery. We have spare rooms."

Blanc wanted to decline both options gracefully until he saw the kids looking at him expectantly. "I'll take a tent," he said. "Just in case."

He was rewarded with a smile from all three. Léo, the oldest, went over to the Peugeot and opened the trunk. "For you, Monsieur," he announced proudly and handed him one of those flat-packed extremely modern backpacker tents that you could put up with a single pull but never properly fold back up again. "I could put the tent up in my bedroom," Blanc said indecisively, "or maybe it would be better to spend the night outside the house in case one of the rotten beams falls on my head."

"The larger branches of your plane tree also need to be cut back or they'll come down of their own accord," Fuligni added calmly.

Before Blanc could say anything in reply, his Nokia rang. The number on the display was one he knew by heart, Aveline's cell phone.

"Maybe we could meet up today? Your place?"

Blanc took a few steps away before answering in a whisper: "My house looks like the scene of a terrorist attack." His mind was racing. His lover almost certainly had mysterious preferences he was unaware of, but he was fairly certain that an hour making love in a ruin was not among them. "How much time do you have?" he asked her.

"I don't have to be in the Palais de Justice in Aix-en-Provence until tomorrow morning. I'm free all afternoon." Then, after a brief pause, "And all night."

"In that case, let's meet in Saint-Gilles," he suggested. "We can meet outside the church in two hours' time, look around the town, find a restaurant, and book a hotel room."

"We'll take two separate rooms. I'll book them." Aveline hung up. She hadn't even asked why he had picked that place in particular for them to meet.

"Important call?" Paulette Aybalen said casually as Blanc slipped the Nokia back into his pocket and came back over to the Manitou.

"Yes," he said. For a second or two he wanted to add a rider such as "An important official business call," but he was reluctant to lie. But given that he could hardly tell the truth, he gave her an apologetic smile and then nodded to Fuligni. "Do whatever you have to."

"By the time we've finished you won't have to worry about any future damage to your roof," the builder promised him.

"If it's not too late already, that is," Blanc muttered.

His affair with Aveline was insane. Sooner or later it would all come out. And what would happen then? He said good-bye to the Michelettis with a wave and to Paulette with a kiss on both cheeks. For a second he held her by the arm and realized that what he was now planning to do was even more hopeless than what he had already done. What he ought to be doing was staying here, watching the crazy workmen, clearing out the oil mill, and asking Paulette to stay with him a little longer. Instead, he went into the house, amazed to find out how bright it was without the roof. He fetched a toiletry bag and a few pieces of clothing, packed them into a sports bag, and went out again. Even in the steam horse he would make it to Saint-Gilles on time.

En route, his Nokia buzzed: a long text message from Fabienne: *I've managed to hack the first of Cohen's computer's encrypted files. They include a few blurry images of the Van Gogh documents from Arles. I think he took them with his cell phone in the police archive. Proof that he went to Arles. And an indication that he was NOT the thief: if he had intended to steal the documents, he wouldn't have bothered to photograph them first, would he? I'm now looking at MCE, Action Directe, and Saint-Gilles. It's a pity you aren't here to pat me on the back, I could do with some praise. Where are you anyway? Kisses.*

Blanc went to answer while driving, but he had barely typed three letters before he almost crashed into an oncoming truck. So he pulled over to the side and typed, *Merci. Can't you feel the pat on the back? I'm following up on a suspicion. See you tomorrow in Gadet.*

The 2CV groaned as Blanc drove it over a narrow hump-backed bridge across the Rhône. The river here had been channeled into a straight bed. The water was ink-blue; the warm westerly wind raised tiny waves that glimmered like glass sickles in the sunshine. Passing over the bridge that led to Saint-Gilles, he glimpsed through the side window a long row of houseboats moored to the stone quay, beyond which stood the flat façades of houses of an indefinable age, their bright plaster peeling away in various stages of damp decay. A confusion of jet-black electricity and phone lines hanging dangerously low from their poles led into the buildings. It looked like a village in the third world. There were no pedestrians to be seen on the quay, just a few elderly mountain bikers who had just gotten off their bikes and were wandering up and down with stiff legs. In contrast the road was quite busy. Blanc was honked at frequently because his 2CV couldn't go fast enough. He took the main street into the town center. A storefront on his left was decorated in red, white, and blue; it was the local headquarters of the Front National. Blanc finally remembered when he had first heard the name of the little town. Even years ago the Front had gotten more votes here than anywhere else in France. So many that, while he was still working in Paris, newspaper reporters and television teams had turned up down here. Paris! Don't even think about it. *Merde.*

He parked the 2CV on an irregularly shaped square underneath the massive medieval stone wall that held the old town as if in a fist. Blanc wondered if Saint-Gilles was really such a good place for a lovers' secret tryst. He walked through a narrow gate that was so claustrophobic he involuntarily ducked. Two alleys. Heat. Nobody to be seen. A rusted sign on the church. Blanc took just a few steps in the direction it suggested, then stopped. The alleyway opened out onto a small, dull square, which was more accurately an old street intersection blocked off to cars by metal barriers. No trees, no shade, no cafés. But opposite him was a staircase as big as that for the entrance to a soccer stadium. It led up to an ancient church, huge and curiously unfinished-looking: a massive façade in front of a gashed, undecorated nave. There was an ugly tower on the right-hand side, its lower half narrower than the upper, a denial in stone of gravity and proportion. On the left was just a stump as if some giant sickle had sliced off a tower just above the ground, then three entrance doors beneath curved archways in the façade, like a stage set for eternity.

Within the curved arches were stone images of Jesus in judgment, Jesus being kissed by Judas, Jesus being scourged, with the empty tomb, saints, sinners, false prophets, strong kings. A twelfth-century comic book, a bestiary, a world of myths carved in stone. Blanc approached it in amazement, staring up at the rectangular, interconnecting patterns that he would have considered more likely to be Celtic decoration than Christian bas-relief. At the foot of one of the pillars near the main entrance he spotted a camel, a terrified man being eaten by a monster, and a centaur: a half man, half horse, heathen bowman, only a few feet below Christ the Redeemer and the pantheon of Christian kings.

A tour guide with some twenty or so tourists behind her emerged from an alleyway opposite the church. They were the only people around and even though they were talking in whispers, they seemed to Blanc like an enemy army. The tour guide was still young, tubby and sweating through her brightly colored blouse. On her left breast was a badge with the arms of the Commune de Saint-Gilles and her name. "Virginie Berenger,"

Blanc read. He stepped aside to let Madame Berenger lead her group past him as she ushered them through the central entrance into the church interior. He paid next to no attention to the tourists until he breathed in a familiar aroma: Chanel No. 5 and Gauloises.

Aveline Vialaron-Allègre was walking behind three Asian tourists and an elderly French couple. She was wearing dark sunglasses with a black frame, concealing her face. Her short black hair glinted at the edges of a baseball cap printed with the words NOVA SCOTIA. It had belonged to Blanc until he had accidentally left it at her house. The olive-colored skin of her slender arms fit in with the peach-colored polo shirt and her pale blue jeans. Her white boating shoes meant she made no sound on the stone floor worn smooth by the innumerable faithful. Aveline was the most elegant person in the group. She paid not the slightest attention to him.

Blanc waited a moment until two other female Asian tourists had scuttled past him, then he inconspicuously tagged on to the group.

He listened to the explanations of the tour guide who had said the same words so often it seemed as if she was walking and talking in her sleep. The echoing nave meant that Blanc didn't manage to make out why Saint-Gilles had become an important pilgrimage site in the Middle Ages, but he gathered that a thousand years earlier it had had three times as many inhabitants as it did today. The Huguenots had devastated the church during the "wars of religion," which was why it had the irregular appearance it had today: the cobbled-together remnants of a building that had been plundered time and time again. Blanc edged closer to Aveline so that he could at least inhale her perfume. She was paying attention to the guide's explanations and taking notes in a thin black Moleskin notebook. Maybe it was her passion for art that made her take notes? Or maybe she hadn't even noticed how close he was standing to her?

They were led down a narrow stairway into the crypt. The undercroft was dank and cool and smelled damp. Even though it was murderously hot outside, the stone floor here was even dark with moisture in a few places. Salt crystals were gleaming on the walls where water that had soaked in had settled. Blanc stared at the tomb of Saint Aegidius, the church's patron saint—Gilles being the French form of the Latin—a modest stone sarcophagus in the middle of the crypt. He saw votive tablets, flowers, a huge processional candle skewed with age; on the wax he could make out just the year it was bought: 1956.

He was glad to get out into the open air again. The tour guide opened a gate and sent them past toppled columns and overgrown steps to the back of the nave. This was the collapsed remains of the choir, she explained. Then she pointed to the stump of a tower partly eaten away like a rotten tooth. The staircase inside had to be remarkable because for the first time Madame Berenger was registering something close to enthusiasm. But Blanc was paying not the least attention. He had spotted the base of one particular pillar. All the others were decorated with flowers or patterns. This one stood atop a crippled man.

Blanc moved closer. He could make out a hunched stone figure, barely as long as his arm, and eroded by a thousand rain showers. It was the figure of a man hugging the ground in pain because the pillar, which was a hundred times larger than him, stood on his right leg. For nearly a thousand years this pillar had been squashing his calf, without a minute's respite. Olivier Guillaume limps, it suddenly occurred to Blanc. On his right leg.

A little later the tour guide led the group back through the church nave to the entrance. Aveline scribbled something in her notebook, ripped out the page, and left it on a bench. She made not the slightest attempt to conceal the action, which was probably why nobody paid any attention to it. Nobody except Blanc.

He sat down on the bench and put his hand over the page until the last of the tourists had disappeared outside. Only then did he read what was written on it. Her handwriting was very clear but also very tiny, so he could hardly make out what it said in the semidarkness of the church. *The Italian restaurant on the Rhône, in one hour. Table on the veranda by the river booked. Name of Vincent. Be there before me. I hate waiting.*

Blanc looked up as a ray of light fell across his hand. The door had been opened and the tour guide slipped back in. It was cooler inside than out on the square. She was on her own, exhausted, but probably not too exhausted to answer a couple of questions, Blanc suddenly decided. He had nearly an hour to kill.

"Madame Berenger?" He was speaking normally, but in the church nave his voice sounded at the same time loud and almost incomprehensible.

She turned around and recognized him, clearly afraid she had stumbled upon one of those know-it-all tourists who want to round off his tour with endless questions about details. Blanc could see the effort it was taking her just to force the ghost of a smile on her face.

"Gendarmerie," he explained, whispering this time. "Capitaine Blanc. Might I ask you a few questions?"

"Well, at least that's new." He could hear from her voice that she desperately needed a glass of water.

Blanc pulled out a photo of Olivier Guillaume. "Do you know this man?"

"Has he done something?"

"Would that surprise you?"

She laughed. "He's in the church so often, he must have

done something!" Virginie Berenger shook her head in amazement. "Not that I can even tell you really who he is. He's not from Saint-Gilles, that's for sure. But he's here often, at least once a week."

"What does he do in the church?"

"What do you do in a church? Pray, sleep? Every time he sits down on a bench, he closes his eyes and stays for an hour or so, then leaves."

"Always on his own."

"I couldn't even recognize his voice because I've never heard him exchange two words with anyone else. Strange bird."

"Does he never make notes? Or wander around? Outside to the ruined choir maybe?"

"The staircase is superb, isn't it? Every stone perfectly laid and. . . ."

"I was thinking of the man with the crushed leg underneath the pillar."

"Oh, him?" She flicked a hand dismissively. "A worker from the Middle Ages who had an accident while the cloister was being built. His colleagues, the stonemasons, did that to commemorate him. Or at least that's the legend. In reality nobody knows anything about the figure or why any artist would make a figure like that. To be honest nobody cares. At least none of our treasure hunters." She noticed Blanc's surprised expression, sighed, and said, "Come along, I'll show you."

Madame Berenger led him down the narrow staircase back into the crypt. "Saint-Gilles used to be an important stop on the route to Santiago de Compostela. Pilgrims from all over Europe stopped off here. The church used to belong to an abbey. Saint Aegidius, whose last resting place this is, performed many, many miracles. This was a very successful business. The monks became rich and the church was full of treasure. Then the Huguenots came and ever since then there has only been one treasure left: the church façade. But there are people who don't believe that." She indicated a wall without decoration beneath the summit of the staircase. "This crypt is almost as big as the nave above it. But do you see this wall? It really shouldn't be here because there is a part of the nave above it. And it is a fact that the wall isn't as old as the rest of the crypt. So was part of it walled off at a later stage? And is there an underground room hidden behind it? And if so, what does it contain? It's obvious: the treasure of the old abbey of Saint-Gilles. Except that to date nobody has found it. Nor the mysterious room. The wall is simply there. God knows whether there is a hollow space behind it or just rock and earth. Or look here."

Virginie Berenger led Blanc over to the gable end of the crypt, which also ended in a straight wall with no decoration. "There's an entryway here," she explained, pointing at a gate made of heavy dark beams. "That really does lead into a vault, one that supports the main staircase that leads up into the church. A room beneath a staircase. *Mon Dieu*, isn't that symbolic in the extreme? Why is there this hollow chamber under the stairs? It's obvious, this is where the monks' treasure is. Except that, unfortunately, this hollow space is as empty as the brain of my demented grandmother."

"But there are people determined to believe that there is something hidden here?"

"We've had to change the lock on this gate several times because every now and then somebody turns up with a crowbar and tries to break in. We've even had nutcases with dowsing rods, metal detectors, and miniature cameras who got to work on the wall beneath the crypt staircase. Once we just managed to catch someone who had smuggled in a sledgehammer in a sports bag intending to smash through the stones."

Blanc was thinking of what Olivier Guillaume had told Marie-Claude Elbaz about the Van Eyck altar in Ghent and the stolen picture that was believed to be hidden in the church itself. "Did this man," he asked, nodding at the photo of Guillaume, "ever come down into the crypt?"

"I've never seen him here, but then I'm not always in the church. And hardly ever in the crypt. It's far too damp, I get goose bumps."

Blanc fished out a photo of Marie-Claude from his briefcase. "Do you know this woman?"

"Never seen her."

He tried the same with Ernest Leroux, Nora Leroux, and Daniel Boré. On each occasion she simply shook her head. Then Virginie Berenger spotted the photo of Albert Cohen among his papers. "I've seen him on TV," she declared. "And he was here. Just recently."

Blanc stared at her. "When?"

She thought a moment. "A good week ago. Yes, last Tuesday. My afternoon tour."

Tuesday, August 2, Blanc thought. Two days before his fatal encounter with the bull. "What was Monsieur Cohen doing?"

Virginie Berenger laughed. "The same as you, as it happens," she replied. "He joined my group and then afterward caught hold of me and began to ask questions."

"About the church?"

"Yes. He knew more than you, I have to admit. He asked me about the secret rooms. He had bought a booklet about the church with a floor plan in the souvenir shop, the same one all the treasure hunters buy. He was determined to get past the gate in the vault under the staircase and was very disappointed to know that we tour guides don't have a key to it. He would have to get that from the town council. He said he would."

"And did he?"

She shrugged. "I never saw him again."

Back out on the square, Blanc wrestled with his cell phone until he got hold of somebody from the Saint-Gilles town council. Five minutes later, an official he'd managed to wake up despite the heat and the late afternoon hour told him that Albert Cohen had submitted an official request that someone from the local authority should open the gate for him.

"Did he mention why he wanted to get in there?" Blanc asked.

He could hear the man shuffling papers. "All it says here is 'journalistic research,' whatever that means."

"And did you grant his request?"

"So it seems. My boss agreed. We gave Monsieur Cohen a date. This week. Wait a minute." He flicked rapidly through his paperwork. "Yesterday, ten A.M. But Monsieur Cohen was no longer able to make it. I read about it in the newspaper. Ran into a fighting bull. He didn't sound that stupid."

"*Merci*," Blanc replied and ended the call.

The restaurant was called Le Coin Secret. No wonder Aveline had specifically picked it out. He wondered how well she knew Saint-Gilles. The table she had reserved was in the farthest corner of a wooden terrace in the shade of a reed-thatched roof. Between the building where the restaurant was and the terrace was a narrow riverbank road of broken asphalt that a car ran along every ten minutes or so. There were no pedestrians except for the waiters running back and forth from the restaurant to the terrace like tireless ants. There were lots of customers, gentle background music, yellow light from oil lamps. From their corner table he looked out onto the Rhône. Two kayakers were paddling silently against the current, their narrow yellow boat creating V-shaped waves in the water that disconcertingly reminded Blanc of the fins of the white shark in Spielberg's film. All that was missing was the pounding beat of the music. Ridiculous. What could be threatening here? A discreet place by the water's edge, barely visible from an almost empty street. Warm light that tended to cover faces rather than illuminate them. A town where he at least had never been before. Nobody would notice them. And even if they did, was it forbidden for a *juge d'instruction* to go for a meal with an officer of the gendarmerie? All they were doing was visiting a restaurant together.

Aveline didn't leave him waiting for long. She was still wearing her sunglasses when she turned up at the terrace, greeted him with a brief peck on the cheek, and sat down opposite him. Only then did she remove her dark glasses. She took a long cold look at him and in a slightly ironic tone said, "Did you like the church, *mon Capitaine*?"

"I learned a lot."

"Then maybe you'll explain to me why we had to meet here?"

A waiter came up to them and was about to hand them the menus, but Aveline declined with a friendly dismissive wave. "Two *riz rouge aux calamars* and a dry white wine," she ordered. As soon as the waiter disappeared, she whispered to Blanc, "The fewer times he has to come to the table, the better."

"How did you know I like squid?"

"I wasn't thinking so much about the seafood as the red Camargue rice." Blanc smiled to himself. "I'm more interested in the farmer than the harvest. A lady farmer in this case." Then he told her about the all but erased past of a young woman called Marie-Claude Elbaz. About a file held by the DST, although without mentioning how he had gotten hold of it and who had helped him.

And about a long-forgotten theft and a curious janitor. About the altar in Ghent and the mystery of the cathedral.

At that point Aveline interrupted him.

"I know the story about the vanished Van Eyck," she murmured. "Van Eyck–Van Gogh–Ghent–Gilles, a church there, a church here. Do you think Guillaume is inspired by some sort of symmetry? He stole the beach drawing two decades ago and hid it here in Saint-Gilles, is that what you are suggesting? I'm glad we're talking about it here rather than in my office. Any gendarme who came to me with a story like that would be shown the door immediately. Saint-Gilles of all places! This is probably the most searched church in the whole of Provence. A legion of art historians have gone over the entrance portal with a fine-tooth comb. And to them you can add hundreds of treasure seekers, looking for the monks' hidden room. I wouldn't even try to count how many people have gone over every single stone in this church during the last twenty years! And none of them found anything."

"In Ghent they've spent a century with no better results," Blanc said in his own defense. "A man like Guillaume is fascinated by just that. He explicitly sought out the church that the most people imaginable paid attention to. Any idiot could hide a sketch in some godforsaken chapel. But in Saint-Gilles? That would take a genius. In the meantime he's been coming here regularly, observing the visitors who without knowing it might be walking along only a few inches from his hidden Van Gogh. The fact that they don't know would please him, make him feel superior to them. It would be one little triumph in his pathetic existence."

"It could equally well just be that he's pious and comes here to pray. Saint-Gilles is a pilgrimage site. And now that more believers are doing the trek to Santiago de Compostela than there used to be, the church gets full of sore-footed salvation seekers.

Not exactly a bad place for a man with a religious side, don't you agree? And it's not exactly illegal to spend hours squatting on a church bench."

The waiter came back and carefully set down two deep dishes steaming with the aroma of white wine, seafood, and spices: squid rings, onions, and slices of lemon glistened amid the dark red rice. The white wine came in an unlabeled bottle and was so cold that the glass was frosted. Blanc suddenly realized how hungry he was. "Madame Leroux insists that you can taste the sun and the mistral in the local rice."

"The woman has a poetic vein. But she knows when something's good. Try it."

Blanc took a first bite and closed his eyes with a gourmet's enjoyment. "*Très bon.* From now on I will let you order every time we eat together in a restaurant."

Aveline didn't reply but just lifted her glass and smiled.

They ate in silence for a while. Blanc wondered what the woman in front of him was thinking. So near, and yet so impossibly distant. When he was with Aveline, he would always have to think of the present and never of the future. He drank only a little of the white wine. He was going to lose his head tonight either way.

Only when the plates had been cleared and they were relaxing over two espressos did Blanc mention his case again. "Cohen was also here in Saint-Gilles just a few days before his death." Aveline listened with interest as he described the few details he had discovered. There was no longer any trace of sarcasm on her face. She was looking at him with an expression he knew only too well. He only had to look in the mirror: curiosity and stubbornness.

"Vincent van Gogh never came to Saint-Gilles," she interjected. "Cohen must have come here more or less secretly because he didn't mention it to his publisher and certainly not to the man's wife, who happens to be an art historian and a fan of the painter. If he had told either of them that he was coming here, then they would have immediately realized he was no longer following in the footsteps of Van Gogh."

"Nor did he say a word about it to Boré, at least according to Boré. Cohen had also agreed to an appointment with Guillaume, but he never met him and had mentioned no details on the phone. So who could have known that he had been here in Saint-Gilles? Or that he planned to come back?"

She lit up a Gauloise. "Maybe nobody knew? Maybe his visit here has absolutely nothing to do with your investigation. And maybe his planned second visit here had nothing to do with his sudden death."

Blanc shook his head. "Why does Cohen turn up here? The only explanation can be that he somehow found out what we have only found out since: that Olivier Guillaume is obsessed with Saint-Gilles. That Guillaume was the chief suspect in the old theft. That the story of the vanished Van Eyck in Ghent might have inspired him. Cohen was looking for the drawing! He hadn't told anyone because he wanted to surprise the world with a spectacular comeback. That's why he came here and why he wanted to get into the sealed vault beneath the staircase. He was following Guillaume's trail. And who knows, maybe Guillaume was already aware of it? Guillaume who spent lots of time sitting on a church bench—a figure in the semidarkness. Cohen might not have noticed him when he came into the church. But Guillaume, who had hidden the picture here and watched keenly the behavior of all visitors, would have spotted him . . . and maybe he's not as unworldly as we think. Maybe he watches television every now and then? Maybe he recognized a celebrity like Cohen? And then when the journalist called him he put two and two together: a reporter, trying to find his hiding place? He would have to neutralize him before the journalist found out everything. So Guillaume becomes a murderer."

"And a mommy's boy like him decides to use a fighting bull as his murder weapon, in broad daylight?" The familiar sarcastic look appeared in Aveline's eyes. "How was Guillaume even to know that Cohen regularly rode around the Camargue on his mountain bike? And what route he took? And that precisely on that route there was a field with a fighting bull in it?"

"We don't have enough to make a formal case out of it," Blanc conceded. "At least not yet."

"At least I haven't had a boring evening," Aveline said consolingly, and waved the waiter over. "Pay cash. Cards leave too many traces."

"I'll do the same for the hotel check."

She stroked his hand unobtrusively. "I already checked in at the Logis Rene earlier today, the best place on the square, not that that's saying much. It's a little yellow-plastered building just a few paces along the riverbank. You can't miss it. I shall head there now. Stay here a quarter of an hour or so. You have a room booked on the same floor."

"In the name of Vincent, I suppose?"

Aveline just smiled.

When he finally held her in his arms, he wanted to think of nothing more than her naked body. The hotel room was small and the bed only just big enough for a couple to make love. When he checked in, the old lady at the reception desk hardly looked at him. No one was in the lobby or on his floor. And then Aveline had knocked on his door.

He kissed her cheeks, her neck, her shoulders, carefully exploring her body with his lips. He had all the time in the world.

Not just a stolen hour, a meeting between two appointments. He had the whole night.

Then his phone rang. The ringtone was partly muted as it was coming from his pants pocket, where he had left it in the impatience of his lust: a penetrating little melody from the black tangled bundle of clothing on the floor next to the bed. Blanc wanted to ignore it, but Aveline stroked his face and whispered, "Take the call."

He growled a curse, untangled his jeans, and pulled out the phone: Fabienne's work number.

"*Salut*," he greeted her, trying to breathe calmly. Aveline was stroking his chest and stomach with her fingertips.

"Roger? Sorry to call you so late, but can you come in to the gendarmerie?" His colleague was speaking barely louder than a whisper, as if she was afraid somebody in her office could hear her.

Aveline was so close to him that even though she couldn't make out what was being said, she could hear that it was a young woman's voice coming from the phone. She smiled triumphantly and let her hand wander lower. Blanc closed his eyes. "I'm afraid not," he managed to say. "Can't we talk tomorrow?" His voice sounded strained.

Fabienne was so worked up that she didn't notice how breathless he was. "*Bien*," she replied. "Then I'll have to tell you the story on the phone. I need to get it off my chest or I won't get a wink of sleep tonight."

Blanc sighed.

"Anyway. The man who was killed back then was a rice farmer. He owned the biggest rice fields in the whole of the Camargue. You know his farm. You were there last Thursday."

Camargue Rice

Thursday, the fourteenth day of the heat wave. Blanc was in the gendarmerie by eight o'clock. He felt exhausted and ecstatic at the same time. The first night they had spent together! On the very edge of his consciousness the hope had kindled that just maybe, somehow, sometime, he might have a future with Aveline. The whole way back Blanc had wondered what it might be like to wake up every morning in his oil mill with her next to him. He couldn't quite manage it. But no more could he manage to put the memory of the past few hours away in some closed compartment of his mind.

He only really returned to the real world when he was standing in the shabby hallway outside Nkoulou's office. The commandant greeted him militarily, as if he was in a parade in front of the president on the Champs-Élysées. At the same moment Blanc was thinking about his forced move from Paris, his ruin of a house, his hopeless affair with a married woman, his mysterious case about a murderous fighting bull, a vanished Van Gogh, and a long-forgotten assassination. Pathetic, he told himself, everything I do down here is just pathetic. He returned the salute wearily, sat down in his office, and left the door open, so he could see down the corridor. He hoped he wouldn't have to wait too long before Fabienne arrived.

It was ten minutes before he noticed that a report from the forensics team about the scene of the accident was lying on his desk. Just two sheets of paper, which didn't look exactly promising. Blanc skimmed through it. There were photos and drawings of the plaster casts of all the tire treads near the gate to the bull's field, but there were no details to allow them to be identified. There were a few fingerprints on the gate, mostly too blurred to identify, but the few that could be identified were not Cohen's. The photos taken by the officer at the site might have been an example from the gendarmerie training school in how not to do it. The bits that Blanc had found underneath the gate were scraps of dyed-black crocodile leather and half of a stainless-steel buckle from a watch strap of indefinite brand. All in all, a confirmation of everything he had already supposed.

Blanc closed his eyes and in his head went over the men he had had dealings with in the past few days. Ernest Leroux—a steel Rolex with the same sort of watchband. Daniel Boré—an elegant Jaeger-LeCoultre with a narrow brown leather strap and a gold buckle. Olivier Guillaume—an unusually heavy diver's watch, allegedly inherited from his father. The strap of a high-tech synthetic material.

Not that any of it necessarily meant anything. A man might have more than one watch; any one of the three of them could have ripped a strap of one and put on another watch instead. Boré and Guillaume would both have had time to get new straps for their watches. Tonon was right: It was simply ridiculous. The whole thing was ridiculous. Blurred tire tracks, a light-colored car in the distance, fragments of leather, shiny metal on dusty ground. *Merde.* He had only fixated on these "clues" because he'd had nothing else to do and was going mad in this heat. He would never get out of here, never have a serious case again, never stand outside his house with his wife looking to the horizon while the sun set the sky on fire.

Blanc was already at the door of his office, about to go into Nkoulou's office and tell him to close the file on Cohen's death. It had been a damn accident. Why was he bothering with the disappearance of a Van Gogh and an assassination that nobody even remembered anymore?

"You look like Zidane's just head-butted you."

All of a sudden Fabienne was standing in front of him, kissing him on the cheeks, smelling of perfume and shampoo and the leather of her motorbike jacket. She smiled and looked at him expectantly, eager to tell him the results of her further research. Suddenly Blanc could no longer bring himself to go in to see Nkoulou and tell him to file the case away in the cellar. He couldn't bring himself to extinguish her smile, to make her taste of the hunt seem ridiculous.

"In the end it was the victim who won out, not the assailant," he said, replying to her joke about the French soccer star who had head-butted another player and been sent off the pitch. He waved her into his office—to hell with Nkoulou and his doubts, and the damn heat.

Fabienne closed the door before sitting down on Marius's empty chair. "César Durand was a young farmer from Saint-Gilles when the war began, no older than twenty-two. Can't think why he wasn't called up straightaway. Anyhow in 1940 he was still on his farm when the workers from Indochina were beached in Marseille. Durand was one of the first here to think of sending the Vietnamese into the former rice paddies. Up until the nineteenth century his family had grown rice, or at least that's what his grandfather had told him. Maybe that's what gave him the idea.

From 1944 on, Durand's farm yielded a lot of rice. Durand bought more land, including the farms that had long since been abandoned, and in 1947 he moved from Saint-Gilles to a big house in the middle of the Camargue, which he turned into the family seat."

"I think I know where that might be."

Fabienne nodded. "By then Durand had long since sent the Vietnamese home. With no bonus, no pay, no reward, not the slightest recognition. Durand got married, produced two sons and two daughters, and after 1958, when the old general de Gaulle became president, he became involved with the local Gaullists. And all the time he kept bringing in the harvests. It could have gone on like that forever."

"Until Action Directe got involved with direct action," Blanc suggested.

"The terrorists didn't only target cops, they were also deadly enemies of 'capitalist exploiters.' At least that and other fine phrases were what they used when they claimed responsibility."

"They didn't just talk the talk, they murdered the chief executive of Renault."

"Among others. He was just the most prominent 'exploiter.' Durand, for example, was shot three times as he left the Gaullist office in Saint-Gilles after a New Year's Eve party. The gunman, according to witness statements, was a young man on the pillion of a motorbike with Paris number plates. It was winter, cold and dark, and there were few people out on the street. But everyone insisted that the motorbike was driven by a young woman. She was wearing a helmet, but everyone described her as slim and fit."

"It's a good thing you weren't born back then or the DST would have had you down as a suspect."

She gave a thoughtful laugh. "I wouldn't have made the

mistake that motorcyclist made. Five days before the assassination a young female motorcyclist filled up at the Saint-Gilles gas station. The assistant remembered her because it was unusual to see a female motorcyclist down here in the middle of winter. On a motorbike with Parisian number plates. The guys at the DST bought the gas station assistant a big mug of coffee and sat him down in a quiet room to look through their files. They had already put together a file of hundreds of young female sympathizers of Action Directe. The gas station assistant flicked through them and *Bingo!* there was Marie-Claude Elbaz smiling up at him."

"Who featured in their files because she had been arrested at a left-wing protest demonstration."

"And who had a motorcycle license. And had not been seen in her apartment since the end of 1983. *Oui, mon Capitaine*, and all of a sudden you're a suspect in a murder case."

"In the circumstances I would have made her a suspect, too."

"Me, too. The shooter who had been on the pillion seat was arrested two years later for that murder and several other crimes and jailed for life, not that it lasted that long. After less than twelve months inside he hanged himself in his cell with his own trousers, which he had ripped up and tied together to make a rope. Up until the end, in 1988, he never revealed the identity of his accomplice."

"And the search for Marie-Claude Elbaz simply came to nothing."

"And it remains so today."

"Even though Marie-Claude Elbaz has returned as Marie-Claude Leroux more or less to the scene of the crime," Blanc said in amazement.

"One of Durand's sons took over the farm but made a mess rather than a success of it. Officially Ernest Leroux bought it off Durand's children in the end—on September 21, 2001."

Blanc whistled through his teeth. "Ten days after the attack on the World Trade Center."

"While the whole world was concentrating on new terrorists, and nobody gave a thought anymore to the old left-wing urban guerrillas. The Islamists were the best thing that could ever have happened to the former revolutionaries. When you've seen the twin towers in New York collapse, you don't pay much attention any longer to Action Directe. And even if you should perhaps recall them, then those ancient assassinations no longer seem so shocking. What does a rice farmer shot dead in the Camargue matter compared with the massacre in the World Trade Center?"

"Even so . . ." Blanc muttered.

Fabienne nodded. "Even so . . . after September 21 an alarm bell should have rung in some office of the DST. An alleged murderer gets her hands on her victim's property. But it would seem that the DST remained deep in slumber."

"Or maybe nobody wanted to hear the alarm bell," Blanc went on. "Forget about it. Let's draw the line below those inconvenient olden days."

"Do you think Ernest Leroux might be involved?" Fabienne asked.

Blanc thought back to the rumors he had heard about the publisher. "Definitely. A man like him who made his fortune publicizing every single scandal in *L'Événement* lets this story stay in the closet? Why? Maybe because he really does genuinely love Marie-Claude and keeps silent to protect his wife. Or maybe it's just cynical calculation: Marie-Claude cuts an elegant figure as his wife, while he can go on groping every other woman he can lay his hands on. Leroux doesn't even have to bother about hiding his affairs from his wife. The last thing Marie-Claude wants is a public divorce scandal that could end up in court."

"In any case you said yourself that Leroux had set out on a

political career, which suddenly came to an end for unknown reasons. And now he's got similar ambitions again. Would you vote for a politician whose wife is a murderer who's never been brought to trial? Perhaps Monsieur Leroux thinks that now might be the time to split up with his wife?"

"In that case, surely he'd have unleashed the fighting bull on Marie-Claude rather than his friend Albert Cohen."

"Maybe it was a case of mistaken identity? Marie-Claude has a sporty figure and if she was wearing a helmet and sunglasses . . ."

"Can you really imagine the elegant Marie-Claude Leroux on a mountain bike in neon Lycra?"

Fabienne thought for an instant, then shook her head. "In that case, what's the answer?"

"We've lifted the veil a bit on Marie-Claude Elbaz's past, at least a little. But we have no link between the earlier murder in Saint-Gilles and the death of Albert Cohen. No link as yet."

"But are you satisfied so far even so, *mon Capitaine*?"

"You rescued me from the depths of doubt, Second Lieutenant Souillard."

Fabienne laughed; she must have thought Blanc was joking.

Marius Tonon didn't turn up until midday. He was wearing a freshly ironed blue shirt with a pattern of Provençal flowers and a spotless pair of white linen trousers, his hair had been cut, and he smelled of the sort of aftershave that granddads used to wear when Blanc was still a boy. He didn't say a word about the day before and Blanc was clever enough not to ask about it.

He had agreed to have lunch with Fabienne at Le Planet and took his colleague along, bringing him up-to-date on the current state of play in the investigation. When they had sat down at the table in the shade of a plane tree, Marius ordered a pastis even before the waiter had brought the menus. Fabienne and Blanc exchanged glances. Then she ostentatiously nodded at the table next to them where a young pair was trying to feed their twins. The boys were about one year old, and judging by the amount of food on the ground, their parents hadn't managed to get much food between their lips.

Fabienne sighed. "Roxane and I would like to have children," she announced unasked.

This time it was Blanc and Marius who exchanged glances. Blanc said nothing but wondered how that was going to happen. Adoption? Artificial insemination? Fabienne worked hard. She would probably have to go to court to get the right to marry. He didn't think it would exactly be a good idea then to start worrying about having children, but what sort of expert on family matters was he?

In the hot midday sun, none of them had an appetite for a hot meal. Blanc and Marius ordered cold ratatouille; Fabienne made do with a small salad. Blanc told Marius about Marie-Claude's dark past and the Action Directe murder.

"If even the DST has closed the file, then nobody else in Paris will want to get their hands dirty," Marius said.

"That doesn't mean we can't try."

"Even your *juge d'instruction* won't take the case," Fabienne interjected.

Blanc gave an embarrassed cough. "Officially we're investigating Cohen's death. Should we succeed in finding a link to Action Directe, then the courts will have to deal with it. That makes it official whether the people in Paris like it or not."

"Let's run through our suspects," Marius suggested. "Madame Leroux, did she have an opportunity to carry out the killing and is there a motive?"

"She had the opportunity," Blanc replied. "At the time of the accident she was allegedly on the farm in the Camargue. But she has no witnesses, no alibi. And no scruples. She's been involved in a murder before. Anyone who's committed a crime like that once doesn't have a problem doing it again. And her motive? She was afraid the reporter was looking into her past and wanted to make a story of it."

"For which we have found not the slightest evidence on either Cohen's computer or his phone," Fabienne reminded them.

"Apart from the hint in the letter Cohen sent to his publisher."

"Intended to send," she insisted. "It was only a draft. We have no evidence that either Leroux or his wife, to whom the letter was not addressed, ever saw a single line of it. And even if they had, Cohen's hint is so vague that you can't be sure that he was even referring to Madame Leroux."

"Marie-Claude Leroux, alias Elbaz, had the opportunity and was cold-blooded enough, but so far we haven't found a convincing motive," Marius summed up. "And what about her worthy husband?"

"At the time in question, Ernest Leroux was allegedly on his yacht in the harbor of Port-Saint-Louis-du-Rhône," Blanc said. "We've asked the officials down there to look for witnesses who can confirm that."

"The harbor authority uses video cameras to monitor their expensive little boats," his colleague added.

"The gendarme on the phone told me that," Blanc confirmed. "They're still going through the tapes, and they promised me they'd be finished today."

"Until they prove different then, Leroux has an alibi." Fabienne leaned forward and pointed in the air with her fork, as if she was training for a fencing contest. "But Leroux had lots of motives. Motive number one: Perhaps he had found out about Cohen's protest letter? It would be seriously annoying if the publisher were to face criticism from one of his closest friends for firing journalists—especially if the publisher was planning a career in politics. Who's going to vote for someone who fires people? Motive number two: Cohen's sleeping with his wife."

Marius laughed. "Roger's accusing Cohen of exposing Marie-Claude's dirty laundry, you're accusing him of sharing her bed. Poor Cohen! But you can't prove either of them."

"Maybe Leroux had heard that Cohen was researching his wife's terrorist past?" Blanc suggested, unperturbed. "He kills his old friend to protect his wife. And to prevent his political career from being wrecked by a scandal about his wife, wrecked for the second time before it had even taken off."

"This is getting more absurd by the minute."

"*Bon*," Fabienne said. "Let's leave the publisher couple for a minute and examine our other two candidates."

"Daniel Boré?" Marius asked. "He kills Cohen because the reporter has unearthed the story about the old theft and Boré is nowhere near as innocent as he let on to us."

"I've been thinking over our interview," Blanc replied. "I happen to know," he hesitated briefly, "a female art historian who happens to have Boré's book on her shelves. Along comes a journalist like Cohen to ask for Boré's help in his research. In passing, Boré discovers that Cohen might have found a photo of the artist, which would be sensational. Boré puts Cohen out of the picture in order to claim the discovery himself and secure his fame."

Fabienne shook her head. "There's a problem with that story. Yesterday, after you took off in a panic about your oil mill, Marseille police got in touch. Boré had insisted that on the day of Cohen's death he had been in the MuCEM. Their cameras show Boré entering the building about eleven A.M. and only leaving again after five P.M. There's no way Boré could have set the bull free from its meadow. His alibi is rock solid."

"*Putain*," Marius mumbled. "I would have enjoyed arresting a man who knocks back pastis in front of me, without thinking of offering me one."

"That leaves us with Olivier Guillaume," Blanc said.

"Cohen was researching the art theft. Guillaume would have known that at the latest when Cohen called him to arrange a meeting. Guillaume, who had been the chief suspect back then, fears that he will once again be unjustly accused. Or he really was the thief and fears that he will at last be found out. One way or the other, it's a good motive for murder. Guillaume felt threatened by Cohen." Fabienne leaned back in her chair, looking satisfied. "And he doesn't have an alibi. He was at home with his mother. But that old witch would tell any lie imaginable for her son."

"Even so, she is still a witness whose testimony would have to be challenged. And until then Guillaume also has an alibi," Marius replied, knocking back the last drop of rosé in his carafe. "Also the problem you have to solve is how Guillaume could know precisely that Cohen would be cycling on a borrowed mountain bike at a specific time along a particular *route départementale* past a field with a fighting bull in it."

"Maybe Guillaume had been watching Cohen for days," Fabienne replied. "He only worked evenings in the bar, he said so himself. And a witness saw a light-colored car speeding away from the scene."

Blanc sighed. "There's something not quite right here. Cohen's curious death; the ambitions of the publisher Leroux; his wife's relationship with Cohen; the theft of a Van Gogh years ago; the Action Directe murder even longer ago. It can't just be coincidence that we've stumbled on to all this. They all fit together somehow. But how? We're missing a piece of the jigsaw."

"We're missing a whole handful of jigsaw pieces," Marius declared, waving over the waiter to order three espressos.

At just that moment, Blanc's cell phone rang. It was a gendarme from Port-Saint-Louis-du-Rhône. "We haven't been able to find any useful witness statements from down at the harbor," he told Blanc. "It seems as if Monsieur Leroux was on his yacht. But he's so often on it that nobody could exactly recall last Thursday. He was there, okay, but nobody knows exactly when. But we do have a clip from the camera at the yachting harbor parking lot. Monsieur Leroux's Volvo left about two P.M., but the clip doesn't show who was driving."

"You say two P.M.?" Blanc checked. That was an hour before the bull's attack on Cohen. He ended the call and looked at the others. "How long does it take to drive from Port-Saint-Louis-du-Rhône to the scene of the accident?" he asked Marius.

Marius shrugged his shoulders. "Maybe three-quarters of an hour."

"Monsieur Leroux's alibi has just gone up in smoke," Blanc declared, telling the pair of them what he had just found out.

"And he, too, drives a light-colored car," Fabienne added.

"It's not one hundred percent proof. Somebody else could have been driving the Volvo. But it does at least look as if you've found one jigsaw puzzle piece that fits," Marius said, rubbing his belly. "What's happened to that espresso?"

When they were all back in the office, Blanc waited until Marius disappeared into the washroom before calling Aveline at the court.

"*Mon Capitaine?*" Her voice was cool and sounded a little on edge.

Blanc could hear nothing in the background, but he had the impression she wasn't alone. He had wanted to whisper sweet nothings in her ear but instead went straight to the issue at hand. He had to tell her about Fabienne's discovery the night before—afterward, when they were lying exhausted next to each other and Aveline had asked him who the woman on the phone had been and whether she often called him late in the evening. Now Blanc told her as briefly as possible how the former Marie-Claude Elbaz had come into possession of her victim's farm.

"In order to open a formal investigation I have to have official proof that Madame Elbaz alias Leroux is being sought in connection with an old murder case," Aveline reminded him. "And seeing as the file on the Saint-Gilles murder has disappeared into the DST's armor-plated filing cabinet, my hands are tied. What basis have I to open legal proceedings? How am I to explain my suspicion that Marie-Claude Elbaz murdered a rice farmer in the Camargue three decades ago? I haven't a single solid document in my hands. Can you provide me with one?"

"No, *Madame le juge.* But I do have the DST file."

"Which you are not legally allowed even to have seen. If my husband himself doesn't demand your head on a plate, then every single mediocre defense lawyer will be calling for slaughter."

"I have a probable murderer, who bought up the estate of her victim and presents herself as the patron saint of Vietnamese refugees. Should I just ignore all of that and go back to my daily routine?"

"That is a very good idea, *mon Capitaine.*"

This is the very same woman I was holding in my arms just a few hours ago, Blanc thought in amazement. "I am a cop, *Madame le juge*, I'm not programmed just to let criminals go free."

"Nor am I. But nor do I get involved in hopeless cases."

"I thought you loved risk?"

"I love winning. I don't get myself involved in something that I am bound to lose. That's not loving risk, that's just stupid." She was silent for a second. When she opened her mouth again, her tone of voice was still formal but just a tiny bit warmer. Maybe she was on her own now? "*Mon Capitaine*, I am not forbidding you from getting involved in this dirty business. But you're going to have to find me a lump of gold in the midst of the mud or else you'll get me into difficulties. Your own head has already been lying on the chopping block for several weeks now, and if you continue as you're doing, you'll be bringing the guillotine down on it yourself."

"You'd turn down the case to save my neck?"

"I quite like your neck."

Blanc had to smile. "What sort of lump of gold would you like?"

"Forget the DST file. We'd never be allowed to use it. But you're still investigating the Cohen case and Madame Leroux was the victim's host. You've stumbled on to the old Van Gogh theft—and Madame Leroux was interviewed as a witness in that case. You therefore have reason to look into her past. Absolutely officially. I give you permission. And who's to know what you might come across in her past when you've begun to look into it?"

"A lump of gold with the Action Directe logo on it."

"If you find that, then I'll pull your head out from underneath the guillotine."

"I hope we both find ourselves in court soon."

"You may call me anytime, *mon Capitaine*."

Sometime later Blanc was driving around Salon, frustrated because he couldn't find a parking place. The 2CV's roof was rolled back, but the town lay at the bottom of a great sump that held in the heat like a wok. The air shimmered over the asphalt and cars were crawling fender to fender between the rows of houses. If Blanc had found a parking place anywhere on the edge of the town, he would have parked the 2CV immediately and walked the rest of the way. It would have been quicker. In the end it took him half an hour to find a spot. In a loading bay. *Merde*, he thought, as he stuck an official GENDARMERIE sign on the windshield of his rickety jalopy. Nobody will believe it anyway, he thought resignedly. He just hoped no angry local would call a tow truck; the steam horse wouldn't survive rough handling.

He cursed the sun, the traffic, the clogged alleyways, and even to some extent Dr. Fontaine Thezan, who was the cause of all this: she had sent a text just after his phone call with Aveline. *Can we meet in the Case à Palabres to exchange gossip?*

It had taken Marius to explain to Blanc that she was referring to a café in Salon. "That's a weird place," his colleague had muttered, showing he knew of it, but skeptical of Blanc's intention. "What's taking you there of all places?"

"A pretty woman," Blanc had replied, though he was really asking himself the same thing. Why had the pathologist decided on meeting there? Why not in the hospital?

"Because it is absolutely certain that here we won't run into any of my colleagues who might listen in," she answered his question five minutes later. The façade of the Case à Palabres was bright yellow and red with little tables inside in two rows in a room shaped like a tunnel. There was a bar at one windowless end and homemade cakes sitting on it. Shelves held bottles of organic wines. There was an aroma of exotic herbs, and all the tables were occupied by people who didn't exactly look as if they might be Front National voters. The only free place was that opposite the pathologist. Fontaine Thezan had been aimlessly stirring a cup of green tea when she spotted him. She fitted into this universe perfectly. Blanc, on the other hand, felt completely out of place.

"You'll get used to it," Fontaine Thezan said, to bolster his confidence when she saw him looking around uncomfortably.

"I feel as if I'm in an office of the Green Party," he admitted.

"Ever since the last election that's a less happy place than this. You drink coffee, I assume?"

He nodded and let her order. After the first sip, he felt his mind clear a bit. "So," he said, "what's up?"

Fontaine Thezan raised her thumb as if she was about to count a series of things. "All the doctors in Paris and in the south have prescribed Viagra for Ernest Leroux at least once. No real clinical need, but there are a lot of men who take the blue pill for, shall we say, prophylactic reasons."

"Which is, strictly speaking, not legal."

"Don't tell any other cops." She raised another finger. "If everybody was as healthy as Marie-Claude Leroux, every doctor would be a pauper. She even brought her daughter into the world in her Paris apartment with the aid of a midwife, no doctor. Her rules seem to be: no treatment, no convalescence, no broken bones, no prescriptions."

No trace of any records on the electronic system of the Sécurité Sociale, Blanc thought. Maybe Madame Leroux did fall ill from time to time but knew a discreet doctor who took payment in cash.

Fontaine Thezan raised a third finger. "Nora Leroux seems to be somewhat unstable. Drugs. Hysterical fits. She's been in therapy with a psychiatrist ever since she started school. I haven't been able to find out anything more precise, but to be honest I wouldn't tell you even if I had. Medical confidentiality has to begin somewhere. But it looks as if the kid deserves sympathy."

Blanc chatted a bit more with the pathologist, then realized he was drinking his coffee more slowly than usual. It was not only doctors who wouldn't set foot in the Casa à Palabres, you wouldn't find a cop here either. He took note of the address. When did he last have the chance to talk about God and the world? When he was a student? He didn't even like to think how many years ago that had been. In the end it was Fontaine Thezan who got to her feet first with an apologetic smile. “I’m going back to the office to smoke a joint before I have to bend over my next patient. In this heat it’s best not to drag the corpses out of the cooler until evening.” She kissed him on both cheeks. “You can pay for this consultation.”

Blanc nodded and settled the check for the coffee and tea. He sat there for a while and then pulled out his phone, even if he was the only one in the room using one. Just a brief call to Madame Leroux.

He hoped the lady of the house would pick up. Then he could arrange an appointment with her for a lengthy discussion about her past. But the voice on the other end sounded almost like that of Madame Leroux but not exactly: it was younger, more lively.

“You’re the cop with the crappy car,” Nora Leroux called out, right after he had given her his name.

“Can I speak with your mother?”

“What do you want with my mother? It’s me you should be talking to, *putain*!” The last sentence sounded as if it were a cry for help.

“I’ll be there in an hour,” Blanc promised and hung up. All of a sudden he was in a hurry.

A Rendezvous Before a Death

The Camargue lay in the violet dusk as if beneath a velvet blanket with veils of mosquitoes hovering over the marshy ground. Nearly 90 degrees Fahrenheit. It was quiet on the *route départementale*, but nearly every driver who approached Blanc's slow steam horse from behind flashed their lights into his rearview mirror before overtaking him. Even an elderly lady in a large Peugeot 607 took pity on him. As she overtook him, she slowed down, slid down the tinted side window of her air-conditioned limousine, and bent toward him as far as her seat belt allowed. "You're driving without taillights, Monsieur," she called out to him over the noise of the wind, "I nearly rear-ended you." Then she put her foot down and shot off into the twilight.

Blanc swore and parked the 2CV on a narrow strip between the tarmac and the drainage ditch. He climbed out and looked all around the 2CV—the lights in front were working, the taillights weren't. He found a little toolbox fastened in the trunk by an elastic cord. Riou would have been able to take the entire car apart with the contents, but Blanc was just happy to find an old-fashioned square tin flashlight and a roll of duct tape. He turned the flashlight on and used the silvery tape to attach it to the rear so that it shone down onto the fender. He just hoped the batteries would see him home. For the rest of the way nobody flashed him from behind. They all seemed to consider it normal for the driver of a 2CV to be trundling along by night with a flashlight to indicate his position.

"Couldn't you even afford a few euros to buy a real flashing light?" Nora Leroux asked as he rolled up to the family *mas*. She was standing outside the house and had clearly been waiting for him for some time.

"France is going to pieces," Blanc replied. "Next time I'll be turning up on a bicycle. What can I do for you, Mademoiselle?"

The publisher's daughter turned pale. She crossed her arms over her chest with her hands on her shoulders as if trying to hug herself. Then she noticed what she was doing and let her arms quickly fall back to her sides, angrily saying, "Let's go sit by the pool."

"Wouldn't we be better in the house?" said Blanc, thinking of the swarms of mosquitoes.

"It's suffocating in there."

"*Alors?*" Blanc said as he lowered himself into a basket chair. The water of the swimming pool turned the beams of two spotlights into blue light shining into the night sky. Apart from that there was no other light save for the red glimmer of Nora Leroux's cigarette. He hoped that at least the smoke from her cigarette would keep the insects at bay, but he would have preferred more light in order to make out the expressions on her face.

"That Boré was here," Nora suddenly blurted out.

"In the past few days?"

"Just the day before Albert's . . . before Monsieur Cohen's death."

"On Wednesday, August 3?" Blanc had to restrain the impulse to get his notebook out; he felt that would disconcert the young woman.

"I'm not good with dates," she told him brusquely. "I can't even remember whether August has thirty or thirty-one days. But that guy was here the day before the accident. Sitting just there, where you are now."

"Did you talk to him?"

"One more question like that and you're out of here. I don't talk to that guy." She took such a deep breath that for a moment Blanc was afraid she had a hole in her lungs. "He was here to talk to my mother, who else? Papa was down at his yacht. My mother thought I was out with friends. But I . . . I wasn't feeling well, I was lying down in my room." She pointed up to a window at the rear of the *mas*, just a few yards from the pool. "Not exactly the front row, but I could see them well enough."

"Your mother and Monsieur Boré . . ." Blanc hesitated. "Talked to each other."

"You want to ask if they were fucking, don't you? No. At least not that time. When you think that my mother and Boré used to . . . Imagine if it had gone on longer. Boré could have been my father." She gave a hysterical laugh.

"How long have you known about your mother's past affair with Boré?"

"As long as I've been able to remember anything. Everybody in Paris knew about it. The art guy and the publisher floozy. That gets around."

"Does your father know about it?"

"Of course."

"Did he also know that Monsieur Boré was here that Wednesday, Mademoiselle Leroux?"

She leaned forward. "Would you go off down to your yacht if you knew your wife's former lover was coming around?"

"I don't have a yacht." Or a wife, he thought to himself. "Why are you telling me all this, Mademoiselle?"

"Because I want to get you cops out of my hair. Ever since Albert's death, you've been crawling all over the place."

"This is only my third visit. And you practically invited me to come see you."

"Cops and I are on different levels in the food chain," she continued, as if he hadn't said anything. Maybe she really hadn't heard him. "You eat things and I don't want to be one of them. I want you to leave me in peace. Me and Papa. If there's something dodgy about Albert's death, then it's Boré who stinks. Do something about it."

"Why would your mother's former lover want to kill one of your father's reporters?" Blanc asked.

"You're the one who's supposed to have the answer to that question! As far as I'm concerned, Boré's always been just a bit of meaningless crap. An unpleasant memory you forget, most of the time, that is, if you know what I mean?" For an instant the glow of her cigarette illuminated her face. She glanced at him as if looking for help. "One time Papa had a tooth infection, back when I was six or seven years old. It was really bad. He had to be taken to the hospital in the middle of the night. I can remember it perfectly, if I have to, but most of the time, I hardly remember it at all. It's the same with Boré and my mother. He's a boil on a rotten tooth from the past."

"And then suddenly the boil bursts."

She stopped and for the first time gave him a look of recognition. "Yes. All of a sudden, the guy's sitting next to my mother by the pool."

"No advance warning? No phone call? No letter? No other meetings over the past few years?"

Nora shrugged. "Maybe. Maybe not. My mother keeps herself to herself to the extent that she probably wouldn't say a word to anyone if a spaceship landed on her beloved rice fields. Least of all to me. If I hadn't secretly been lying there in my room, I would have had no idea that Boré had been here. Who knows how many times he might have visited her? He certainly didn't seem to have any difficulties finding our *mas.*"

"But the two of them just talked. About what?"

"About Cohen."

"What in particular?"

"No idea."

"Mademoiselle Leroux, I spent an hour driving through the marshland to get here, and you . . ."

"Don't preach to me, okay? I told you my room isn't close enough. I hardly understood a single word, even though the pair of them got more and more angry and louder. At one point Boré jumped to his feet and started counting something off on his fingers: first of all, second, third. And each time he mentioned Cohen's name. First of all, Cohen this . . . Second, Cohen that . . . Third, Cohen whatever . . ."

"And how did your mother react?"

Nora Leroux hugged herself again without being aware of it this time. "She seemed to be scared. All the more so with every new thing he brought up. Then she whispered something. And at that point the guy took her in his arms. It looked as if he was consoling her." She shook her head in disgust.

"And then?" Blanc asked mercilessly. He expected Nora was going to tell him that her mother did take Boré into the house. Or that maybe even by the poolside . . .

"Boré got up and left. He took my mother in his arms again, cuddled her again, consolingly. But I could see his face as she was crying on his shoulder. The guy was smiling, looking pleased with himself. He couldn't have had a more self-satisfied grin if he'd been screwing her then and there."

Blanc's mind was racing. Boré and Marie-Claude had both

kept quiet about this meeting. When they had first interviewed him, the art historian had claimed, *I haven't seen her for years.* And Marie-Claude had said, *I'd have to think how many years ago it was.* But in fact they'd met only days earlier—to talk about Cohen, whom Boré had allegedly only met once before and otherwise only knew from his television appearances. "Did they mention any other names?" he asked.

Nora shook her head. She seemed drained. Vulnerable.

"Olivier Guillaume?"

"I've told you all I know. *Merde.* So that you would leave me in peace, not for you to ask me a thousand other questions. I'll tell Papa to speak to his friend, the minister. To tell him about you!" She gave him a challenging look.

"Monsieur Vialaron-Allègre and I are old acquaintances," Blanc replied drily. "Where were you on the afternoon of August 4, Mademoiselle Leroux?"

"August 4? No idea. What day of the week . . ."

". . . the day when Monsieur Cohen found himself impaled on the horns of a fighting bull, Mademoiselle."

She coughed out cigarette smoke. "What is this shit?" she spluttered.

"A witness saw a light-colored car being driven away from the scene of the accident at high speed. I would like to speak to the driver. As a witness. Your Polo is white, you live near the scene of Cohen's death, so I'm asking you. Not even the minister would have any complaint about that," he added with a thin smile.

"In the morning I was on the beach at Saintes-Maries."

"Do you have witnesses?"

"There were a million people there. But none of them will remember me. Nobody ever does."

"How long were you on the beach?"

"Until I got too hot. I had something to eat and a coffee. On my own."

"In Saintes-Maries-de-la-Mer?"

Nora Leroux shook her head. "Too many tourists. I went to Saint-Gilles. It's not as busy."

"Which restaurant?"

"No idea. Somewhere by the canal or the river. You really have to go now. My father won't be coming home tonight, because he . . ." Her voice died away, then she resumed. "But my mother could be back at any moment. And I don't want her to see you, okay?"

"*Bon*," Blanc replied and got up.

"And take the other direction when you get onto the *route départementale*," she begged him. "I know it's a huge detour, but I don't want my mother to run into you. She would be bound to recognize your funny little car."

"I have next to no lights," Blanc replied, but even so he took the other route to do Nora Leroux a favor.

The improvised light over his fender got ever dimmer, but luckily there were few other cars about and most of them coming from the other direction. Jigsaw pieces, Blanc thought to himself. I have another couple of them in my hand, but where do they fit in? Nora Leroux had called him to set the cops after Boré. And to distract their attention from her father. Or from herself. Or from her mother. Was Marie-Claude really so secretive, even toward her only child? Or did Nora know about Action Directe and the murder in the Camargue that had taken place years before she was born? Was her story about the meeting between Boré and her mother even true? Maybe Boré had been telling the truth and Nora had just made up a fairy tale to put him in the frame?

Because she herself was the culprit? She referred to the victim instinctively by his first name when she wasn't paying attention. Maybe because he was an old family friend. Or maybe because . . . lust and jealousy were also very good motives for murder. Maybe Cohen had gotten involved with the young Leroux? Or maybe he had been in a relationship with her for years and now that he was changing his lifestyle had split up with her? Nora Leroux was nonetheless wearing a plastic Ice-Watch on her wrist. Was she wearing this already damaged cheap watch because she had lost another one? Or was it something she always wore, as a fashion statement? Blanc tried to think of what his own daughter might wear, but in the end came to the conclusion that he hadn't a clue if Astrid even wore a watch band.

Assuming for a moment that Nora's story was true, then Boré and Marie-Claude Leroux had a secret they didn't want to share with anyone else. Former lovers, former colleagues in a provincial museum, who had given evidence in the investigation into an art theft. An art theft that Albert Cohen had become interested in. Cohen, whose name the pair of them had said so loudly that Nora heard it from her bedroom window. Boré, worked up. Madame Leroux, nervous, anxious. So anxious that Boré had to console her, which perversely seemed to have made him happy. And barely twenty-four hours after this secret rendezvous, Cohen was found sliced open on a *route départementale.*

If the story was true, then Blanc had to do precisely what Nora Leroux hoped he would do, which was to put Boré under his magnifying glass. But the unstable young woman hadn't reckoned with the fact that that meant he would also have to concentrate on Marie-Claude Leroux. More than ever. But was Nora in a position to make a complaint to the minister? And if so, what would Vialaron-Allègre do about it?

When the 2CV's tiny engine eventually screeched to a halt

outside the oil mill, Blanc sat there behind the steering wheel a while, lost in his thoughts. Eventually he spotted from the corner of his eye a shadow near his neighbor's house and flinched: Paulette's ex-husband? His right hand felt for his gun while his left slowly opened the driver's door. But then he realized it was Paulette Aybalen herself, standing outside her house about to hose down her old VW. Surprised, Blanc climbed out, unstrapped the flashlight, still just about glowing, and went over to her. There was rock music coming from the open door of her house: Led Zeppelin. Paulette didn't hear him approach until he was right next to her. Then she flinched and gave a small cry.

"Hey, don't worry," Blanc said to calm her down, "I'm one of the good guys."

She gave a nervous laugh and pushed back a strand of her black hair. "I should have known," she said. "You couldn't possibly have been my ex. He's scared of the dark."

"What are you up to?" Blanc asked.

"The wind's from the south," she explained with a laugh, relaxed this time as she noted the puzzled expression on his face. She dragged two fingers down a part of her blue car's bodywork that she hadn't hosed down yet, and even in the dull light Blanc could see that the tips of her fingers were yellow. "Sahara sand," Paulette said. "If the wind gets strong enough, we'll have enough of it to fill entire cars."

"And that's why you're out washing your car in the middle of the night?"

"If I didn't I wouldn't be able to see through the windshield tomorrow morning. I didn't have the time earlier. I was in Aix. At the hospital." She saw Blanc's worried look and smiled. "I'll take your concern as a compliment," she said reassuringly. "I was visiting Sophie Micheletti."

"She's unwell?"

"It's her chemo again this week. I just wanted to give her a bit of company. We just chatted on and on."

"I'm sorry," said Blanc. "I didn't know."

"She doesn't exactly advertise her cancer. She's been battling it for years, to the extent that it's become routine, for us, too. You can laugh or cry, but you mustn't treat her with kid gloves."

Blanc nodded wearily. "I'm off to bed."

"Don't make too much noise with your vacuum cleaner."

He looked so flustered that she kissed him on both cheeks and whispered, "The Sahara sand. Your house doesn't have a roof, remember? *Bonne nuit.*"

Blanc spent the first half of the remaining hours of the night sweeping and dusting very fine yellow sand out of every room. He had turned the radio on to keep himself awake. An irritatingly wide-awake DJ interrupted every second song to give a warning about the *canicule*, the heat wave, and how dangerous it was to do any work in these temperatures. *Merde*, Blanc thought to himself, thanks for the encouraging words. He turned the radio off.

When he finally lay down on his hard bed, he stared up at the sky through the skeleton of his roof. Stars like glass pinpoints. A yellowish shimmering moon as big as in a science fiction movie. Shadows of bats. The high hunting cry of an owl, the death cry of a mouse. Three lights in the night and a distant grumble: an aircraft flying south. Africa, somewhere beyond the horizon. No, he thought to himself, damn it, not beyond the horizon. Here I am already in the middle of Africa. In the middle of the Sahara. It would have been perfect if he had a woman to hold in his arms and stare with her into the endless night sky. Unadulterated happiness. But at the same time he suddenly longed almost physically for Paris and rooftops and the noise of cars and the flickering neon signs and rain and the sirens of ambulances and the stench of dog shit on the sidewalks.

When he eventually fell asleep, he dreamed of Geneviève and Aveline, Paulette and Sylvie, Nora Leroux and his own daughter, Astrid—and Marie-Claude Leroux, calling out Cohen's name, again and again. Then he dreamed of the Sahara and its fine sand, which he kept shoveling away, but it kept coming back. And then, eventually, he stopped dreaming.

Collectors and Painters

Blanc woke up as the first gray light of dawn trickled into the house. His body had gotten so used to the heat that for a minute he found himself shivering in the dew-drenched air coming in from his missing roof. It was a Friday in August, not yet 5:30 A.M. It would be at least three hours before there would be anybody in the gendarmerie station in Gadet. It was market day and the early risers would be doing their shopping for the weekend before turning up for work. Too early for him to call Riou and ask him to change the burned-out bulbs in his taillights that had made his 2CV invisible at night, unless, of course, it turned out to be something much more complicated. So he took a shower—even the water was the color of Sahara sand—and hunted around the house until he found batteries that would fit the tin flashlight.

There was one man he wanted to try his luck with even at this early hour: Olivier Guillaume.

When his 2CV rolled into the courtyard, the first frogs were already croaking—or maybe it was the last—Blanc had no idea whether the animals conducted an all-night concert. The house's façade looked even more washed out than on his first visit. The green wooden shutters were closed. But there was a white light shining onto the asphalt from an open gate to an extension that was too large to be a shed and too small to be a garage. A few seconds later Olivier Guillaume came out. He probably heard my car, Blanc thought.

The man stared at the car as if it were a provocation on four wheels. Maybe he thinks I'm not taking him seriously, turning up in a crate like this, Blanc thought with a sigh. Guillaume was one of those people who considered the slightest blink of light in the farthest of galaxies as an insult intended for them.

"Please excuse me for disturbing you at this extremely unusual hour, Monsieur Guillaume. Could you spare five minutes?"

"I never sleep very long. But I have no time."

"Just five minutes."

Guillaume shot a quick glance at the closed upstairs window of the house, then nodded, waving his hand nervously. He limped on, saying to Blanc impatiently, "Come in here and speak quietly."

Blanc entered the shed only to stop in amazement by the door. A halogen spotlight, the sort that was fashionable in the eighties, clinically illuminated every corner of the little room. The concrete floor was spattered with oil, plaster was falling from the walls, and there were steel cupboards at the back, more than six feet high and covered in a film of rust. Their doors lay open and in front of them was a workbench covered in pictures. Blanc found himself staring at abstract compositions, some in gold frames, some in simple handmade frames. Still-life flowers. Three or four watercolors that seemed to him, as a layman, Impressionist in style. Asian woodcuts.

"My father's art collection," Guillaume told him in a low voice. "Ever since he disappeared, my mother has kept them here in the shed because she can't bear to see them in the house anymore. I get them out every now and then. To air them."

Blanc glanced back and forth between the masterpieces and

the embarrassed elderly man in faded clothing, socks, and sandals standing next to them like a schoolboy doing something he shouldn't.

"Our investigations," he began, "have led us to believe that the Van Gogh stolen from the Musée Maly might have something to do with Saint-Gilles. Are you familiar with that area?"

Guillaume had gone pale. "Saint-Gilles has nothing whatsoever to do with Van Gogh," he muttered.

Blanc chose his language carefully. "There are rumors," he said, "that the stolen picture might be somewhere in Saint-Gilles church. Just like the stolen Van Eyck is supposed to be hidden in Ghent cathedral."

"Marie-Claude," Guillaume whispered. "That trollop planted the idea in your head, didn't she? All because once, and once only, I had a conversation with her. Only a conversation. And now more than twenty years later, she sets the cops at my throat because of it."

"Monsieur Guillaume, I have not the slightest interest in your throat. I'm asking your advice as a witness . . ." He struggled to find a fitting word. "As an expert, you might say."

"You have to go now," Guillaume replied. "You've had your five minutes. Mother will be awake at any moment."

Blanc couldn't bring himself to torture the man anymore by refusing to leave or shouting at him. Instead he merely said, "*Eh bien*," and touched two fingers to his forehead, a gesture that said "thanks" and "farewell" simultaneously. Guillaume limped after him to the door, so close that he could smell the man's unwashed clothing. It was as if he wanted to physically push him into his car. But the moment Blanc opened the driver's door, Guillaume turned around: a ray of light had suddenly emerged from the upstairs window.

"Please!" Guillaume whispered. "I have to put the pictures away."

"Have you ever heard of a murder that happened in Saint-Gilles?" Blanc asked him. "A rice farmer."

Guillaume shook his head. It was clear that he hadn't been listening properly and that he had no interest in any murder in Saint-Gilles. "Please go, *mon Capitaine*," he begged.

When Blanc was back on the straight road a few seconds later, he found himself thinking of the fact that Cohen had arranged a meeting with Guillaume and that he was a reporter. What would he have made of the pictures in the shed? "*The Treasure on the Edge of the Camargue—Vanished Modern Masterpieces?*" And what would have become of Guillaume if his mother had read a piece like that? Yet another murder motive, Blanc thought to himself wearily. I have one more murder motive.

It was still far too early for Marius to turn up in Gadet. Blanc grabbed the phone. Ernest Leroux answered so quickly that he might have had his cell phone next to his coffee cup on the breakfast table.

"How well do you know Monsieur Boré?" Blanc asked. He had called Leroux's cell phone deliberately so as not to have his wife or daughter answer. He was tired, the heat was taking its toll on him, and he was feeling rather depressingly down, in no mood for feints, small talk, or any other complicated maneuvers.

It took the publisher a couple of seconds before he answered the question. "I've been at his exhibitions now and again, as have about a million other people in Paris. And I know that once upon a time my wife and he were close. Blanc, what case are you investigating actually? Don't tell me that this has something to do with Albert's tragic accident. You're airing dirty laundry.

Looking for a ticket back to Paris, *mon Capitaine*? Well, I am not the railroad company."

"And I'm not in the laundry business." *Connard*, thought Blanc. Then he added politely, "A witness at the scene of the accident reported seeing a light-colored car driving off. We are trying to find out who the owner is. Just as another witness, no more. Monsieur Boré is in Provence at the moment and is driving a light-colored car belonging to a friend. We have asked him and he told us he was not there at the time in question. But I want to be sure. The *route départementale* on which Monsieur Cohen died also goes past your *mas*. Not many people take that route on an afternoon in August. But Monsieur Boré had been to your house on occasion, so he must have taken that road, and it was possible that he could have seen something at the time in question."

"At my house? Boré came to see me?"

"To see your wife."

Leroux was silent for quite a while. Gotcha, thought Blanc. "If that's the case, then you should speak to my wife," the publisher eventually said. He sounded cautious. "That said, I don't believe a word of it. Boré here at my house, a light-colored car, it's all nonsense. Cohen was cut open by an animal, even you must accept that. Now you've sunk your teeth into a tragic accident because Albert was influential and you want to get into the minister's good books. But junior minister Vialaron-Allègre stands between you and the minister of the interior himself. And I'll do everything I can to keep you out of his good books if you don't call a halt to this ongoing investigation."

"It will come to an end soon enough, Monsieur Leroux," Blanc said with the hint of a threat in his voice.

"My wife is out in the paddy fields. Call back tomorrow." Leroux put the phone down without saying good-bye.

Blanc leaned back and looked out of the window. The flag on the *mairie* was hanging limply on its pole, like a deflated red-white-and-blue-striped balloon. So Leroux didn't know Boré had been to see his wife. That they had talked about Cohen. He didn't even seem to know that Blanc had already been to see Marie-Claude and interviewed her. Clearly they were not a couple who talked to each other a lot. They would now, though. It would put more pressure on Madame Leroux when her husband confronted her with the story. And people under pressure made mistakes. Maybe something new related to Cohen's brutal death would come out.

Or something new related to the all but forgotten murder in Saint-Gilles.

A few minutes later Fabienne came into his office. She glanced at Marius's empty seat. "It might be for the better if we discuss this just between the two of us," she said quietly, pulling the door to and taking her iPad out of her bag. She opened a folder.

"The folder from Cohen's computer," Blanc asked hopefully.

"Cohen's final encrypted folder. Hacked."

"Congratulations."

"The folder is labeled 'specific dates-iPhone.' Not exactly a work of poetry."

Blanc thought of the conversation he had just had with Ernest Leroux. The publisher could wipe the floor with Blanc if he had reason—and now he had. Blanc had lied to him when he told him he didn't know where Cohen's iPhone was. If he now came out with data that came from the phone, Leroux's lawyers would be on him like a gang of hyenas on a dying antelope. "We have to keep this to ourselves," he told Fabienne. "None of it can go into the file."

"Pity. But I'm not surprised." She took out a USB stick and

waved it triumphantly in the air. "I copied the file directly on to this so there is no digital trace on the hard drive of my work computer. But even if we find we have to give up Cohen's smartphone, we still have its data."

"If I'd known how to pull tricks like that a while back, I'd still be working in Paris."

"If you were still in Paris, I would never have discovered illegal investigations." She laughed, put the tablet back in her bag, and the USB stick into Blanc's computer. "It's all yours now. The list of all calls made and received first," she explained. "Nothing special: a few calls to the landline at the Leroux *mas*. A few to the publisher's cell phone, to the editorial office in Paris. One call to Boré and one to Guillaume—just like both of them said."

"Are the cell phone numbers of either Madame Leroux or her daughter on the list?"

"Marie-Claude Leroux called Cohen twice from her cell phone; he didn't call her. Or at least if he did it was on her landline. Nora Leroux doesn't feature."

"What about text messages."

Fabienne smiled sarcastically. "Cohen was too old for texting. There are a couple of text ads from his network provider, which might as well have cobwebs on them: never read. He never sent a text himself. Cohen also had a few messages on his voicemail, from Leroux or other colleagues, nearly all just asking him to call back, a few dated 'get well' messages. No emails. No documents. The only route saved in his satnav app covers some twenty-five miles through the Camargue: a loop. I suspect it's the route he cycled regularly. No other apps downloaded. No music. There was a lot of free space on Monsieur Cohen's iPhone."

"You hardly needed to close the door to my office if that's all there was."

Fabienne said nothing but simply clicked on the folder entitled "Pictures." It contained two items labeled "123.jpg" and "456.jpg." "Cohen hadn't transferred all the photos into the normal folder on his laptop. These two are only in this hidden file. He changed their names, but you can still get a lot of technical data from them. These were taken a week before his death."

"Can you tell if they were taken with his iPhone?"

"Of course. Everything is included in the photos' details."

"Shame," Blanc mumbled. Another reference to this damn phone. He couldn't just change the names of the photos and present them as evidence. Any lawyer who had access to an equivalent of Fabienne Souillard would be on his tail and prove that he had hacked into the phone despite not having had permission even to pick the thing up.

He clicked on the first file: it was a photo of a photo. A blurred shot of an old black-and-white photo lying on an office desk. Badly lit and green-tinged.

"It looks as if Cohen took this in a room lit by neon lights. That would explain the tinge," Blanc suggested. "He didn't have a tripod and he clearly didn't have much time."

Fabienne nodded. "A photo taken secretly. In an office maybe."

"Or in an archive," Blanc murmured, zooming in on the photo so that it filled the whole screen of his ancient computer monitor. It still wasn't easy to make out much: a man, no longer young but not old either, staring back at the photographer suspiciously. The man must have moved while the photo was being taken because the contours of his face were ever so slightly doubled. The photo paper was spotted in places and had a zigzag cut along the edge.

"I'm guessing it's from the nineteenth century," Fabienne muttered. "Looks a bit like a long-dead uncle in my grandfather's photo album."

"I didn't know Vincent van Gogh was your great-uncle."

She stared at him, then back at the photo, then back at him. "Why not Victor Hugo? Or Charles de Gaulle? That could be any old geezer, the picture is too blurred."

Blanc stood up and pulled out from between the files on the shelf Daniel Boré's book, *Vincent van Gogh and the Light of the South.* He got the impression that Fabienne was immediately more interested in the art book than she had been in the blurred photo on the screen. He flicked quickly through the book until he found a page with ten different self-portraits by Van Gogh. He held it up next to the screen.

"It could be him," he declared.

"Maybe you're right," she admitted reluctantly. "But it's not exactly proof. And even if it is him, what does it matter?"

"Boré himself," Blanc said, tapping on the book, "told Marius and me that it would be a sensation in the academic world if somebody found a photo of the painter. It would appear Van Gogh didn't like being photographed."

"No selfies of old Vincent then, who'd have thought it?"

"Don't laugh. Boré got quite worked up about it. He reckoned that in the course of his research Cohen might have come across an authentic photo. And now we've actually found it, on his iPhone. He stumbled across the old photo somewhere and secretly took his own photo of it. The question is, where did he find it? And where is it now?"

"We didn't find it in his room at the Leroux house."

"But maybe he let Boré know where it was. That would be a good enough motive for his murder. Boré kills Cohen, thereby getting rid of the only person who knew of the photo's existence. Then he claims all the credit for finding it. The populist exhibition organizer, scorned by all his academic colleagues, turns up with a genuine sensation in the field."

Fabienne didn't bother to reply, but it was clear that Blanc hadn't convinced her. She clicked on the file labeled "456.jpg." It was of an old document, equally badly lit, photographed from the same angle. Yellow paper, old-fashioned handwriting with an old official stamp. "According to the digital data this was taken the same day," she told Blanc, "just five minutes after the other one. Also probably in the same place."

Blanc zoomed in on the photo and whistled through his teeth. "It's a page from the old Van Gogh file in Arles."

"I can't read the scribble," Fabienne had to admit.

He just smiled. During his years investigating corruption Blanc had learned to decipher all handwriting: signatures on checks, notes on Post-its, comments on files, abbreviated entries in calendars. "It's a report," he told her, skimming through the lines, "from the policeman who investigated the instance when Van Gogh cut off his own ear. It's a recommendation to his superior that they arrest Gauguin."

"The other artist?"

"He and Van Gogh had lived in the same house. But they didn't get along and had an argument just before Christmas 1888. Gauguin spent the night in a brothel, and Van Gogh cut his own ear off. According to Gauguin."

"Did you learn all this at the gendarmerie academy?"

Blanc tapped the book again. "It's all in here." He looked for the relevant chapter, scanning through the paragraphs, then shook his head. "I can understand our colleague from back in those days," he muttered. "I also would have suggested arresting Gauguin on the spot. He was a fanatical fencing fan and he took off in a panic the day after the incident. Suspicious, don't you think?"

Fabienne laughed. "Nkoulou is going to explode if you suggest digging up *that* old case!"

"The two artists have an argument, like they've done lots of times over the previous few weeks. In the heat of the quarrel, Gauguin, the experienced fencer, lashes out at Vincent's head with his rapier, slicing off part of his ear. I bet fights like that happened all the time back then; everybody had a sword or a dagger at home. It sounds a lot more plausible than an artist who cuts off his ear himself one night and then can't explain to anybody why he did it. Don't you think?" Blanc went back over the last lines of the report. "This is just a suggestion by a junior officer," he muttered. "It would appear his superiors just ignored it." He flicked through Boré's book again. "Gauguin had been a stockbroker, and he had powerful friends in Paris."

"You know how that works."

"Vincent van Gogh by contrast was just a poor foreigner and not exactly the most pleasant man in the world. So Gauguin was believed and the Dutchman was more or less thrown into the madhouse."

"Then more than a century later a reporter finds out that Van Gogh wasn't that mad at all. How about that?"

"A lot of books would have to be rewritten. Including Boré's own."

"Boré kills Cohen because he doesn't want the reporter's research to discredit the main point of his own book." Fabienne tapped him on the shoulder. "Your theory doesn't just sound ridiculous, it also has a flaw. Of all the people we've come across so far in the Cohen case, Daniel Boré is the only one with a watertight alibi. He was in the MuCEM in Marseille, some sixty miles from the scene of the incident. There's film of him in the museum. Whoever let the fighting bull out, it wasn't Boré. Which doesn't mean the guy hasn't got something to hide . . ."

She clicked open the final file on the phone—the calendar.

"We obviously don't know if Cohen actually turned up for the appointments in here. But take a look at this: *Tuesday, August 2, 11.00 A.M. Boré.* It looks as if the reporter didn't meet the art historian once but twice."

"Two days before his death. And when we interviewed Boré, he didn't mention a word of this."

A Man with an Alibi

For the rest of that Friday, Blanc tried in vain to get Boré on his cell phone. Marius turned up at some stage and volunteered to go over to Eyguières. But the house was locked up. Blanc's colleague spent the afternoon keeping a watch on it, from the café opposite. He didn't come back until the early evening, with empty hands but in the best of form. "Better than spending the day in the office," he said. "The waitress . . ."

Blanc had waved him off in irritation. Meanwhile, just to be certain, Fabienne had tried the art historian's apartment in Paris and got hold of his housekeeper. But she said that Monsieur Boré was still down in Provence. Blanc swore. They could hardly bring the man in on suspicion just because of a single entry in the calendar of an iPhone that was officially not in the possession of the gendarmerie. Boré could be visiting a museum somewhere, lying on the beach, or opening a gate in the Camargue, but there was no way for Blanc to know.

He tried again to get hold of some material relating to the investigation into Marie-Claude Elbaz, but had no luck. He tried looking for more information about the long-past Action Directe murder in Saint-Gilles. No luck there, either. Into the Leroux family's purchase of the *mas*. Again no luck. The theft from the Musée Maly. No luck there, either. It was as if in this merciless summer even the computers and files were too exhausted to open.

That evening he lay in bed looking up through his dismembered roof at the stars and then suddenly he remembered the pictures in Boré's book. Vincent van Gogh had painted the Provençal night sky: stars in circles of light on a black-blue velvet background behind the jagged silhouette of a cypress tree. The Dutchman had been right, he thought, that's just what it's like in the Midi. The artist wasn't mad, he could just see more clearly than the guys who laughed at him. Or Boré was right. The "light of the south" turned northerners mad. First Vincent van Gogh. Now Capitaine Roger Blanc. Don't make a fool of yourself, he reminded himself, and then he fell into a deep exhausted sleep.

He didn't wake until just before eight and felt guilty until he remembered that it was Saturday and there would be nobody waiting for him down at the gendarmerie station. Or anywhere else. Blanc spoiled himself with a relaxed breakfast after taking a few minutes to rattle over to Gadet in the 2CV: freshly ground coffee and croissants from the bakery so buttery that they made the paper bag transparent, still fresh from the oven. In Paris he would have been slurping down bitter coffee from a ten-year-old machine. He never normally ate anything. He could have his cell phone on the table and the radio on the shelf above it blaring out France-Info. Geneviève had long ago given up having breakfast with him. Here he was being serenaded by the cicadas, hidden in the plane trees, that began their concert once the thermometer crept up toward 90 degrees. And a tomcat creeping along the bank of the Touloubre: brown and white, short-haired, big head, both ears torn from countless fights, an animal on the reverse route of evolution—from domestic pet to beast of prey.

Beast of prey . . . Cohen's murder had something about it of the cold economy of a beast of prey. Kill the victim with the minimum of effort. Just pushing back a metal bolt on a gate, a piece of steel the length of a finger moved a couple of inches in a second, and a few moments later a man is lying on the road with his guts hanging out. Boré, Blanc thought. Tall but weak. Diabetic. Unwell. He would never strangle anybody with his bare hands or push him over a cliff into the sea or smash his skull with a hammer. He would look for help. *Merde*, Blanc said to himself. Forget the goddamn video footage from the MuCEM. Boré was just the type to need help to carry out a murder, even if it was help from a fighting bull. Blanc felt the delicious coffee stimulating his brain.

Time for another trip to Eyguières.

He rang the bell of the house next to the narrow square. He could have parked his steam horse in the middle of the street without troubling anyone. There were no other cars, no pedestrians, just a cat lurking in the narrow strip of shade outside the art gallery. Two doves were sitting on a cast-iron streetlamp, too exhausted even to coo.

Blanc had half expected his journey to be in vain. So he was surprised after ringing the bell to hear a key turn in the heavy lock. Boré gave him a disparaging look, a tall glass in his hand full to the brim with a milky liquid. If I were drinking pastis at this hour of the morning I'd be lying in the shade alongside that cat, Blanc thought. "I have a few more questions about Monsieur Cohen," he began.

"I've already told you all I know about him."

"I doubt that."

Boré stared at him, then glanced up and down the heat-shimmering street as if he was expecting the right answer to come strolling up, then shrugged and let Blanc into the house. "Whatever."

It was cool in the relative darkness, and Blanc was almost absurdly grateful to Boré for letting him get out of the sun. "When did you last see Madame Leroux?" he asked, sitting down in the living room with its depressingly low ceiling.

"I thought this was about Cohen."

"If you don't mind, Monsieur Boré." Blanc was tall, but he was too thin to be imposing. It had taken him years to master the art of positioning himself in a room in a way that signaled "I'm not going anywhere fast."

The art historian sighed. "No idea. Once upon a time I used to note down my appointments in a calendar. I can't check those on my phone." He gave an artificial laugh and took a drink from his pastis glass, which left it half empty. "Eight years maybe? Ten years?"

"How about ten days?" Blanc suggested as if helping him out.

Boré choked on his pastis.

"At the Leroux family *mas*? By the pool? In the afternoon, the afternoon of Wednesday, August third?" Blanc continued as if the man opposite hadn't reacted.

The art historian emptied his glass and got up to refill it. "Whoever told you that story is a liar," he insisted. He was standing without looking at Blanc, but the pastis bottle and his glass were visible and his hands were not shaking. "Marie-Claude and I have had nothing more to say to each other for a very long time, *mon Capitaine*. And certainly not in the afternoon by some swimming pool. I am a very busy man."

"I noticed that when I tried to get hold of you yesterday."

"I was with a private collector. When you set up exhibitions, you always try not to just get pictures on loan from museums but also pictures that are not normally visible to the public. The treasures that really serious art connoisseurs have hanging in their living rooms or locked away in vaults."

"And that's why you keep your cell phone switched off?"

"Collectors are very discreet people. You can't have your iPhone tinkling in the middle of a conversation."

"Could you give me the name of this collector?"

"So discreet, *mon Capitaine*, that I would only reveal the name if I was in the witness stand in front of a judge."

"You might find yourself in front of a judge sooner than you would like," Blanc said as friendly as he could. "A judge who will ask you about your last meeting with Monsieur Cohen. You told me the one and only time you met Cohen was on Thursday, July 28, but Cohen kept an electronic calendar just like you do, and I've found an entry for Tuesday, August 2: a meeting with you. Just two days before his death. Can you please explain that to me? Or should I hand over the files to the *juge d'instruction*?" It was a bluff, because Cohen's entry on his iPhone was not proof, but Blanc was sitting there on his stool as relaxed as if he was looking forward to the conversation lasting for hours.

"A *juge d'instruction*? You're that far, are you? I shall have to talk to my lawyer."

"Why don't you just talk to me, Monsieur Boré?" Blanc asked him.

The art historian was gazing into the middle distance, his hand gripping his glass so tightly that Blanc thought for a moment it might shatter. "Oh, well," Boré finally conceded hesitantly. "There was nothing illegal about it. Our meeting was just . . ."—he searched for the right word—"so grotesque that I would have preferred to keep it quiet. Out of respect for Monsieur Cohen's reputation."

"I can be every bit as discreet as your art collector friends."

Boré coughed. "*Bien.* Cohen came here to see me on that Tuesday in the morning, I can't remember the precise time."

"Eleven A.M.," Blanc told him with a smile.

There was a trail of sweat beads on Boré's forehead now. He glanced over at the black case with the medical equipment in it, then at his Jaeger-LeCoultre wristwatch.

"Take your time if you need insulin," Blanc said.

Boré gave him an irritated look. Behind his outsize spectacles, his flickering eyelids were as visible as if they were under a magnifying glass. "I'm all right for now," he mumbled.

"Did Monsieur Cohen advise you in advance of his visit?"

A shake of his head. "No, he just burst in, the same way you did."

"So it must have been something very important to Monsieur Cohen."

All of a sudden Boré thumped the little table unexpectedly hard. "Nonsense. He told me the most stupid story I've ever heard."

"So stupid that you failed to tell it to me and even about the meeting."

"Exactly."

"Could you tell it to me now, please?"

Boré sighed. "Cohen came to me claiming that Vincent van Gogh hadn't cut his own ear off in Arles, that the injury had been Paul Gauguin's work."

"That's it?"

"Isn't that enough?" The art historian took a few seconds to pull himself back together. "Look," he said excitedly, "whatever psychologists or art historians or quack doctors want to tell you, it is not where an artist was born or brought up, what sex they are or even the sum of their talents, that make an artist an artist. It is their genius. It is the inexplicable in their soul. The vision that only he and he alone has, that is what makes him different from other mortals, what lifts him out of the herd. And every genius is born from illness. All of them. It is only the struggle against their illness that gives birth to genius!"

Blanc tried not to look at the diabetic. He was remembering that Olivier Guillaume, the former janitor in the Musée Maly, had thought quite the opposite: that artists were strong.

"There is no question about the fact that Van Gogh was a tortured soul. A man tormented by his own internal demons," Boré continued. "The most painful expression of his genius and his madness was that night before Christmas Eve when he mutilated himself. This act of self-harm, as radical and incomprehensible as it seems to us, is what made Van Gogh Van Gogh! And then this. . . ."—he took a deep breath—"this scribbler charges into my house and tells me Van Gogh was just the victim of a thug. Two painters who had knocked back too much absinthe and laid into each other. It's like saying Chartres Cathedral is nothing more than a lookout tower."

"Did Monsieur Cohen say how he had arrived at his conclusion?"

"He would have done if I'd heard him out. But I threw him out instead. It was just absurd. I didn't want to waste my time listening."

"Do you think there might be some documentation to back up Cohen's hypothesis?"

"Nonsense. There are documents, of course. The report of the hooker Van Gogh used to visit has survived. He gave the girl his sliced-off earlobe wrapped in a piece of cloth. And then there are the doctors' reports, including one from the head of the Saint-Rémy sanatorium that Van Gogh had a tendency to nervous breakdown. From the tart to the doctor, they all agree, that Van Gogh was not in his right mind."

"What about the police?"

Boré waved his hand dismissively. "The cops in Arles were glad to get the crazy painter off their hands when he was put into the Saint-Rémy sanatorium. You can read that in the police files today."

Blanc cleared his throat. "Did the police back then not even interview Gauguin?"

"I'm telling you how crazy this all is. Anyone who had the slightest acquaintance with Van Gogh took it for granted that his act of self-mutilation was an accident waiting to happen."

Blanc wondered what Boré would have to say about the photo of the police file on Cohen's iPhone. It couldn't have been kept alongside the normal Van Gogh file or any art historian would have discovered it long ago. But Cohen must have gotten his hands on it somewhere in Arles. It was quite possible that the report had accidentally found its way into some other police file; things like that happened, even nowadays. But Blanc didn't mention the document because if he had, Boré would have moved heaven and earth to get a glimpse of it. And then it would have inevitably come out that Blanc had found the photo in the memory of Cohen's phone, a phone that he had gotten hold of unofficially. Instead, he asked, "Do you think Monsieur Cohen might have mentioned his theory to anybody else?"

Boré shrugged. "I don't know. Nothing he said to me hinted that he had."

"Do you think he wanted to make a big deal about it in an article for *L'Événement*?"

"You'd have to ask his publisher that. Or Marie-Claude. She's the Van Gogh expert in the Leroux family."

Blanc drove slowly back from Eyguières to Gadet. Saturday or not, he had nothing better to do than drop by the gendarmerie station. Cohen would be buried soon, that couldn't be delayed any longer. He had the weekend because nobody was going to do anything in this heat. But next week Nkoulou would take him off the case, which wasn't officially a case anyhow. The file would be closed. Done with. Blanc was fairly certain that Boré had been lying to him when he had denied meeting with Madame Leroux, but he wasn't absolutely one hundred percent. It was one person's word against another's. A mentally fragile teenager known to the police versus an exhibition organizer known all over Europe. If he had nothing else against Boré, then he might as well give up the investigation now. And Boré's last meeting with Cohen that the art historian had kept quiet about? A minor economy with the truth on their first interview. The story about Vincent van Gogh's severed ear. If he told that to his colleagues in Gadet, they would be slapping their thighs in laughter, except that it was too hot for that.

Blanc wanted to spend the quiet Saturday hours putting together and secretly copying into a personal private file everything he had on Cohen, the Leroux family, Boré, Guillaume, the long-ago theft from the Musée Maly, the missing Van Gogh file in Arles, and the Action Directe murder in Saint-Gilles. That was what he used to do in Paris: build up his own archive of dirty, incomplete stories that nobody wanted to know about, that nobody took seriously, that nobody even believed. Sooner or later there came a time when all the dirt surfaced. And then the stories suddenly made sense. He had to quickly suppress the thought that it was precisely this that had caused his downfall in the end.

• • •

There were only a few of his colleagues in Gadet, and all were in a bad mood. *La canicule.* The heat wave had been going on for long enough to claim its first victims. Commandant Nkoulou was there and had ordered all his younger officers without exception to turn up and under strict orders in uniform. Every few minutes there were emergency calls. The engines of the patrol cars were never turned off because the second one team got back, another had to shoot off. Tourists with sunstroke who could hardly answer a question. Small fires, started by discarded bottles whose glass had acted like magnifying glasses. Children left locked in cars in supermarket parking lots. And old people, all the time old people whose families had decamped on vacation leaving them stuck in houses and apartments, buildings that had grown old with their inhabitants or so cheap that the rent wasn't quite enough to cover the costs, and they had no air-conditioning. Old people who were too weak or too indifferent to keep the air flow going, or to close shutters, or to drink water. Neighbors calling the police to break down the door of somebody who hadn't been seen for three days.

"You'd think it had never been hot in the South of France." Nkoulou sighed. He was sitting at his desk and coordinating the teams, reassuring the callers, the doctors, concierges, and sometimes even the mayor, who also rang up to deal directly with emergency cases, while he himself exhausted his officers in endless tasks. Cool and efficient, a general holding his army together in a war already lost. Blanc wondered in passing whether behind that immaculate dark forehead passionate feelings of disgust or resentment were at work. Whether somebody who had barely escaped from deepest Africa didn't somehow disdain a world where a few days at over 100 degrees was enough to invite the grim reaper into a house where an old man had been left alone. Or whether Nkoulou genuinely saw the chaos as a game plan for the gendarmerie. A demand on his intellect and logic, one that, if he managed it in record time, would bring the next rung on his career ladder an inch or two closer.

Blanc locked himself in his office, then turned on his computer and printer, which was also a scanner and photocopier. Then he took a new empty file and a USB stick and set to work.

By the evening he had an inconspicuous box file on the passenger seat of his 2CV and a USB stick that made the tiniest of bulges in his pocket. Nobody had even noticed Blanc leaving the gendarmerie station where the uniformed teams were still hurrying back and forth on missions that were gradually diminishing in number as the worst of the midday heat finally passed. When he turned into Sainte-Françoise-la-Vallée, he noticed a few figures standing outside the house of his neighbor: Paulette Aybalen was talking to the Michelettis from the Bernard winery. And a man Blanc had gotten to know on his first murder case in Provence, Lukas Rheinbach.

The German painter with the wavy red hair and the pirate's beard was in an energetic conversation with the others, in particular Paulette. Blanc, driving up slowly, noticed from a distance the way the pair of them were smiling at each other. He parked the 2CV and joined them, greeting the men with handshakes, the women with kisses on both cheeks. He approached Sylvie Micheletti as carefully as if she was made of fine glass. Cancer. Don't make a fuss, treat her the same as ever.

"Nice to see you in a nonwork situation," Blanc said to Rheinbach.

"The pleasure is all the greater for me," the artist replied. The German earned his living by painting Mediterranean pictures that were turned into jigsaw puzzles. There were people who spent their lives doing things that were even more meaningless;

sometimes Blanc had the feeling he was one of them. He wondered how Paulette Aybalen had gotten to know the unsuccessful painter from the north who had several years ago settled like an immigrant in a stone house in the middle of the forest near Caillouteaux. And how well they knew each other. And whether . . . *Connard.* Don't be an idiot.

"Have you been making Provence a safer place again today?" Sylvie Micheletti asked him.

"We've enough to do at the moment stopping people dying of thirst," he answered evasively.

"Dying of thirst is the right expression," Bruno Micheletti interjected, going over to his battered Peugeot and scrambling around in the trunk until he produced a *fontaine à vin*, a plastic gallon canister of red wine. "Our sole remaining top wine from the year before last," he announced proudly.

At that point Paulette fetched a few wooden folding chairs from a shed. Blanc suddenly felt happy; he laughed and fetched some baguettes and Banon cheese from his roofless house. Then they all sat down on Paulette's stone-tiled terrace in the shade of a mimosa tree still glowing from the heat of the afternoon.

"I have a case that will interest you more than anyone else," Blanc said to Rheinbach, as the others were all chatting about the heat wave.

The painter invited Blanc to address him with the familiar "*tu*" rather than the formal "*vous*," while he poured wine from the *fontaine* into the glasses. In the evening light the wine itself looked like red glass.

"You in particular," Blanc resumed. He didn't reveal all the details and made no mention of the connection to Action Directe. He gave no names, but it felt good: the more he talked, the clearer his head became.

As the evening went on, the conversation turned to everything under the sun. They didn't get to their feet until the evening hours had almost come to an end and the exhausted cicadas had finally ended their concert. Only the crumbs of the baguettes and the oak leaves from the Banon cheese remained, with a few white strips of rind attached. Paulette had set a raffia bowl of peaches on the table next to the folding chairs and that, too, was already half empty. Meanwhile the *fontaine* was nothing more than an empty shell of paper and plastic. Lukas Rheinbach closed the paper pad on which he had been making charcoal sketches all evening long without showing them to anyone. I wonder if we'll all end up as jigsaw puzzle pieces, Blanc asked himself in amusement.

As they were leaving, Paulette smiled at everyone, though Blanc had the feeling her smile was really for him in particular. He walked a few paces away from the gate that separated her garden from the road and waited in the dark until the Michelettis had climbed into their Peugeot. Lukas Rheinbach had opened the door of his Renault Clio but not driven off yet. Blanc emerged from the darkness quickly and rapped on the passenger window.

"On duty after all?" the painter asked, somewhat alarmed.

Blanc answered him with a reassuring whisper, "You never give up drawing or painting, do you? I'd be grateful for an expert opinion."

"About Van Gogh?"

"About Daniel Boré. Between the two of us."

"I won't tweet his name."

Blanc nodded in relief, then told him what role the art historian had played in his case so far.

"Boré is the André Rieu of exhibition organizers, if you know what I mean," Rheinbach said cautiously. "Very successful."

"And very disparaged by those in the same business."

"All the painters hate him, but nobody would say that out loud. Every now and then Boré organizes exhibitions of contemporary art. Anybody he turns the Paris spotlight on suddenly becomes a favorite of the art collectors and a recipient of the contents of their wallets."

"What are the chances that Boré might discover you?"

"Thanks for even asking."

"How has Boré managed to acquire such influence? He started out as curator in a tiny museum."

"He has a talent for selling artists, Vincent van Gogh in particular."

"His book on the painter is a best seller."

"Boré owes everything to old Vincent. Nobody celebrates the cult of the sick mad genius more than he does. The Van Gogh exhibition was Boré's breakthrough in Paris, the book may as well be his visiting card and guaranteed pension, with good royalties, year after year."

"Van Gogh is the foundation for Boré's whole career?"

"Not just the foundation, the ground floor, the upstairs, and the roof. Neither critics nor artists have much time for Boré, but as far as the greater public is concerned, he is *the* Van Gogh specialist, which makes him a famous man."

Blanc stared into the dark, the patterns of branches and pine needles, all against a violet shadow. "Boré's reputation is based solely on what he wrote about Vincent van Gogh," he muttered to himself.

"It's based on what he pushed to the public in general: the image of the mad genius."

"You've been a great help."

"If I run out of luck with the jigsaw puzzle paintings, I can draw composite sketches for you cops. There's just one more thing." Rheinbach hesitated.

Blanc bent down to the car window. “I won’t tweet that,” he said.

“The art market is full of sharks,” Rheinbach muttered. “If you want to organize exhibitions or get collectors onside, talent alone won’t get you very far. There are lots of talented people out there, but not many stars.”

“If you’re about to go swimming with sharks, it’s best to have a few sharp teeth in your own mouth?”

“Boré has the biggest teeth of them all. If he wants something done, it gets done. He gets hold of paintings for his exhibitions from private collections that nobody else has been able to manage. He finds castles and churches to host his exhibitions that nobody else has been able to rent. He gets publishers who’ve already got thousands of unsellable art books out there to publish his. Just watch out if you’re planning to put your swimsuit on. You could end up as fish food.”

“A few big sharks have already had a go at me,” Blanc replied, and tapped the window lightly to say good-bye.

A little later Blanc was lying in bed and as usual glanced at his Nokia. Normally he had no signal in the oil mill, but on this occasion he had received a text. Possibly because there was no roof to get in the way. It was from *Sous-brigadier* Accoce, the colleague from Arles he had given his cell phone number to.

The v.G. file still missing. Only experts had access over last 10 yrs. All checked out. Nothing.

Blanc called Accoce. He had the impression that the second sergeant was one of those cops who’d been on nights so long that he no longer knew what the sun looked like.

“Do the experts include a certain Boré? Daniel Boré?”

“Just a minute.” Blanc could hear the rustle of paper. “He’s a regular. Been here at least nine times in the past few years.”

"When was he last there?"

"On Wednesday, August 3."

"We need to have a coffee together one of these days."

"Or maybe a pastis. *Bonne nuit.*"

August 3. The day before Cohen's death.

The Letter

The next morning the earth shook. Blanc stumbled half asleep to the window and breathed in huge clouds of diesel fumes. They were coming from the exhaust pipes of the Manitou, which Matthieu Fuligni was trundling up to the oil mill.

"It's Sunday morning!" Blanc shouted hoarsely.

The young building contractor just waved cheerily from the cabin of the great machine. "From August 15 we're on vacation, Monsieur, and I promised you we'd be finished before that." A truck was following him; it was stacked high with towers of new *tuiles*, a virtual mountain of red, ocher, and pale pink, like so many colored clamshells.

"*Merde*," Blanc muttered. By the time he'd made it to the coffee machine, he could already hear the heavy workers' boots on the roof beams. Fine mortar dust had already penetrated into the kitchen. Blanc went out with a bowl of steaming coffee.

"The house will be intact again by midday," Fuligni promised him, clambering down from the machine and handing Blanc a crumpled piece of paper: the invoice. Blanc felt faint. "I'll get my checkbook," he said wearily. He fumbled around in his desk until he found it. There were disconcertingly few checks left. One more renovation project on this scale and he wouldn't have enough money left to pay the divorce lawyer.

"Will you be in Caillouteaux this evening, Monsieur?" Fuligni was almost irritatingly wide awake.

"What would I be doing in Caillouteaux?" he asked. His brain was refusing to spring into gear.

"Tomorrow is August 15. The Feast of the Assumption. Lots of towns put on a big fireworks display the night before in honor of the Holy Virgin. From the top of Caillouteaux hill you can see as far as Salon-de-Provence and over the Étang de Berre. Half the town will be there: fireworks, music, rosé, and pretty women!"

The prettiest woman in Caillouteaux won't be there, however, Blanc reflected. Aveline had gone to spend the weekend with her husband in Paris.

"In my job you never know whether you have the evening free or not," he answered.

Fuligni laughed and gave him an encouraging slap on the back. "There'll be so many bangs going off this evening it'll seem every *voyou* in Marseille's letting loose with his Kalashnikov at once. Don't let it make you nervous."

"I'm gradually getting used to life down here in the south."

Half an hour later, Blanc pulled on his running gear and went out jogging.

"Keep to the roads," Fuligni called after him. "Fire could break out in the woods and then you'd be in danger."

"I'm in danger here," Blanc called back, nodding toward Fuligni's workers going around with piles of roofing tiles more than three feet high. He had no intention of heeding Fuligni's advice, given that the asphalt in the sunshine was as hot as a stream of lava. And in any case the *route départementale* reminded him of another, with blood and stench and plump bluebottles. He turned onto the forest footpath. The shade of the Mediterranean oaks at least gave the impression of tolerable temperatures. The noise of the cicadas all around. Red hard-baked sand under the soles of his feet. He might be an astronaut on Mars. The scent of rosemary in the air and just a hint of oleander from somewhere. The path suddenly went steeply uphill along a set of natural steps made up of stone and scree. It was mad running uphill in this heat, and he didn't even have a bottle of water with him. After a few minutes he wasn't sweating any longer; every pearl of water that materialized on his skin evaporated immediately and every breath filled his lungs with air from a baker's oven. He ran even faster. Blanc felt great.

He ran for an hour or more. The more exhausted he was, the clearer his head became. It was as if every step took him further away from thinking about the case, about Paris, about his ruined career, about Geneviève and the children, as if even his painful lust for Aveline would burn off, as if his soul would be as cleansed as in the flames of a pyre.

When Blanc finally turned onto the last few yards toward his house, breathing heavily, he spotted Paulette Aybalen in her front yard. She noticed him, too, and without saying anything went into her house and came out with a plastic bottle of mineral water. She had to have taken it out of the fridge because it was ice-cold with condensation gathering on the outside. Blanc smiled gratefully, incapable of speech, and drank and drank and smiled again.

"You have a few habits you're going to have to lose down here in the south," she said, when she thought there was any point in speaking to him. She gave him her cheek to kiss in greeting.

"I'm not exactly presentable," Blanc spluttered, lifting his hands up apologetically.

Paulette just laughed. "I even kiss my horses sometimes."

Blanc touched her smooth cheeks with his dried lips for a second and was briefly tempted to take her in his arms. He took a step back in embarrassment. "Are you going to Caillouteaux this evening for the fireworks?" he asked.

"I'm afraid I'm already booked up," she said apologetically. "For one of the other fireworks."

He didn't ask where and with whom.

Blanc completed the last few yards to his house, outside of which stood a battered white Fiat Marea. Marius was leaning against the hood looking up at the roof and shaking his head. He was wearing a checked shirt, jeans, light-colored canvas shoes, and a straw hat so perfect the individual straws could have been still in the field that morning.

"You look like shit," he called out as soon as he noticed Blanc. "In this weather going running is about as clever as cycling past an unlocked gate with a fighting bull behind it."

"My guts are still where they belong."

"Jump into the shower and put on a clean shirt. I'm going to take you to a *course camarguaise.*"

Blanc took a moment to understand the invitation. "A bullfight? In the middle of the summer? You told me it was only in autumn that they . . ."

"Last week the president of the Club Taurin in Eyguières died. And seeing as they had to miss a fight in the spring because of bad weather, they're holding it now, in honor of the deceased. It's not exactly the Cocarde d'Or they have in Arles, but it's the best chance you've got of seeing one in the next few weeks."

A quarter of an hour later, Blanc removed the empty bottle of rosé from the passenger seat and climbed into the Fiat. "I didn't even know they had an arena in Eyguières," he said as his colleague bent down beneath the dashboard and held two loose wires together to start the engine.

"It's only a little one but nice and shady," Marius explained. "Next to the cemetery. It means they don't have so far to take the *raseteurs* who aren't quick enough."

Another twenty minutes later the Fiat pulled up in an inconspicuous side street in Eyguières. A ring of weathered concrete stood on a patch of high ground. The arena, Blanc reckoned, could hold at most a thousand spectators. The crowd by the entrance was mostly male, with not a single tourist. A few pretty young women in traditional dress were welcoming them and a band of musicians in red frock coats were playing a sort of circus music. There was a stench of cattle in the air. The concrete rows of spectator seats had been built around some old plane trees, which gave them a bit of shade. But the sand of the bullring glinted golden in the sunlight.

Marius led him to the first row of seats, barely six feet from the ring itself. The bench was narrow and hard. Blanc found himself looking down at a sort of corridor because a red-painted wooden barrier some five feet high separated the sand of the fighting ring and the concrete of the arena. White beams like steps and metal bars were attached to the concrete and wood leading right up into the spectators' seating.

"That's what the *raseteurs* have to climb up to get away from the bulls," Marius explained, noticing Blanc's gaze.

"Up into the public?" Blanc queried, slightly uneasily.

"Right up to your nose. And here they come."

Eight fit-looking men strolled out of a gate at the side of the arena and began doing stretching exercises. Four of them had their names in dark blue lettering on their backs. They had bandages wrapped around their hands and were carrying metal objects in their hands that Blanc assumed to be tools of some sort, until Marius told him they were the *crochets* that they would use to pull the ribbons from the bulls' horns. The other four had their names in red on their backs and had nothing in their hands.

The next half hour was taken up with speeches, songs, and greetings. The women in traditional dress paraded proudly through the arena and then were led up to places of honor. Then the circus band started up noisily. Blanc cursed the hardness of the benches and his dry mouth reminded him that he hadn't had enough water after running. It was going to be a long afternoon.

But five minutes later he had forgotten his worries. A gate to the side of the arena marked TORIL opened and a black colossus hurtled into the arena, its great tongue hanging from its half-open muzzle, dribble flying from its huge lips as it shook its head. The animal pawed the sand with one hoof, lowering its head ready to attack before raising it again and sniffing the air. For a moment it stared at Blanc, whose heart nearly stopped as he glanced at the animal's tiny black eyes. Then the *raseteurs* sprang over their red beams, screaming and whistling and hooting and calling the animal by its name.

Blanc felt as if he had suddenly become a witness to an ancient ritual, some demonic, heathen dance from prehistoric times, the sort of thing preserved forever on the walls of the Minoan palaces. A dangerous game, long forgotten or banned elsewhere but here passed down from aficionado to aficionado and celebrated. The men provoked the animal until it growled with anger, first throatily and then more quietly, which sounded even more threatening to Blanc. Then it charged at the first *raseteur*. The man waited until the last moment, then flitted light-footedly out of the way up the beams and from there onto the red barrier, until as surefootedly as a cat he grabbed the first bars just before the public seating area. Blanc instinctively recoiled, as the *raseteur* flew through the air right in front of him. Fine pearls of sweat glistened in the man's hair; the expression on his face was frightened, relieved, excited, and angry and at the same time in a bizarre way happy. Blanc was certain that the *raseteur* hadn't even noticed him. A split second later the animal crashed into the wooden beams with a thud that resounded across the arena.

Again and again one of the men ran toward the bull while the others screamed and prodded the animal, then ran off. Gradually Blanc began to get the hang of the game: he realized that there were always two *raseteurs* at a time charging at the bull. The one with his name in red on the back of his shirt was a sort of second who distracted the bull's attention. The other *raseteur* waited for the right moment and charged at the beast from the other side of the arena, effectively ambushing it. Fast as lightning he would poke the *crochet* between the animal's horns and pull it out again. The bull roared and kicked up sand, its branded black pelt shaking, and left a trail of spittle more than a foot long behind it.

From time to time the public took a collective intake of breath, a *raseteur* would raise an arm like some ancient gladiator, and somebody said something incomprehensible over the loudspeaker—the *raseteur* had succeeded in catching the rosette between the animal's horns and pulling it loose.

Within a few minutes the animal was exhausted, confused. It stared at the men in white swirling around it like aggressive wasps. The animal was too tired to fight back anymore, too resigned from chasing into thin air. Finally music broke out and the animal was led out the gates it had come in through.

"They have seven bulls today," Marius told Blanc. "The older and more experienced the bull is, the later it appears. And at the same time the *raseteurs* are more exhausted by then. So the finale is always the most exciting."

Blanc saw older bulls who no longer stormed in a blind rage into the arena, but came in slowly, taking a look around. They knew that sooner or later the *raseteurs* would turn up. They were saving their energy and would only attack when their targets were close enough. Bulls that had learned how to use their horns to rip the beams on the edge of the arena out of their iron posts and fling them into the air. They acted as if they would let the unarmed man in red provoke them, but at the last minute they would turn their heads and attack the *raseteur* rushing toward them head-on. Blanc saw one *raseteur* reach the barrier a second too late and get hit on his foot by the horns, then limp back into the arena. He saw one of the men in white lose his hold on the hand grip and leap into nowhere, crashing into the concrete. A few minutes later even he was reeling toward the animal again, this time with his white pants ripped and his arm bleeding.

The last, most experienced of the bulls never crashed into the red barrier when it was chasing a *raseteur*. Instead it leaped over it. Blanc's pulse raced when he saw a creature with half a ton of muscle and two horns as long as a man's arm leap over a five-foot barrier like a show jumper. All of a sudden the bull was running down the narrow corridor on the other side of the barrier and all the *raseteurs* and their assistants had taken cover behind the concrete protectors while the bull hunted them around the arena like the Minotaur itself. Blanc could smell the animal's sweat, share its anger, feel the clattering of its hooves as it raged along the corridor just six feet below him. It was only with difficulty that two men managed to get the beast through the gateway and back into the middle of the arena.

Later, when the dusty, bleeding *raseteurs* were being rewarded with kisses and enamel bull's-head badges by the women in traditional dress, the public was applauding, the red coats were playing the Coupo Santo, the breeders of the best bulls of the afternoon were being praised, when Marius was happily slapping him on the back, only that much later did Blanc notice his shirt was sticking to his shoulders even though he had thought there wasn't a drop of moisture left in his body.

The ancient skill and the wildness of the animals had entranced him. His hands were shaking as if he himself had spent two hours facing down the black monsters with no more than a laughable iron hook in his hands. Immediately Blanc understood that whoever had opened the gate in the Camargue had to have already seen these animals fighting. Nobody who hadn't experienced this could have imagined their ferocity, their aggressive intelligence. The culprit must have sat in an arena, just like he had just done that afternoon. Once at least.

Boré? He came from Paris and had previously lived on the Côte d'Azur, not exactly places where there were bullfights. Guillaume? He was a homebody who would never have gone to a heathen spectacle like this, not with his witch of a mother. The Leroux family? They lived at least part-time in the Camargue, the heartland of French bullfighting. They had taken on board every typical local custom and tradition. Ernest Leroux, Marie-Claude Leroux, even their daughter, Nora Leroux—they would know what happened when a bull like that snorted and dropped its head ready to attack. They knew how fast they were. And they knew exactly what damage those horns could do.

Later that evening after he had said good-bye to Tonon and poured him a pastis "for the road" outside his oil mill, Blanc sat on his own amid relaxed rosé-drinking men and women on the small square between the church and the bell tower in Caillouteaux, trying not to think about bulls and eviscerated bodies for a few hours. His house now had a roof of new *tuiles*, a solid expanse of regular waves of fireclay. He had admired the tiles, then admired them again, then put a record on his ancient Technics turntable and played *Graceland* right to the end. Nobody would hear. The roof now swallowed noise. He had made tabouleh with couscous, cucumber, onions, and tomatoes, and admired the *tuiles* again, then he had climbed into the 2CV and driven up the hill to Caillouteaux. Next to the side wall of Saint-Vincent stood a red and yellow pizza truck and the aroma of mushrooms, tomatoes, and charcoal would have made even the fullest of people hungry again. Loudspeakers were playing movie music: *Titanic*, *Pirates of the Caribbean*, *Amélie*. The sound wasn't quite synchronized with the fireworks. Sometimes basses and violins boomed or droned when the sky was dark and sometimes they were quiet when the most beautiful flowers of light were exploding in the sky. But most of the time it worked well enough and the finest passages of music rang out when red, green, or blue lights were bursting above the bell tower and the heads of the spectators who all sighed together.

Kitsch, Blanc thought, it's obvious kitsch compared with the ancient ritual in the arena of Eyguières, or witness to piety and devotion like the church in Saint-Gilles. This was not a work of art wrenched from light and madness, like a painting by Van Gogh. But it was still perfect. The air was mild at last. Stars and fountains and veils of light rising with muted roars over the Étang de Berre, its water glittering like a sheet of silver in the dark. On the horizon the fireworks displays of neighboring towns blossomed while children ran rampant, realizing that their parents weren't going to send them to bed as early as usual. By the fountain next to the church two teenagers were smooching. Blanc turned his head away; it reminded him of the happiness he missed.

The music from the loudspeakers changed. Now it was Beethoven's "Ode to Joy." This must be the finale, Blanc thought, amazed at his own anticipation, staring up at the sky.

Then the Nokia in his pants pocket vibrated.

Don't answer it, he told himself. It's Saturday evening. *Merde.* Saturday evening! But he would only get a call on his cell phone at this time if it was something important. Really important. Blanc hurried into the nearby alley, which swallowed the sound like a ditch, getting there by the fifth ring.

"I'm sorry to disturb you, *mon Capitaine*, but we've got a suicide on our hands." It was Baressi.

"Who is it?"

"Our colleagues didn't make that clear, but they said the victim had left a sealed letter." Baressi cleared his throat. "Addressed to you."

It was the first time in the old 2CV that Blanc had put his foot all the way down, not that it helped. Not anymore. The 2CV swayed into the curves, with the tires squealing occasionally as he raced down Caillouteaux hill. He hadn't bothered to turn on the flashlight at the rear, but the fireworks meant that there was next to nobody out driving so there was little danger of somebody crashing into him.

Bel Air. The neglected house. The frog concert from the drainage ditches, their croaks now a funereal mass. There were two patrol cars parked in the grubby courtyard but their blue and red flashing lights had been turned off. Next to them stood an ambulance, its driver leaning on the hood smoking. And right at the end stood the white Jeep of Fontaine Thezan. The pathologist herself was nowhere to be seen, nor were the gendarmes. The house door was open and there was a dim, orange-colored light coming from inside, with a hint of flickering blue as well: a television. He could hear laughter from a studio audience. Olivier Guillaume's mother stood in the doorway like some monstrous statue on a Gothic cathedral. Only her eyes showed any sign of life. They followed Blanc and in them he saw no sense of grief or mourning, just pure animal hatred. Be professional, Blanc reminded himself, be professional. *Merde.* He felt he was sleepwalking into the courtyard but still seeing every detail as clearly as if it was an operating room. But he felt nothing. The shed. There was a halogen light shining out of it. And the voices inside were not coming from a television.

The battered Fiat Marea turned into the courtyard, braking so fast that the shock absorbers screeched. The door was thrown open without the driver even bothering to turn off the rattling diesel engine. Tonon was wearing checked Bermuda shorts and a less than perfectly clean undershirt. He was so drunk that Blanc couldn't help wondering how he'd managed to find his way to Bel Air. And how he'd managed to put away so much alcohol in such a short time. He nodded to him. Tonon stared at him. It wasn't clear he recognized him.

Fontaine Thezan came out of the shed just at the very moment Blanc had been about to enter it. She pushed her glasses back into her hair and rubbed her eyes. "I need a smoke first, *mon Capitaine*," she said wearily, by way of greeting. "I think you can work out what happened without any help from me. I'll be right back." Then she glanced over at Tonon and said, "Come over to my car with me, Lieutenant, and I'll give you something to keep you awake."

"Dope?" Tonon asked, grinning.

For the first time since Blanc had known her he saw Fontaine's elegant mask of cool self-control explode for an instant to be replaced by a godalmighty anger. She said not a single word, but Tonon had noticed. He straightened up and followed her silently to her Jeep.

Blanc went into the shed, nodding to the other officers already there. He looked around carefully, his mind and his senses still as neutral as a radar scanner. The steel cupboard's doors were open. There were pictures laid out on the shelves, the workbench, even on the floor, making a luminous carpet of canvas and color. Olivier Guillaume's body lay in front of the workbench, a leather belt around his neck and fastened to a vise on the workbench. A ribbon of dribble from his mouth had turned white; his tongue, poking out slightly from between his lips, was already turning black.

"Unusual way to hang yourself," Fontaine Thezan said, having come in behind Blanc without him noticing. Tonon was nowhere to be seen.

"I had never thought it was possible to hang yourself from a workbench."

"You can hang yourself anywhere, *mon Capitaine*, you just have to make sure the noose is attached to something higher than your head." She pointed to his throat. "In a typical hanging, the noose is knotted around the neck. Here it is to the right side. Guillaume put the belt attached to the vise around his neck, then sat down in front of the workbench. You can't break your neck like that, but it's enough to cut off the flow of blood. It takes a while though."

Fontaine Thezan pointed out the corpse's closed eyes with little red dots around them. "Petechiae. Bleeding beneath the skin because of a blockage. The veins taking the blood away close up first, but the arteries still briefly deliver fresh blood to the head."

"Guillaume would have had the time to free himself?"

"Definitely. He wasn't dangling helplessly from a tree branch. He could have tried to get to his feet. To relieve the pressure on his veins."

"He must really have wanted to die."

"I wonder why he didn't just attach the belt to one of the beams in the ceiling. Then he wouldn't have had to suffer so long."

Blanc thought back to his last conversation with Guillaume,

in exactly the same place. And then he thought of the rigid figure in the lit doorway. "He didn't want to make any noise," he guessed.

One of the other officers came over and gave a snappy salute, which Blanc found somehow unsuitable. "There's a letter on the workbench," he announced. "Next to the vise. It has your name on it." He said it as if he considered Blanc a suspect.

"I'll go and see how Tonon is," the pathologist said. "You'll get my report later."

Blanc nodded absently, lifted the letter, and took it over to the halogen lamp so that none of the other officers would be able to read it over his shoulders. It was an old-fashioned envelope, with his name and rank typed on the front with an old manual typewriter. His hands did not shake as he opened the envelope.

Capitaine,

You will never give up, I know that. People like you never, never, never give up. And you know why you never give up? Because you haven't a clue, not the merest ghost of a clue. People like you are always looking in the wrong place.

You want to find the Van Gogh? Then look for the heathen hunter by the feet of the saint. You don't understand that? See, you'll never give up because you never understand anything.

I had thought that at last I could have some peace after all these years. Do you know what it's like to spend a night behind bars without being charged? When you're fired from your job because you're suspected of being a criminal, but nobody dares say that to your face? All I wanted was just to be here, among my father's paintings, in peace. But then you had to show up and torment me with questions. Me!

Why don't you ask that Boré? That sanctimonious, superficial, completely clueless connard who declares every artist to be useless because he himself is useless. Ask him about Van Gogh rather than asking me about the missing picture!

Why do you see Cohen as just a victim? If you had done your work properly, you'd have realized that scribbler only wanted to unearth dirty rumors, that the guy enjoyed digging around in other people's past! I only spoke to him once, on the phone, but I still know more about him than all you cops put together!

And why does Marie-Claude Elbaz get treated with kid gloves? You must know she has blood on her hands. But you're not interested in that, because she's a pretty woman, isn't that right?

But you won't get me. I want peace. So I'm going to get peace the only way I can. Try to ask me some of your questions now!

O.G.

P.S. Please ask my mother not to have me buried in the family grave, but anonymously. Anywhere. I don't care. She'll scratch your eyes out when you tell her that. But you caused me so much trouble that I think you owe me the favor.

Blanc read the letter twice. He was exhausted, but he forced himself to be like a computer and impartially analyze every word. No feelings. Anything but feelings.

Was this an admission that Guillaume had stolen the Van Gogh from the Musée Maly back then? You could understand the letter to mean that, but you could also understand other lines in it to mean that Guillaume used his last words to deny having been the thief. He's laughing at me, Blanc thought. No feelings. Analyze every word.

Boré? Guillaume hadn't told Blanc anything he didn't already know. Cohen? He had confronted Guillaume with the theft story and because of that the man had felt under pressure! But was there any suggestion in the letter that Guillaume had let the fighting bull out? If this was an admission, then the writer of the letter was correct: Blanc knew nothing, nothing, nothing.

Marie-Claude Elbaz? Guillaume must not only have known that she belonged to Action Directe. He apparently knew about the alleged murder in Saint-Gilles. Or was the "blood on her hands" just a throwaway allegation because for Guillaume every terrorist was a murderer? But if he had known something . . . For how long had he known? Perhaps since their time together at the Musée Maly? How would he have found out? And had he kept silent about it all these years? And . . . was that maybe why Cohen had gotten on to him? Perhaps what the reporter had wanted from Guillaume was not just information about the stolen picture but about a murder in the distant past in which the wife of his friend had been involved?

Fontaine Thezan had come back into the room and was looking at him. "Should I give you something, too?"

"Do I look that bad?"

"Worse than Frankenstein's monster, but not quite as bad as your colleague outside."

"In that case I don't need anything." Blanc tried to smile, but his face was frozen into a mask.

"The hearse has just drawn up," the pathologist told him. "I'll look at Guillaume in the morning. I'm going home now, and that's what you should do, too, *mon Capitaine*."

"In a minute. There's something I have to do first." Wearily

Blanc made his way the short distance to where a rigid little figure seemed to be waiting for him.

Shortly after, a procession made its way along the bleak street of Bel Air: the hearse, the two Renaults with the gendarmes, and Tonon's Fiat, driven by one of the other officers Blanc had ordered to drop his colleague off at his house—explaining to him first the trick needed to get the old jalopy to start.

"This guy's on our conscience," Tonon had whispered to him, as he heaved him into the passenger seat.

"Not *our*, *mine*. I'm the one who fucked up, just me," Blanc had replied, but he wasn't sure if his colleague understood his meaning. Tonon had dozed off almost the minute his back touched the seat.

At the first roundabout, the vehicles took different directions. Blanc alone crept on along the *route départementale* in his 2CV, thinking of Guillaume's mother. He hadn't even attempted to convey his condolences with one of the old clichés but simply informed her of her son's last wish. She didn't even do him the favor of answering. Nothing. No reaction. Not a single word. Just that look. As the coffin was pushed into the black van and his colleagues closed the doors, he just turned around and left the courtyard. He wondered how long the old woman would stand there in the door frame, and whether or not she would heed her son's last wish.

When at last Blanc was in bed back at his old oil mill, he told himself he could stop acting like a robot. He could give in to his feelings now. He should feel sorrow and anger and shame. But he felt nothing; he just lay there on the mattress staring into the darkness, waiting for the light of the next morning.

A Clear Track

It was a quiet Monday morning, August 15. A holiday. Headaches in every office at the gendarmerie. Blanc hadn't mentioned the contents of Guillaume's letter to anyone, but he was afraid word would soon get around that a suicide had addressed his last letter to him. Nkoulou might even ask him to put the document in the file, where every single one of his colleagues would have access to the bitter allegations against him.

Blanc had been expecting people to avoid his glance and whisper comments behind his back.

There was nothing.

Nobody even mentioned the previous night. Nobody seemed interested in the dead man. There were still endless emergency callouts, but more volunteers had been found in the towns, and the hospitals, doctors, and local administrations were all better prepared to deal with the heat-wave victims, with the result that the hectic state of affairs over the weekend had ebbed, so everything was more or less back to normal and hour by hour got back to summer acceptability. What did a suicide matter?

Tonon hadn't turned up yet; Fabienne had also taken the day off. Nkoulou had given orders not to be disturbed because he had been at the shooting range earlier that morning and didn't want to be disturbed while he was cleaning his weapon.

Blanc shut himself away in his office, relieved at least not to have to look his colleagues in the eyes. He stared at his monitor, as if the solutions to all his problems were to be found in the slipping and sliding of his screen saver.

Olivier Guillaume. What a botched life, Blanc thought. And: I fucked it up for him. And: I had no need to do that, not even for a Van Gogh. And: I should have foreseen it. A failure of a man. A hate-filled mother. The pictures locked away in the cupboards. The old story of the theft. Cops outside the house. Fear of being arrested. *Merde*, I must have been blind.

Then Nkoulou called. "Come over."

So there it is after all, Blanc thought resignedly as he got up from his desk. Standing in front of his chief, he noticed creases in the man's uniform for the first time. He wondered if Nkoulou had spent the entire fireworks weekend in the station.

"I've had a call from Paris," Nkoulou began.

"From Minister Vialaron-Allègre?" Blanc was relieved that it wasn't about Guillaume. "The minister wants a nice funeral."

"Save me the sarcasm. I have reassured Monsieur Vialaron-Allègre that despite the holiday today the body of Monsieur Cohen will be transferred to the capital. You don't have any objections, do you?"

The commandant pushed a form across his desk: "Sign here," he ordered.

Blanc nodded, resigned to his fate, and scrawled his scribbled signature at the bottom of the form. An accident, he thought. A suicide. An old assassination. An old art theft. With one scrawl he had turned all of these into things of the past: forgotten, meaningless. Nobody will ever again have the idea they might all be connected.

"Monsieur Leroux also wants the return of the computer that you, if I recall correctly, took from his house. By the way, I can't recall any regulation that permits such a thing. But I'm sure you'll remember it if and when you're asked."

"But of course."

"Then I look forward to seeing the computer and the file on my desk as soon as possible."

"Absolutely."

"Have you any questions, *mon Capitaine*?"

"No more questions, *mon Commandant*. None at all."

Back in the office Marius was already waiting for him, showered and as happy as if nothing at all had happened the night before.

"Do you remember much of yesterday?" Blanc asked him.

"I preferred the bull before the last. The one that always pretended not to see the *raseteurs* and then in the last second . . ."

"I was thinking of yesterday night."

His colleague raised his hands self-defensively. "I was celebrating, like every other normal person in Provence. Wine, fireworks, mild air. I could have spent the whole night like that except that I'd forgotten my cell phone was still in the pocket of my pants. How peaceful life used to be without these things! An officer called me and said I might be interested that my partner had been the recipient of a suicide letter. He sounded as if he was going to make a joke of it. But I got there all the same to give you moral support."

"Which you did brilliantly."

Marius gave him a sideways smile. "Don't take it so hard. I had the same thing happen once: you start asking a guy questions and then zap! he's booked himself a one-way ticket to a country where there's absolutely no chance of an extradition order. It feels like shit. But it's not your fault. That Guillaume was a loser."

"I still should have seen it."

"What should you have seen?"

Blanc made a helpless gesture.

"Listen," Marius went on. "You saw a pathetic life. But you didn't see the dangling rope, because there wasn't a dangling rope. None of us could have guessed what was going to happen."

"Guillaume hanged himself because he felt I'd put him under pressure."

"And why did you put him under pressure? Because the guy had something to hide. You just did your job. He had skeletons in the closet. That's just the way it goes."

"This job is over. I've just come from Nkoulou. File closed. It was an accident. You were right. I should have treated it like that from the beginning."

"I was wrong. The whole business stinks." Marius slapped the table with the flat of his hand.

"I've signed off on it."

"That simply means the file is lying on Nkoulou's desk. He's got a lot on his hands with the *canicule.* He won't forward the file until tomorrow at least, after the holiday. That means we've still got a few hours. If we find something, we can pull the file back from the boss and reopen it. To hell with your signature."

"You were the one who thought from the first the whole business was nonsense! And now . . ."

". . . now some poor bastard is lying dead in front of his workbench, and I was too drunk even to be able to cut the noose free. I have a debt to settle."

Blanc gave a weak smile. "I have no idea what to do with the next few hours."

"Which pile of shit stinks the most?"

"The Action Directe business. Murder is worse than theft."

"Then let's interview this crackpot terrorist again."

Blanc pulled the papers together, grabbed Cohen's laptop, and carried it all into Nkoulou's office. Was he imagining it, or were there disparaging glances from the other offices? When instead of taking your files to a *juge d'instruction* to bring a case to court, you're giving them to your boss, then you've fucked up. He wondered what he was going to tell Aveline. While their colleagues were out dealing with dehydrated walkers and abandoned old people, Blanc and Marius sat there hunched in front of their computer screens, going through old documents. Anarchists and the linked autonomists had founded Action Directe in 1979, and only much later had linked themselves with left-wing terrorist groups in neighboring countries such as the Netherlands, West Germany, and Italy. At first their actions were more propaganda than bloodshed. The first murder was in 1983, the year Marie-Claude Elbaz disappeared from the radar screen, Blanc reflected.

There was a bomb attack on the Rhein-Main Air Base near Frankfurt in 1985, which according to expert opinion was jointly carried out by the West German Red Army Faction and Action Directe. A few months later a pamphlet signed by both groups appeared entitled "The Most Important Tasks for the Communist Guerrilla in Western Europe." Blanc skimmed a few scanned-in pages from an old police file: madness on a large scale, stubborn, cold, as if written by an SS officer with a sociology degree.

"Maybe our friend was in Germany in the eighties?" Blanc said, nodding toward the document.

Marius came over and shook his head. "Our German colleagues know even less about the Red Army Faction than we do about Action Directe. They wouldn't even have a clue whether Marie-Claude Elbaz had ever been in their country or not."

"What about afterward? After 1989, when she pops back up legally?" Blanc sat for a quarter of an hour at his computer, but in the end only shook his head. "Madame Leroux was abroad a lot with her husband: Europe. America, Africa, Vietnam."

"She does have a weakness for rice growers in Indochina."

"But she was never in Germany."

"I've never crossed the Rhine, but that doesn't mean I'm not a former terrorist. Doesn't mean anything."

"Monsieur Leroux was in Germany frequently. Why didn't she accompany him? Because she was afraid that there was still an open file on her from the eighties?"

"Who in Berlin is going to be interested in a bomb attack carried out thirty years ago? And it was aimed at the Americans anyway, not at the Brandenburg Gate. There wasn't even anybody killed. The reason Madame Leroux doesn't visit Germany is because there's no rice growing there. Find proof that's not the reason."

Blanc didn't reply, just sat there hammering away on his keyboard. He felt his friend and colleague looking over his shoulder, half skeptically, half sympathetically. January 21, 1987: Jean-Marc Rouillan, Nathalie Ménigon, Régis Schleicher, Joëlle Aubron, and Georges Cipriani arrested at a farmyard in Orléans. Nine months later Max Frérot was arrested in Lyon. That was the end of Action Directe. The follow-up: trials, sentences, life sentences. But what came after that? Hunger strikes, protests, appeals. In 2007 Frérot got twelve thousand euros in damages from the state because he had been treated humiliatingly while under arrest. In 2008 Ménigon was the first leading figure of Action Directe to be set free. That was the end of the chapter, everything tidied up, nobody interested in the terrorist group anymore, neither those who had sympathized with Action Directe nor the state. And absolutely nobody was interested in their victims.

Finally Blanc leaned back, exhausted. Sweat was running down between his shoulder blades. The a/c unit, which one of his colleagues had repaired, was blowing out tepid air that stank like a mushroom cave. The cooling fan on his ancient computer was under so much stress that Blanc turned the machine off before the processor melted in the heat.

"That was an interesting history lesson," Marius murmured.

"I'm no archaeologist!"

"Think about it. Even the murderers who got life sentences have been free again for years now. The whole business is over and done with."

"Murder has no statute of limitation."

"In that case, you may as well also send out 'wanted' alerts for the murderers of Julius Caesar."

"You don't think we're going to nab Marie-Claude Elbaz?"

"She got her act together. Didn't get arrested in the eighties. Her name was never mentioned in any of the numerous trials. And her convicted former comrades are now all free again. She pulled it off, Roger. We've done all we can, but we're not going to get her."

"This is one shitty day."

"It's the heat. You'll get used to it."

That evening Blanc was too exhausted to roll back the roof of his 2CV before driving back to Sainte-Françoise-la-Vallée. The air in the car was as stale as in an oven, but he found a perverse masochism in torturing himself. It had gotten hot and humid. In the light of the already sinking sun he could see great mountains of clouds piling up in the western sky. But they had not yet reached the sky above his head. The moon was full, watery with pale blue patches on its scarred face. Once people had thought they were seas. He wished he could fly up to the moon and see the Earth disappear behind him becoming ever smaller and less important.

"*Merde*," he muttered as he turned in toward his oil mill. On the other side of the Touloubre his neighbor Serge Douchy was sitting on his tractor with a huge camera in his hands. The flash on the SLR split the night. Blanc wondered what sort of pictures the guy was taking.

"Your roof is too light," Douchy called out to him when he noticed he'd been spotted. "The *tuiles* have to be ocher-red, that's building regulations. That clown Fuligni has put any old tiles on there, lots of them far too light-colored: it's not even light red anymore, it's almost white. You don't notice that in the daytime, but at night those white *tuiles* shine like a neon advertisement. You'll have to change them."

Blanc thought he had heard wrongly. It must be the tiredness, he told himself. "You think you can go to the mayor with a few photos of light-colored tiles and make a formal complaint?"

"Anyone who cares about an old rubbish Roman road needs to be careful about his brand-new roof, too!" Douchy shouted at him. "Those white stripes are annoying."

White stripes . . . Blanc thought to himself. "*Merde*," he growled all of a sudden.

Douchy gave a derisory laugh for a moment, thinking Blanc had meant it for him. Then he went quiet. Because Blanc was no longer even looking at him, but had dashed into the house. The farmer shouted another curse at him, then rumbled off on his tractor. A few minutes later Blanc came running out again, jumped into the driver's seat of the 2CV, and roared off into the night, unseen by anyone.

A Confession

It took him just a few minutes to get to Saint-César. It wasn't getting any cooler; the air felt like a damp blanket lying heavily over his shoulders. He flinched as a lightning bolt flashed in his rear-view mirror. A few seconds later he heard an endless rumble. As he passed through the high bridge that ran high above the town, the first drops spattered on the 2CV's canvas roof.

Two lightning bolts hit the ground not far away on either side of the edges of town, like the left-right combination of a powerful boxer. The next couple of thunder rolls merged into a roaring that was so loud Blanc couldn't hear if his engine was still running. He felt around the steering wheel until he eventually remembered where the windshield wiper control was. The two little rubber blades just moved the drops around in two semicircles on the windshield; his headlights shone little yellow beams in front of him. He felt almost blind. He raced on, praying that nobody would be so mad as to set out driving on a night like this.

He couldn't find a parking space by the curb so he stopped in the middle of the road, directly outside of Marius's house. He got drenched just walking the few yards to the door. The raindrops were huge and warm; it felt as if jellyfish might start falling from the sky. Blanc couldn't find a doorbell, so he hammered on the wooden door. He just hoped Marius hadn't drunk too much.

By the time his sleepy colleague finally opened the door, Blanc's T-shirt was sticking to his body and water was flowing from his hair down his face.

"You've looked better," Marius said when he recognized him. He didn't seem in the least surprised. "Is your house roof not rainproof? Come in."

"I've got a roof over my head. We need to move!"

Marius pulled on jeans and a shirt and set a frayed straw hat on his head, the most ridiculous protection against rain Blanc had ever seen. "Do I need to take my gun?" he asked dutifully.

"Better not."

Marius smiled in relief. "Where are we headed?"

"Into the Camargue."

"In this weather? In that car? *Putain*, we'll never get there! My Fiat won't start in the rain. It's not something they expect Italian cars to have to do. Can't it wait until tomorrow?"

"By tomorrow the file will be gone."

Marius closed the door, sprinted off, and squeezed his huge frame into the 2CV's passenger seat. "Is what we're about to do legal?" he spluttered. Just running those few yards had already exhausted him.

"If we're successful, nobody's going to be interested," Blanc replied, putting his foot down. His spinning front wheels sent showers of water from the cracks in the asphalt. His colleague didn't ask again who it was they were looking for at night. He leaned forward until his inflamed eyes were almost touching the windshield, but he restrained himself from giving warnings in a quiet voice whenever their slithering vehicle came too close to a drainage ditch or whenever there was a fallen branch in the road.

The lightning bolts were now falling so rapidly one after another that it was no longer either properly dark or light. It was as if they were in some huge discothèque. Blanc felt as deaf as in a nightclub, except that it wasn't music hitting his ears but interminable rolls of thunder. The windshield wipers were dancing with hectic staccato movements across the glass, but even so it was like driving through an aquarium. When they left Saint-César and the last streetlights had disappeared into the gloom, Blanc had to cut his speed to about fifteen miles an hour because he could hardly see beyond his own fender. Both the tarmac and the road markings on the *route départementale* had vanished beneath a film of water. It felt as if they were swimming in a stream. Then suddenly gusts of wind began to shake the car.

"We're going to have to drive the next forty to fifty miles with no protection from this," Marius reckoned.

"If I remember well enough, the roads in the Camargue are dead straight," Blanc replied stubbornly and put his foot down again.

"*Putain*," Marius muttered, wiping away with his hand condensation that had formed on the inside of the windshield.

They raced on silently through the night storm, until Blanc at some stage felt drops of rain running down his back. "The roof is leaking!" he cursed.

"This isn't exactly a United Nations Land Cruiser," Marius replied. It suddenly seemed as if he was enjoying the ride. "There's rice growing by the edge of the road. It can't be far now."

Blanc suddenly braked hard. The 2CV slid right across the road before coming to a stop. Marius's forehead bashed into the windshield and he cursed aloud. "I didn't say we'd already gone past!" he complained when he got his breath again. "No reason to slam on the brakes!"

Blanc stared into the lightning-bolt fireworks. The air smelled of electricity, and he could taste something metallic in his mouth. His heart was pounding. "A bull," he whispered. "There was a bull in the road . . ."

Marius, who was still rubbing his forehead, only ventured to flick up the side window and risk a quick glance under the open glass. "Ridiculous," he said. "Even a stupid bull finds somewhere to shelter in weather like this. Drive on. But do me a favor, keep it in second gear. I don't want to land in a ditch in the last few yards."

Blanc forced himself to breathe calmly. Pull yourself together, he told himself. This is your idea, after all. He set off again, at a gentle pace, until eventually he spotted the entrance to the Leroux family *mas*. Streams of heavily silted water were gurgling over the rough path. "Let's just hope we can get through that," he muttered determinedly.

"First gear now, please," Marius said, unimpressed. "And apart from that it's high time you told me which member of this respected family we're coming to visit."

"Madame Leroux, I'm so pleased to see you," Blanc said a few moments later, after they had knocked on the door of the *mas* and were standing in front of the surprised lady of the house. She was wearing a T-shirt and cloth pants with a blue and white Provençal flower design on them. She looked as if she'd been sleeping. She gave a long look at Blanc, then Marius, and then the 2CV parked in a puddle in the yard, and for a moment her features softened as if she was going to burst out laughing. Then she took control of herself, nodded briefly, and invited the two gendarmes in.

"My husband," she hesitated a moment, "is on his yacht. He wanted to make sure nothing happened to it after he'd read the weather forecast. And my daughter is out at a party, I think."

"It was in any case you we wanted to speak to, Madame," Blanc replied, waiting for an invitation to take a seat in the living room.

"The wet soles of your shoes are darkening the wooden floor," Marie-Claude Leroux said as if in answer to his remark.

"That shouldn't be your main cause for concern right now," Blanc said in a serious voice. "Have you ever been to see a *course camarguaise*?"

"Many a time. Usually in Arles, but what . . ."

"Do you happen to have a computer handy?"

She looked at him as if she was beginning to wonder if these two cops had completely flipped. "I hope my old netbook will do," she replied, handing him a pocketbook-size computer with a screen saver sliding across the monitor, showing black and white photos of the Camargue. Blanc pulled a USB stick out of his pants pocket and plugged it into the netbook.

"I'd like to show you a few photos, Madame," he explained in a friendly tone. "Monsieur Cohen took these with his phone and transferred them to his computer."

"I thought Albert's cell phone had vanished."

"Please concentrate on the photos, Madame."

"What have a few private photos taken by poor Albert got to do with his tragic death? Don't you think you might be going a bit far here? In any case I don't think it's even legal to—"

"Just look at his picture," Blanc interrupted her gently.

Cohen standing between Monsieur and Madame Leroux, laughing. A holiday snap. Her arm around his neck, her left hand almost touching Cohen's ear. The white lines on her wrist. Blanc zoomed in on that area.

"That's none of your business," Marie-Claude Leroux whispered. She had gone pale and was using her right hand to massage her left wrist.

"Quite right," Blanc reassured her. "It's none of my business where and why you cut your wrists. But take another look at what's on your wrist. At least in this photo, taken shortly before Monsieur Cohen's death."

"A watch," Marius whispered, whistling through his teeth. "With a leather strap and a steel buckle."

Madame Leroux said nothing. She stared at the little monitor as if she would prefer to be looking at something else.

"Could you please show us this watch, Madame?" Blanc asked.

"I threw it away."

"Just like that? It looks like an expensive model."

"Very expensive, I imagine. A present from my husband, and Ernest never scrimps." She pulled her eyes away from the monitor and looked long and hard at Blanc: cold, wearied, but somehow at the same time relieved. "Actually," she whispered eventually, "I'm even grateful to you for finding out."

"Keeping quiet always seems so much easier than a confession. But in the end it takes too much strength."

Marie-Claude began rubbing her pale scarred wrist again, then noticed what she was doing and smiled apologetically. "I tried to come to terms with it. Believe me. Silence until death."

"You shouldn't keep silent any longer."

"Is that why you're here, a soggy Don Quixote with his Sancho Panza, galloped up on a mule with four wheels? To hear this old story? Because you're not just interested in the details of Albert's death, are you? I've done my research on you, Capitaine Blanc, through friends of my husband's in Paris. Very discreetly, never fear. I was told, how shall we put it, to beware of your stubbornness."

"I'm also interested in the Action Directe story . . ."

". . . and the story of a Saint-Gilles rice farmer, no? Ernest and I should never have bought this place. Very careless of us. But I had no choice, believe me. I simply had to have this *mas*, I had to farm rice, as a form of atonement, do you understand that?"

"No matter how much you try to atone for the past, you won't bring the dead back to life."

"No." She sighed and with an almost careless gesture opened a drawer in a sideboard crammed full of thrillers and threw Blanc the watch strap. Torn leather band, broken buckle. "I imagine your forensics lab will be able to link the pieces."

"I would also like to link up the pieces of this story."

"You've already done that, *mon Capitaine.* Back then I drove the motorbike, on which the comrade who'd been chosen by us to carry out the sentence against the rice farmer sat. At least that's the way we saw things back then. We were naive. Whether you believe it or not, I sincerely believed that a few weeks later the revolution would break out. Action Directe! It was different from the bourgeois conversation among my family. All those so-called actions and impotent demonstrations my fellow students wasted their time on. I went illegal: 'safe house' apartments, fake papers, attacks on police stations and banks, to get money and weapons. All in the name of the repressed people! After the Renault boss was taken down, we sat together to think up new targets. Which capitalist bosses needed to be taught a lesson? I had already by chance come across the story about the rice farmers from Indochina and brought it up. Exploited Vietnamese! If there was anything that was going to win us recognition from the Vietcong, that was it. They wouldn't let me do the shooting, because I was too young. But I had a motorcycle license."

She closed her eyes and was silent for a minute.

"Should I make us all some tea?" Marius offered with a calming smile.

Marie-Claude Leroux opened her eyes and nodded thankfully. Soon they heard the hissing of the kettle in the next room, and the living room filled with the aroma of black tea. Marius came back in with three delicate cups with Asian patterns with clouds of steam rising from them.

"It's one thing to demand the liquidation of an exploiter. Another thing altogether to see an old man lying in a gutter bleeding to death. It was just a picture in the round shaking rearview mirror of the Suzuki as I accelerated away. But I will never forget it. I took the shooter to our hiding place but didn't stay there myself. I don't know to this day where I drove around that night. The darkness was unending. It was so cold. I cut myself off from the comrades, didn't even return to the 'safe house.' I called," she stuttered, "my family. Maman and Papa hid me away, and you don't need to know how and with whom. Most of the members of Action Directe were arrested shortly after. My parents waited two years before they, as they put it, 'filtered me back into the system.' I have no idea how they got all the papers, all the testimonials and forms and recommendations that you need in a bourgeois life. It must have cost a pile of money and a lot of nerve. We never spoke about it. Strange, isn't it? They managed to secure for me a new start on the Côte d'Azur, not a bad rehabilitation into society, don't you think?"

"Even so, somehow or other, Monsieur Guillaume at the Musée Maly somehow found out. He told me you had blood on your hands."

She shrugged indifferently. "I hardly ever spoke with that guy at the museum, like I told you. Who knows if he really did know something or it was just crazy talk?"

"Was Monsieur Boré in the know?"

Marie-Claude Leroux laughed and shook her head. "The only thing he was interested in was art. And my legs. There were no pillow stories. But afterward, after we split up, he might have heard something."

"Because the important people in Paris were aware of the dark years of your life."

"You might say so. I did notice after I met Ernest and he introduced me to his circles. Everybody knew, but nobody knew and nobody wanted to know. The whole purpose of those Parisian good-for-nothings is to decorate the bright lights of the capitals with their own scantily clad bodies. All those half-understanding, half-disparaging looks, those false and"—she looked for the right word and lit up a cigarette—"those bloodthirsty double entendres in the middle of a conversation in a restaurant or museum or ministry. I was so fed up with belonging to it all that for years now I haven't turned up at receptions. None of those people, I suspect, actually knows the details, but everyone has some idea or other about my dubious connections, everyone except for my daughter. I hope that at least I can keep that secret from her forever."

"Your husband, on the other hand, is in the know."

"At the magazine he has some journalistic bloodhounds on the payroll who do nothing else but dig around in dirty laundry. I would be amazed if he hadn't set them on to me as soon as he got to know me. Ernest found my involvement in Action Directe from the first . . . let's say, attractive. He's always had a weakness for dangerous women." She laughed mirthlessly, then bent her head so low over her teacup that her face was invisible.

"Monsieur Cohen knew, too. At least there are serious hints to suggest so."

"Albert, of course. Albert was a reporter. But he knew how to be discreet and friendly in his own way. A rather reticent way, which unfortunately I found out only too late. He let me know he had heard the story, but that he understood and was even somewhat sympathetic, but beyond that not interested in it. Neither privately nor professionally. He was also a lefty. It was years ago that he told me that. And only once. I think he wanted to reassure me that he would be silent on the subject forever. And from that day on he never once mentioned a word about it. At least not to me . . ." She laughed again.

"But he said something to someone else?"

"Daniel Boré." She spat the name out. "Look, Albert had had a health crisis, which in reality had less to do with his heart than his fondness for illegal substances. You obviously know that after this crisis he came to us. I gave him the idea that he should write about Van Gogh, and I swear I had no evil intent. A harmless little summer story. A favor for an old friend. Then all of a sudden one day Daniel Boré turns up here, sitting almost exactly where you are now, *mon Capitaine*. I was not happy to have a long-since-ditched and I can assure you totally forgotten lover turn up in person in my house. Daniel dithered about embarrassedly for a while and claimed that Cohen had sought him out because he was chasing down the old story about the theft from the Musée Maly. I had more or less forgotten about that, too, although I suppose a gendarme like you, who never forgets anything, won't believe me.

"In any case Daniel was talking rather crazily about Albert's visit to him and about the old theft, and I wondered, Why has this guy come here at all? Then he came out with it: Albert hadn't just talked to him about Van Gogh, he'd talked about me, too. Albert had somehow found out that once upon a time Daniel and I had been close. Daniel had been my first lover after I resurfaced in society. And Albert had asked him what I did back then. What I thought, what I said, and what I had done before he got to know me."

"He was researching your past and your involvement with Action Directe," Blanc said.

"What else? After his collapse, Albert was determined once again to become the good, upstanding reporter he had been. And how better to prove to the world how good and incorruptible he was? In the middle of a crisis in the media, with journalists being fired all around, he would nail the wife of his publisher. And not just with a story that would be devastating for me, but that would also embarrass the whole Parisian elite."

"So why did Monsieur Boré tell you all this?" Marius asked.

She made a vague gesture with her teacup. "Because it would appear that in all these years, Daniel had thought of me a lot more than I had thought of him. Old love, old blindness. You might have come across that."

Both Blanc and Marius cleared their throats. "And then?" Blanc asked. "What happened then? Did Monsieur Boré perhaps suggest"—he weighed his words carefully—"a certain means of action against Monsieur Cohen?"

"Oh, *mon Capitaine*!" This time she didn't try to conceal her amusement. "Are you implying that Daniel suggested I should kill Albert? Daniel has been living for years on pastis and insulin, but that doesn't exactly make him a cold-blooded killer, does it?"

"But you've already proved that you yourself could be cold-blooded," Marius interjected. It sounded as if he almost admired her.

"It's true that killing is easier the second time," Marie-Claude confessed. "When Daniel left, I sat in a stupor for half an hour, an hour, beside the pool next to the house. I was almost frozen with horror. At one point I thought it would be best for me to simply slide into the water and surrender: a short battle with death in the swimming pool and then peace. Then I said to myself: Why should I die? For that old story? On the one side, it was ages ago, and on the other, who would gain by me paying for my deed? What's the sentence for accessory to murder? Ten years? Twenty years? I would be an old woman when I came out of jail. What would have happened to the farm and the rice? And my daughter? I'm already losing Nora, can you see that? What would happen if I ended up behind bars?"

"And that's when you thought it would be for the best if Monsieur Cohen was silenced forever." Blanc felt weary all of a sudden and somewhat disappointed. "Couldn't you just have talked to him about it? You'd known him for years."

"But that's just it. I didn't really know Albert!" Marie-Claude Leroux shook her head as if she was astonished by the question. Or by Albert Cohen, or maybe even by herself, Blanc thought. "All these years I thought I knew him," she continued. "I never thought that one day he would be digging around in my past. I felt"—she took a deep breath—"safe with him. How naive I was! How could I trust Albert anymore after Daniel's revelation? I couldn't have trusted a word he said, no matter what he told me."

"So you didn't even give Monsieur Cohen the chance to say a word."

"Albert had no family. We were his family! It was him or me, that was the only choice. Anyone would have done the same."

"Nonetheless, not everyone would have chosen a fighting bull as the murder weapon."

She shrugged, as if the means of murder was irrelevant. "I already knew that Albert went out for a ride on his mountain bike regularly. I know every corner of the Camargue, including the fields where they keep the fighting bulls. I've seen the animals in the arena often enough. Ernest is a big fan of the spectacle. If they have a chance to go for a human being, they take it. It's as reliable as a bullet flying through the air once you've pulled the trigger. I set off in the Toyota the minute Albert got on his bike. I overtook him. Whether he recognized me or not, I don't know. I didn't care because he wasn't going to have the chance to tell anyone. I waited for him next to the field where the bull was. I had already partly released the bolt on the gate by the time I saw him coming. Then another car appeared on the horizon."

"The electrician's car," Marius growled. Even he sounded exhausted by now.

"I panicked, because I had to get out of there before a witness turned up. It must have been because I was so nervous that I ripped my watch strap when I opened the gate. I didn't have time to pick up the broken parts; I just jumped into the car and sped off. Who would suspect me?"

"Yes, who indeed would even think of it . . ." Blanc mumbled, getting to his feet. "Madame, would you please accompany us to the gendarmerie station?"

On the long route back the occupants of the 2CV were silent. The thunder had silenced, but lightning bolts still flashed on the horizon. Now that the gusts of wind had died down, the rain was falling straight down, solidly enough that Blanc still had to drive carefully, but at least the car wasn't in danger of flying off the road every time he turned the wheel.

In Gadet they filled out a protocol form and then put Marie-Claude Leroux into the gendarmerie station's solitary cell. Blanc went into Nkoulou's abandoned office and laid the protocol form next to the other file and Cohen's laptop.

"That'll be a surprise for the boss," he said to Marius. The light of dawn was creeping over the floorboards from the window outside. Blanc glanced at Marius's red eyes, his wrinkled T-shirt, his hunched shoulders, his bedraggled straw hat, with raindrops falling now and then from individual straws. "I'll drive you home," he offered.

His colleague dismissed the offer. "One of the officers on duty can do that in a patrol car. I have no desire to be squeezed into your tiny steam horse again." Then he smiled and patted Blanc on the back. "That was a good bluff you plated tonight! How did you get the idea to look at the photo in enough detail to recognize the watch?"

"My crazy neighbor gave it to me. He was cursing the light-colored lines of the new roofing tiles on my house. Light-colored lines? All of a sudden something clicked. My mind immediately went to Madame Leroux's wrist, which also had light-colored stripes. I had only concentrated on the scars. But the light-colored skin had to mean that she had until recently been wearing a watch. So I looked back through Cohen's photos and *voilà*."

"What would you have done if even so Madame Leroux had denied it all? If she hadn't practically thrown the damn watch strap at our feet? *Mon Dieu*, you had just shown her a creased vacation photo where you could see a watch on a scarred wrist. That would just have been dismissed as a joke in court."

"I simply hoped she was ready to confess," Blanc admitted. "She's exhausted. She's tormented herself for years over the murder she was involved in when she was young. Her daughter, about the same age as she was then, is being pulled apart by all the unsaid things. Her husband makes use of the great taboo to act like a pig. Sooner or later it becomes unbearable. Sooner or later you become thankful when somebody gives you an excuse to free yourself from your history."

"Even if they come in the form of Don Quixote and Sancho Panza in a soaked steam horse?"

"Particularly in that case."

Marius laughed. "You should let your steam horse dry off outside the gendarmerie station and get a lift home. I think we've earned ourselves a limousine taxi service."

Blanc nodded inconclusively and waited until Marius had vanished with one of the young uniformed officers. Then he grabbed the keys to the 2CV. He was dead tired.

But there was still one thing he had to do.

No Confession

He drove through a fairy-tale world. The sun was up, and the ground was beginning to sweat off the storm water. White clouds were rising from the ground as if the Camargue had turned into an Icelandic volcanic crater. Above, a mist the color of skim milk rose to the sky. The cicadas were silent, and the storm had ripped off branches of pine and cypress trees and left them lying on the road like fallen soldiers. Blanc had to take extreme care. It was Tuesday morning, August 16, and despite it being the height of summer, it was a normal working day for many people. Some were driving with their lights on against the morning mist, but most just followed the sacred national rule to turn off your headlights by 6:00 A.M. at the latest, and to hell with anybody who only noticed you when it was too late.

Battered vans and minibuses of suppliers were rushing over the vaulted Rhône bridge into Saint-Gilles, and in front of the shops their rear loading platforms were already down. There were no tourists on the sidewalks. Lots of free parking spaces. Blanc parked the 2CV next to the city wall. There was only one other car parked on the square next to it. One that Blanc had noticed before.

The storm the previous night had drenched a poster on the

wall for a local rock band concert to such an extent that the musicians looked like zombies looming out of the stone. Blanc felt as if he was in a dream that had begun harmlessly but was getting more sinister from second to second.

The strangely unfinished church. The massive entrance. Stone figures that in the mist looked even more alive than in the southern sunlight. *You want to find the Van Gogh? Then look for the heathen hunter by the feet of the saint. You don't understand that?* That was what Guillaume had written in his suicide note. A man who underestimated his fellow human beings. It wasn't exactly hard to solve his riddle: the centaur with the bow and arrow on the Saint-Gilles entrance.

The heavy wooden doors were still closed. There was nobody on the square in front of them save for a cat that was crawling beneath the steps in an attempt to get at some quarry Blanc couldn't see. He walked over to the right side of the façade and then along the fissured side wall of the building. There was barbed wire in front of this area, but it wasn't hard to squeeze through a gap in it. The stink of cat's piss. Footsteps in the softened red earth. A man's, Blanc reckoned, a heavy man.

He reached the far side of the church. The ruins of the choir. The remains of the tower and staircase looming up into the sky. Blanc reached for his Sig Sauer, felt the weight of the cool heavy metal in his right hand, checked the ammunition in the magazine, and put the gun back in its holster.

"*Bonjour*, Monsieur Boré," he said, coming out of the half shadow of the church wall.

The art historian spun around in shock. His eyelids were fluttering, grotesquely magnified through the lenses of his old-fashioned spectacles. Then he took control of himself. "Has the gendarmerie delegated you to the treasure hunt section, *mon Capitaine*?"

"I'm still working on the Cohen death case. I arrested Madame Leroux last night."

For the tiniest of seconds the art historian smiled before making it look as if he was about to cough. "I take it you're not going to give me the details, and I also take it that you aren't here hoping I'm going to congratulate you for having put my former lover behind bars. What happened? And why are you here in Saint-Gilles instead of giving a press conference to announce your success?"

"Leave off the sarcasm. Why are you here in Saint-Gilles, Monsieur Boré? Do you really believe Olivier Guillaume hid the stolen Van Gogh here?"

"That makes two of us, doesn't it? The guy was a fool, but the sort of fool that had brilliant ideas."

"Like real artists?"

Boré cleared his throat. Then he nodded at the sculpture of the tortured man with his leg crushed beneath the giant pillar. "Every time I'm here I poke and probe around that figure. It would make a good hiding place, don't you think? But it would seem it's too obvious for a lamebrain like Guillaume." He sighed. "The Van Gogh is scarcely bigger than a sheet of writing paper. Guillaume could have hidden it behind a loose stone or a gap somewhere or under an altar plate. Or maybe even in the sarcophagus of Aegidius, Saint Gilles himself? Pictures by Van Gogh are the modern equivalent of holy relics. Wouldn't it be suitable to hide such a holy relic amid the bones of a saint from the Middle Ages? But how could Guillaume have opened the sarcophagus without anyone seeing him? And how could I get there without anyone seeing me?"

"You could have asked Guillaume. While he was still alive."

Boré looked at him skeptically. "What is it you really want from me, *mon Capitaine*?"

"A confession."

The art historian laughed. "I confess to having gotten into the ruins of the church choir without an entry ticket. But you've done the same thing. Do you want to arrest me for that?"

"I have a better reason."

"I'd be astonished."

"As an accomplice in the murder of Albert Cohen."

Boré gave a nervous laugh. "I thought what we were talking about here was a hidden Van Gogh. You've already arrested Cohen's murderer, a woman."

"We're talking about a murderer who didn't get his hands dirty." Blanc let his right hand drift down to the grip of his Sig Sauer, but the man opposite him looked like he would neither be attacking him nor fleeing into the mist. "You went to see Marie-Claude Leroux," he added. "Your former lover. Cohen's host. The former terrorist. Perhaps you found out about that last detail when you worked together at the Musée Maly. Maybe you only found out about it when you got into the circle of the powerful people in Paris, where everybody knows the large and small past sins of everybody else, but nobody talks about them publicly. Although in private, of course they do . . ."

"None of that makes me into a criminal."

"It puts you into the perfect position to commit a crime. Monsieur Cohen never mentioned Madame Leroux's past to you. He knew about it, of course. But he had no intention of writing a story about it. Nothing in the documents we have of his indicates that.

"Instead, Albert Cohen was researching Van Gogh. His computer is stuffed with documents that prove that. Researching your saint, Monsieur Boré. He came to see you as the great expert, as well as a witness and possible accomplice in a long-forgotten theft on the Côte d'Azur. Cohen was hunting down the vanished Van Gogh somewhere here in Saint-Gilles. And he had come across an ancient police file in Arles that could have been an academic sensation. But you could have at last won the approval of your fellow art historians if it were you, and not some reporter, who could have published photos of the adult Van Gogh!

"And then there was the police report that hinted that Van Gogh hadn't cut off his own ear but that it had happened in a ferocious argument with his fellow painter Gauguin. Brutal and bloody, but also rather banal, no? So banal as to do irreparable harm to your thesis about the mad painter. And your entire reputation is based on the cult of the mad painter.

"Cohen mustn't publish one of his discoveries, the photo, because you wanted to do that. And his other discovery, the police report, wasn't going to be published by him or anybody else because it would make you a laughingstock for everything you've written over the years and on which your fame depends.

"It wasn't hard for you to steal the police file in Arles. You'd been going in and out of the archives for years, as an academic. Nobody paid any attention to you. Where did you hide the file? Here in this church, too? Or did you burn everything?

"But Cohen was a reporter who wanted to know what was what, not an easy man to keep quiet. Nobody was going to persuade him to give up this story, the first one in particular, which he was determined to write to rehabilitate himself after his breakdown. And he was nearly there. You yourself told us how well informed he was. He had been to Arles and photographed the documents in the police file before you made them disappear. He had been to Saint-Gilles and looked around the church—and was intending to come back. And he wanted to talk to Guillaume, the alleged thief. The fool who might not have been that crazy after all. The loner who knew a lot about art, not least because his father was a great collector and art was the only thing that connected Guillaume to him: the former colleague who didn't think much of you, Monsieur Boré."

"If a guy like Guillaume didn't like me, I take that as a compliment."

"But it wasn't a compliment, it was a threat. All the research Cohen had done threatened you. He had brought up the old theft story. He was close to the possible hiding place of the stolen picture. He had dug up photos you wanted to have. He was about to destroy the main thesis of your book. He would have had a spectacular story to sit alongside the big Van Gogh exhibition in Arles. All at your expense."

"That's pure speculation."

"But Cohen had unknowingly made the mistake of telling you where he was staying in Provence," Blanc continued unwaveringly. "Maybe he didn't know that his host was your former lover. He probably wouldn't have cared. But for you, Monsieur Boré, this coincidence suddenly offered a way out of your dangerous situation. You suddenly came up with a nefarious idea and you sought out Marie-Claude. Your former lover was surprised and annoyed, but you were hardly unknown to her. Madame Leroux invited you into the house and listened to you—and you told her a story that you had totally made up and that had nothing to do with Cohen's research. But a lot to do with your girlfriend's past.

"You knew she had been involved in an Action Directe murder. You made her believe that was the story Cohen was working on! The scandal of the forgotten terrorist murder and the celebrity who was involved in it. You knew that for Madame Leroux her past was a taboo that had to be maintained at any price. It might already be known in Paris, but it wasn't spoken of, as if it had never happened. Just like all her husband's escapades. If nobody mentions it, it isn't a crime. But if one word, one goddamn word, came out in the press, then all hell would break loose! Then all the politicians and journalists and celebrities would have to show their true colors, would have to pretend to be shocked and demand an investigation and insist she be sentenced. That, Monsieur Boré, is what you told her that day by the pool behind her *mas*.

"You knew precisely that Madame Leroux would think she had her back to the wall and had to do something immediately. And you knew that once upon a time Madame Leroux had been unscrupulous enough to kill someone. Unlike you, she already had blood on her hands. And unlike you, she was physically fit and strong. When you left the *mas* in the Camargue, you knew perfectly well that without having directly ordered it, you had set a killer on Cohen.

"You were the one who pronounced Cohen's death sentence. You talked a woman who had long regretted what she had done as a young girl and tried to make up for it as best she could, into committing another crime. And you are at least indirectly also responsible for the suicide of a lonely, bitter man. Three lives destroyed for a pathetic little piece of fame. That's quite a price, Monsieur Boré."

"And that's quite a story, but with little to it, *mon Capitaine*." The art historian's hands were trembling, but he continued to look Blanc in the eye. "As you yourself admit, I never once mentioned the word 'murder' to Madame Leroux. The photo of Van Gogh as an adult, which is supposed to make me famous, has so far been seen by nobody. The document that is supposed to prove that Gauguin cut off Van Gogh's ear only exists in your imagination. Nobody knows what happened to the Arles police file. And the fact is: I have no blood on my hands. Not a drop. And you have no evidence to the contrary. Not one shred."

Blanc squeezed the grip of his gun. It would be so easy, here and now, in the mist. No witnesses. Just one shot. One bullet into this self-confident, self-satisfied face, into that sarcastic cowardly grin. A proper sentence, and who would worry about proof, appeals, and complicated trials?

Just like back in the old days, Action Directe.

He took a deep breath and removed his hand from the Sig Sauer. "Carry on looking," he said threateningly, nodding at the church of Saint Gilles. "I'll keep looking, too." And then he turned around. He had a long way back to go.

On the way Blanc stopped at one particular field in the Camargue. By now the sun had evaporated the water on the ground. The horizon had once again vanished into a shimmering haze. Somewhere out there several thousand pink figures were flickering in the silver light. And three or four black giants.

Blanc was thinking of Nora Leroux. Would her mother's arrest give her the chance to escape her own demons? Or would it push her over the cliff? He thought of his own children, whom he never saw and never talked to. Then he did something that he would not have done had he not been so exhausted and so disappointed. He called Aveline on her cell phone even though he knew she had gone to Paris.

"When I saw your number on the display, I very nearly didn't answer," she said immediately. But in her voice, hidden away like a minuscule pearl, there was just a trace of curiosity and maybe even affection.

"Can I speak openly with you, *Madame le juge*?"

"I'm in a corridor in the interior ministry."

Blanc sighed and as quickly as possible told her of the events of the previous night. "I can't prove anything against Boré," he admitted in the end. "And the matter of the stolen Van Gogh will just have to go back into the files. It probably was Guillaume who stole it, but nobody is ever going to prove it. At least not unless somebody finds it in the church in Saint-Gilles. Madame Leroux is going to be your only accused, I fear. For the Action Directe murder all those years ago. And for the murder of Albert Cohen a few days ago."

"For the murder of Albert Cohen, period." He heard the click of a cigarette lighter and then her deep intake of breath. At that moment he longed to take Aveline in his arms. "I already know part of the story," she said. "I had a call this morning from Commandant Nkoulou. And from a Paris lawyer. One of those lawyers you see on television from time to time, if you know what I mean. It would appear that in the early hours of the morning, advised by this prominent lawyer, Madame Leroux, in the words of her lawyer, 'completed' her confession."

It's a dream, Blanc thought. I'm still trapped in this goddamn dream. "That doesn't sound good," he managed to say.

"I have no idea where you are right now, *mon Capitaine*, but you might have done better staying at your desk in Gadet."

"I'm standing next to a field in the Camargue."

For a second Aveline was silent. When she opened her mouth again, her voice sounded a little bit softer. "Madame Leroux does not deny the murder of Monsieur Cohen. Her watch strap is already in the lab. The means of the murder won't be hard to reconstruct in court. But the motive . . ." She took another pull on her cigarette. "Madame Leroux is now claiming that in those final days when Monsieur Cohen was the guest of herself and her husband, he repeatedly harassed her. Sexually. The lawyer says he has the names of other women who are willing to substantiate similar accusations, former colleagues, workers at *L'Événement*. And I have no idea where from, but he has a copy of a medical examination report that clearly confirms Monsieur Cohen's former addiction to cocaine. Madame Leroux, she admitted this morning, felt ashamed before her husband and daughter. But she didn't know how to handle the aggressive attitude of her guest, who after all was her husband's best friend. It just happened that on that particular day she purely by chance overtook Cohen on his mountain bike ride. At that point, completely spontaneously, she decided to give him a scare by letting the fighting bull out. She had in no way intended to kill Cohen; there had after all never been a case of a cyclist in the Camargue being gored by a bull. She just wanted to give him enough of a shock to make him leave Provence. But the animal went so wild she barely managed to save her own skin and was in no position to do anything more for Cohen. It was all a regrettable mistake, if you like. All in all, rather titillating, tragic, and gruesome. All explained by an accused who happens at the same time to be shy and pretty. She will get away with her story and end up doing a few years for manslaughter, not murder. With good behavior she could be out in twenty-four months."

"What about the Action Directe murder?"

"Which murder?"

Blanc closed his eyes. No confession. No documentation. Not a word.

"Madame Leroux's full confession does not mention Action Directe," Aveline told him coolly. "She simply denies even obliquely referring to that old assassination in the presence of yourself and Lieutenant Tonon. Your own career, *mon Capitaine*, is not above reproach. And we should probably better not even spend a word discussing that of your colleague. I surely don't need to spell out the consequences to you. As of this morning there is simply no official connection between Madame Leroux and the death of Cohen on one hand and Marie-Claude Elbaz and the Saint-Gilles killing on the other. That will not even be mentioned in court."

"But you can call me as a witness and I can make the connection."

He waited several seconds for an answer that didn't come. "*Madame le juge*," he ended up saying. "Are you still there?" He sounded foolish to himself.

He could hear her sigh. "If you appear in court, Madame Leroux's lawyer will tear you apart. And then Monsieur and Madame Leroux will do the same. It seems to me I have to protect you from yourself, *mon Capitaine*."

"So the Saint-Gilles murder remains forgotten and unatoned for?"

"You yourself described Madame Leroux's wrists. I think the scars answer your question."

Blanc was battling his exhaustion in vain. The last cooling effects from the storm were wearing off and in a few hours the quicksilver would be back up to the levels that indicated fever in a malaria patient. "This might not have been the most successful case of my life," he said in a flat voice.

"Nonetheless, you unearthed a murder where nobody else suspected one. You put the perpetrator behind bars, if only for the second of her two deeds. And"—her voice suddenly sounded unusually merry, as if she was smiling as she talked—"you've given me an exciting story about a mad painter and a vanished masterpiece. We ought to meet up in Saint-Gilles more often."

"To look for the vanished Van Gogh?"

"That, too, *mon Capitaine*."

Blanc put his cell phone back in his pocket and wandered out to his steam horse. This would be the last time he drove around the Midi with a roof that rolled back. He had promised Riou he would return the car today. His rickety Espace was ready and waiting for him to pick up and drive off in until somewhere or another it broke down again. He would enjoy the new, shiny roof on his oil mill every day, particularly when his neighbor Douchy sat there on his tractor giving him dirty looks. He would empty a few bottles of rose with Lukas Rheinbach and Bruno Micheletti and try not to handle Sylvie Micheletti with kid gloves. He would keep an eye on Paulette Aybalen. He would enjoy Dr. Fontaine Thezan's sarcasm, have patience with Officer Baressi's inertia, and suffer Commandant Nkoulou's correctness. He would admire Fabienne Souillard's courage and try to keep Marius Tonon's demons at a distance. And he would spend day and night thinking of a *juge d'instruction* whose name he would hardly dare mention for fear a trembling of his hands would give him away. And every time from now on that he ate Camargue rice, he would have the metallic taste of blood in his mouth.